I0595071

SEED OF CHAOS

ISBN: **979-8-9992487-0-1**

Cover Design by Jay O'Connell

Bigwaves Publishing

SEED OF CHAOS

Daniel Hatch

PART ONE

PROLOGUE

Like a drop of water squeezing itself from a tap, the research and exploration vessel *Cousteau* popped into existence more than a billion leagues away from an ordinary-looking G4 star.

An instant earlier it had been outbound somewhere between the orbit of Saturn and Uranus, now it was on the outer edges of another solar system 100 light years away.

The *Cousteau* was a small ship for an interstellar spacecraft – barely 400 meters from the sensor pods in the bow to the fusion engines in the stern. It carried two hundred technicians, mechanics, clerks and scientists, a Regular Space Corps officer to command its defensive system, a library filled with two centuries of fine video and two millennia of fine texts, and in the efficient little galley a four-year supply of Spam.

The ship and its crew had came in search of alien intelligence – or its remains.

The visitors from Earth knew there had been an intelligent species here once, almost a century ago – the giant radio ears on the far side of the moon had picked up the gentle whisper of high-frequency transmissions originating in this system. But those signals had started their long journey through the interstellar night more than a century earlier. A century was a long time for a technological society and much could happen in that interval – most of it disastrous. Civilizations that invented radio also invented other things – rockets, nuclear weapons, and nationalism. Twice now explorers from Earth had followed the trail of radio signals back to their source only to find the ashes of a fallen civilization.

The first thing they did upon entering the new solar system, therefore, was to warm up their radio receivers and listen with hopes high and fingers crossed.

They were not disappointed.

A wide range of intriguing sounds issued from the speakers throughout the ship as they scanned across the radio band – codes, telemetry, voices in a dozen strange languages. Cheers rose from the crew in response.

The signals emanated from the second planet out from the sun and a telescopic survey of the world was conducted immediately. It was an unusual world by terrestrial standards – a cross between Mars and Earth, with geological forms resembling those of the smaller planet.

A small portion of the its surface was covered with open water – only a single ocean and a few large seas and lakes. The seas and lakes were among many circular features on the planet – remnants of large meteor impacts early in the history of the planet still visible. The drift of continents that had scoured the surface of Earth clean of these features had never developed here. There were other features associated with a planet below the critical size for plate tectonics – towering volcanoes many leagues high and a rift valley thousands of leagues long.

Superimposed on this were the normal climatic features of a world with atmosphere and life. A rainforest belt wrapped the equator, hot, humid air piling up in endless rain clouds. Two desert strips circled the planet on its flanks where the cool, dry air descended from the tropics. Green temperate zones were sandwiched in between the desert sands and the small polar icecaps. A quick check with the spectrograph revealed that there was an abundance of ground water stored in the soggy lands outside the desert belts. The scientists aboard *Cousteau* were not surprised that life had evolved here – conditions were more than sufficient.

It would take six months for the *Cousteau* to make the long trek in from the outskirts of the solar system to the small world and to gather and assimilate the data necessary to deal with its inhabitants. And even then the time would not be enough to properly prepare.

There were no signs commanding the visitors from Earth to abandon all hope – but they were about enter into a hell the nature of which Dante had never imagined.

And so, without fear or trepidation, blissfully ignorant of the hazards that awaited them, the crew of the *Cousteau* lit off the ship's fusion engines and started their long descent to the world its inhabitants called Chamal.

CHAPTER ONE

Zepp caught sight of the long, razor-edged sword as soon as he rounded the end of the bookcase. He stopped abruptly in his tracks, his tail twitching nervously.

He studied the blade resting half out of its sheath on the floor. It was simple and unornamented, the kind issued to the guards of the Hall of the Seedkeepers. Beside it sat a hand-axe with curved blades and a pistol from a Red Monkey gun shop – also standard guard issue.

For a moment he imagined the sword at work in the confines of the book-lined gallery, hacking through flesh, bone, and bindings. The fur across the back of his neck rose as deep-seated fears of swords, knives, and other sharp instruments bubbled out of his short memory.

For some reason, he had a brief premonition of his life nearly coming to an end on the edge of that sword, but he put it quickly out of his mind.

Zepp was a small green ape with long fur. He stood five hands tall and his tail, less than two hands long, just swept the floor. It was not a powerful or imposing form, but in a world where wisdom came in many shapes and sizes it served Zepp quite well.

A number of features proclaimed his wisdom to the careful observer – the high forehead on his roughly spherical skull, the flexible and facile tongue, lips and jaw that gave him the power of speech, the well-articulated hands, fingers, and wrists that allowed him to manipulate his environment and carry a heavy book with ease, and the dark, sensitive, alert eyes that peered out from under a heavy brow,

He was sparsely dressed, wearing only a brown leather vest with many pockets and a blue loincloth. And beneath the loincloth was a brass chastity belt consisting of a small brass cup held in place by light but secure chains joined above the base of his tail by a tarnished lock – the only part of the assembly exposed to view.

The belt identified him as a member of the tribe of Jobe, and it was a constant reminder of the strict sexual taboos maintained by the tribe – most of which were enforced by a swift application of the blade to the offending member. And that was the root of the keen dread of sharp objects that Zepp shared with his cousins.

But today it was not the only source of Zepp's anxiety.

As a young, unmated male of the tribe of Jobe, Zepp was serving his apprenticeship with the Seedkeepers of Suridash, learning the subtle and chaotic patterns of the seed of the gods. It was not an easy task. There were times in the childhood and adolescence of most chamalians when they devoured and digested new knowledge with vigor and ease – but for Zepp, this was not one of them.

Many months would pass before he could absorb this complex discipline. In the meantime his major goal was to struggle with the duties assigned to him and avoid the embarrassment of failure. He had managed his chores as a clerk in the Hall of the Seedkeepers well enough, but now a new task had been thrust upon him – his first chance to prove his worthiness as a full adult member of the Tribe or to fail miserably and suffer an unknown but certainly undesirable fate.

This new assignment had little to do with his job as a clerk. Zepp was not even sure why he had been chosen. Several days ago Master Tedrak of the Council of Elders had visited the Hall of the Seedkeepers to inspect Zepp and his cousins, going as far as probing into their mouths and examining their teeth – for what reasons Zepp could not begin to imagine.

Tedrak finally picked on Zepp and his cousin Fripp, and after speaking briefly with both of them sent Fripp back to work, keeping the small, green ape.

"You will be leaving Suridash and you will need a bodyguard," Tedrak told him. "For the journey and for the meeting."

Zepp could only imagine why he would need a bodyguard and that imagining had kept him from sound sleep ever since. Now, as the hour of departure neared, his nerves were tight and frazzled.

A deep, rasping snore from a dark corner of the gallery broke the spell of fear that gripped Zepp. There, curled up in a large ball on the dusty stones, was the owner of the grim arsenal, a guard Zepp knew as Snomisch, a tall and heavy beast, near-wise with curving, sloth-like fingers and toes, dirty-white fur, and a flat, pink nose. This must be his bodyguard. No doubt he had slipped into the gallery while Zepp was busy during noon-sleep.

Now Zepp was seized with a new panic. In a few minutes Zepp's overseer, Sheverek, would be returning to work, and Zepp was afraid he would be discovered violating one of the rules of the Seedkeepers – instead of seeking out a cool spot to sleep away the hottest part of the day, the young ape had been secretly prying into his own past in the records of the tribe of Jobe.

His curiosity had been spurred during the meeting with Master Tedrak. While questioning Zepp, Tedrak had mentioned Zepp's uncle. "You're Tapp's nephew, aren't you? I knew your uncle well. You could do worse than to take after him."

Tapp had been claimed by the purple plague when Zepp was much younger, but while he lived, he had been a powerful and respected citizen of Suridash. He was even spoken of as a successor to Tedrak on the Council of Elders. Like Zepp, he was an ape, though blue in hue, and Zepp was examining the records to see if his resemblance to his uncle was more than superficial.

He was disappointed to discover that his own records were incomplete on the subject. There was a surprisingly exhaustive catalog of trivial physical traits – the Seedkeepers had a good knowledge of inherited attributes and kept meticulous records. But there was nothing in his file about character or courage. Even the Seedkeepers had limits.

Now he hurried to return the heavy, handbound volume that held his uncle's genetic history and his own to their proper places before anyone returned to work early and found him out. He was careful not to disturb Snomisch as he climbed the worn wooden ladder to the uppermost shelf and slid the book back among others like it.

The rules of the Seedkeepers were not enforced as harshly as those of the tribe of Jobe, but Zepp had no wish to measure the difference. He was still at the top of the ladder when he heard the sound of approaching footsteps in the corridor – a sound like the distant rumble of thunder in the desert. His hearts squeezed tightly as he realized he could never get down from the bookshelves in time. No matter, it was just was well that he looked busy when Sheverek returned.

The same was true, however, for Snomisch, whose dereliction of duty was all too obvious.

"Hey, Snomisch!" Zepp called from his perch. "Wake up! You want old Sheverek to catch you sleeping?"

The guard stirred uneasily in his resting place, opening his eyes at the sound of Zepp's voice, blinking and twisting his head around as he tried to locate its source.

"Huh?" he said.

Then the storm broke. "Harrgh!"

The roar echoed down the stone walls of the gallery and was barely muffled by the thick volumes that lined the library shelves. Old General Sheverek entered the main chamber of the records section with Kirbum, his assistant, scurrying in front of him, trying to get out of his way.

A scowl was fixed across the general's features, his yellowed eyes bore a thick glaze, and the white bristles around his mouth twitched uncontrollably.

Kirbum, a piebald terrier with tightly curled fur, strayed too close to Sheverek's path, his nose lifted high and a rigid, fearful expression frozen on his face. He didn't move fast enough, and Sheverek hit him across the back of his head with a fistful of swollen knuckles.

"What is this?" he growled. "Snomisch, you still sleeping! Zepp, where are you?"

Zepp said nothing but stirred noisily at the top of the ladder. Snomisch struggled to his feet sheepishly and Sheverek cast a suspicious eye towards Zepp.

Sheverek was a refugee from a tropical kingdom far to the south of Suridash. Back there, he had been the Scourge of Rudabet, the Grand Marshal of the Ivy Horde, and the Wielder of the Golden Lash. Here he was Sheverek, junior clerk of records. In the , he had led his country's armies to disastrous defeat and fled from the victors, leaving everything behind. Suridash had little need for generals, but the Seedkeepers had put his administrative skills to good use,

Both he and Kirbum were permanent workers in the hall, while Zepp was only a transient. Neither of them belonged to the tribe of Jobe. They made Zepp feel unliked and unwanted whenever they could.

"Get to work!" Sheverek commanded as he staggered up the hallway towards Zepp. His aging, bloated body was no longer under the precise control it had once been, and he swayed from side to side, huffing and puffing as he walked.

He passed close to Zepp, watching him all the time. Zepp could see the long, twisted lines of old battle scars beneath a black gauze tunic damp with sweat.

Sheverek disappeared into his office, a small, windowless cubicle in the tower at the end of the hall. Zepp climbed down from the bookcase and returned to his desk.

Kirbum was already there, hunched over a yellowing ledger. He kept his ears pulled in close to his head and his eyes were always half-closed.

"Why do you let him hit you like that?" Zepp asked as he climbed up onto his stool.

Kirbum shrugged, looking away from Zepp. "He doesn't do it that much."

"Yes he does," Zepp said. "I've watched him – he hits you seven or eight times a day."

"I don't mind it," he replied.

Zepp glanced at him dubiously, then said, "He tried it on me when I first got here, but I'm too fast for him,"

"He doesn't hit *me*," Snomisch said, standing behind Zepp,

strapping on his gun belt.

"No, Sno, nobody's going to hit you," Zepp said.

"He's crazy, you know," Kirbum said suddenly. "He's afraid of the revenge squads from his homeland. He's a war criminal."

"How do you know?" Zepp asked.

"I hear him talking in his dreams at noon-sleep."

"I don't believe you," Zepp protested. "He speaks in his own tongue when he talks in his sleep. You couldn't have understood him."

"The guards can. They told me what he says. He thinks we're all spies for the revenge squads. He's afraid they're going to catch up with him for all the things he did during the war."

"What did he do?"

"I don't know. Probably the same kind of things he does now. Did you know he visits the houses where the dead are prepared for the grave?"

"So? What for?"

"He dances with the bodies."

Zepp suppressed a shudder. "Is this what he says in his dreams?" he asked, both skeptical and believing at once.

"No, I followed him last week and watched where he goes at night," he boasted.

Zepp looked at him sideways, then said, "You're just making that up."

"No, it's true," Kirbum insisted. "Ask the guards. They sent me."

Zepp turned to Snomisch, but before the green ape spoke, Sheverek stumbled down the hall from his office.

"What you two up to? What you talking about? I catch you now. You plot against me. Well, I can take care of you. Just you watch!" he bellowed at the two scribes.

"See," Kirbum said. "What did I tell you?"

Sheverek hit him across the face, then glared at Zepp.

"You!" he pointed at Zepp with a clawed hand. "Is time for you to go. But remember, I take care of you, so watch out."

Zepp closed the book on his desk, stuffed his pen into a bottle of sand and hurried out of the gallery, Snomisch following behind.

They padded silently through the long corridors and down the broad stairways of the Hall of the Seedkeepers. The path was not straight or easy, and it was only the experience of getting lost in the chaotic jumble many times that enabled them to find their way. Like all things chamalian, the Hall of the Seedkeepers had not been planned, but had evolved, piece by piece, section by section, gallery by gallery, until the result was a confused riot of architectural designs and styles, jarring to the eye and tedious to the mind. Corridors led nowhere, stairways ended in blank ceilings, gaping pits appeared treacherously in the middle of open plazas, and it was hazardous to wander about the building carelessly.

At last they passed through a heavy wooden door with iron hinges and stepped into a narrow courtyard. A shaft of bright sunlight fell from the opening several stories above, illuminating the cracked stone floor of the yard and the thick dust that hung in the still air.

Zepp had been here several times before, always with an uneasy feeling in the pit of his stomach. He would have avoided this place if he could, but the garage lay on the far side and there was no easy way around it.

Many generations ago, before the time of Jobe, the Hall of the Seedkeepers had been the Hall of the Slavemasters. This courtyard had been the center of the slave pens that rose up, level upon level, eighty-eight hands above Zepp's low head. Hundreds of small, open cages, facing the yard, once filled with the merchandise of slavers, now held a different inventory.

As Snomisch slammed the heavy door behind them, the din of hundreds of babbling creatures ceased abruptly. The air was foul with the smell of living things, dying and decaying things, rotting food and excrement. Zepp gagged briefly and closed his inner nostrils against the stench. Then he stepped into the sunlight.

He was conscious of a thousand pairs of eyes fastening themselves on him, peering out of the dark pens, eyes of every color, size and shape. They seemed to float bodilessly in the deep shadows of the pens, clustering in corners and glaring defiantly.

Zepp felt overwhelmed for a brief moment, and it seemed like the walls of the courtyard were closing in on him. Here was what the Seedkeepers of Suridash kept – all the strains of chamalian life, held in the living creatures who carried them from generation to generation. It was just another form of slavery, no doubt, but one motivated by a higher moral purpose. Pups and halflings could carry the germ of kings and emperors unknowingly for uncounted generations – the valuable seed of the gods mingled with the chaff, almost beyond recovery ... almost, but not completely.

For here lay the task of the Seedkeepers: to sort the grain from the chaff. The chaff filled the pens around Zepp, and their cries of derision and insult filled the air of the courtyard, echoing off the upper levels.

"Hey, Greenie!" halflings shouted from their cages. "Let us out and we'll give you a treat!"

"Are you here to feed us or to eat us?"

"We know what you want, brassbelt "

Then Snomisch stepped into the light and the shouts abated. The guards of the Seedkeepers had a powerful reputation among the lesser breeds who dwelled in the pens. It was not prudent to anger them, and even the half-wit halflings knew that, though the cacophony of the lesser breeds continued. Zepp recovered his nerve quickly and crossed the long, narrow yard, passed through the broad gate at the far end, and away from the screeching, jeering tumult.

He led the way down into the garage where he presented the hand-scrawled travel orders to the clerk in charge of the motor pool and drew a battered electric cart with an open top and a thick coat of dust across the body. Initials, monograms, and obscene slogans written in the dust had faded as the motor attracted layer upon layer of the red desert grit with its strong electrostatic charge.

Zepp initialed the clerk's manifest, and Snomisch climbed into the drivers seat. While clearly wiser than the tree-sloth, Zepp lacked the training to operate the cart and Snomisch did not. He switched the motor on and once Zepp was aboard they wheeled up the ramp and onto the crowded streets of Suridash.

* * *

Suridash was a city of refugees, situated on the edge of the desert, on the eastern shore of a sea at the southeastern end of Chamal's only ocean, far from the more hospitable wetlands where the majority of chamalian breeds had been born. It was the middle of nowhere, the last stop for dozens of tribes, clans, kings, and consuls fleeing from every point of the compass. As a result, the throngs that filled the streets and bazaars of the city were the most variegated conglomeration of creatures to be found in a single spot on the face of the planet.

Fat, red-faced rodents with thick brown fur. Thin, white bears with long, pointed snouts. Leathery-skinned sand-dwellers. Prairie-diggers with puffed cheeks. Orange tree-cats with long, stiff whiskers. Swamp-dwellers with long fangs and spurs on their knees. And that was only as far as the first corner.

It seemed to Zepp as though none of them had ever encountered an automobile before, from the way they gawked and pointed. Few of them probably had – Meshkarian traders had been selling them in Suridash for only a few years.

The going was exceedingly slow on the jam-packed streets of center of the city. Hardly anyone would yield the right of way to the little cart the way they would to a heavy wagon with snorting draft animals. Zepp was at the limits of his patience when they finally reached the roadway out of the central city and the traffic began to move more smoothly.

They wound their way past the high walls of the city's closed enclaves. Behind those walls, the powerful tribes that had founded the city – or had joined it in more recent times – maintained their private and separate lives. They kept up customs and practices that had been overthrown in their homelands, reliving past glories, pretending that whatever tragedies had befallen their forebears were nothing but fairy tales for scaring children. At least they did so until the unique traits that gave each clan its private character were diluted by the inevitable flux of chamalian genetics.

At the north end of the city were the Red Monkeys, all that was left of a mighty race that had once ruled over the Great Rift Valley to the northwest, the developers of nearly every major technological advance in the history of the planet. With the help of the Seedkeepers, they had sustained their breed far beyond its normal life-span.

In the east, the Chorai made their home, having fled from the volcanic highlands where their cousins had persecuted them only a century ago for their incestuous breeding practices.

There were fugitives from the interminable wars of the tropical belt – like Sheverek. Others had come up from Meshkar, losers in bitter trade wars between the commercial cities there. And more recently, waves of refugees had been flowing in from the west, victims of Rikabar's expanding empire and the terror that preceded it.

Meanwhile, the free citizens of Suridash built their homes and shops in the shadow of the walls, filling in the broad spaces between the enclaves with the hodge-podge of urban ecology. That kind of life seemed to have a more enduring quality than the world inside the enclave walls, something the founder of Zepp's tribe had recognized many, many years ago. It was from this group that most of the tribe of Jobe's members had come.

Snomisch stopped briefly at the city's West Gate – the Gate of Jobe's Return. The massive pile of stone arched over the cobbled roadway, with galleries, turrets, and towers poking out at random. Ponderous doors more than sixteen hands high were secured open – and had been for eighty-eight years. Guards manned the entrance, but they were largely ceremonial, of little tactical use in an era where armies and invaders were powerful on a scale never conceived of by the gate's builders.

Over eighty-eight years times four ago, on the far side of Suridash, Jobe had passed through the Eastern Gate – the Gate of Jobe's Departure. Thirty-two years later, Jobe had walked through this gate after circumnavigating the globe, carrying with him the accumulated wisdom of his world. He had used that wisdom to remake his city –

and in many ways the world itself.

Now Zepp trembled at the thought of passing under its stone arch, fearful of what wisdom he might gain from the outside world – a world he had never before ventured into. Snomisch, on the other hand, seemed to suffer no such trepidation.

They waited for a cargo truck from the Tradetown to pass through the gate – a monstrously big machine belching smoke and steam in stark contrast to the tidy efficiency of the electric cart from Meshkar. The guards inspected it and waved it through, then they let Snomisch and Zepp transit the short passage into the world outside. Snomisch maneuvered the cart out onto the asphalt highway that met the cobblestones of the city on the far side of the gate and accelerated away from the city.

A league down the road, as they reached the crest of a low hill, Zepp looked back over his shoulder to see what they had left behind.

"Stop!" he cried. "Stop for just a moment. I want to get a better look."

Snomisch looked down at him with a perplexed expression, but pulled over to the side of the highway and stopped.

From here Zepp could see the sprawling city clearly. The enclaves were distinct sections of dark, square blocks, some standing alone, some bordering closely with others along common walls. In the center of the city, the massive pile of the Hall of the Seedkeepers dominated everything. Zepp studied the organized chaos below him. It was a rare opportunity to apprehend all of his world in a single view.

As he watched, a strange drama began to unfold above the city. A cloud of small, dark shapes rose up from one of the smaller enclaves. Zepp recognized the source of the cloud as the Ravina enclave – the

Ravina, a clan of ancient heritage, had been dwindling in numbers for many years as their gene pool deteriorated.

The shapes – which Zepp now made out to be winged halflings – drifted over the city to the Red Monkey enclave, the largest in Suridash, which bordered the Ravina.

Then little balls of smoke began to rise up out of the Red Monkey workshops and factories, like untethered balloons in the still, afternoon air. A few seconds later, the dull thud of distant explosions echoed across the rooftops of the city.

"What's that?" asked Snomisch.

"It looks like the Ravina are raiding the Red Monkeys," Zepp answered. "Where did they get all those winged halflings?"

Snomisch squinted into the distance, but said nothing. Zepp continued to watch with fascination as the battle developed. Winged halflings were not a common sight in Suridash. The few flying creatures that appeared each year migrated to the south in the spring, returning to their genetic homelands around the rim of the great Arkarian dustbowl.

The Ravina must have been gathering these for a long time in preparation for the attack. Soon the Red Monkeys began to defend themselves, and long feathery streams of water filled the sky along the common enclave wall.

The Red Monkeys had the best fire department in the city and now their fire hoses were being used as anti-air defenses. As the fire brigades swept the halflings from the sky, the dark swarm began to disperse.

Some of the halflings returned to the Ravina enclave, dropping their bombs on their masters, while others scattered to the four winds, taking advantage of their new-found freedom. One small shape seemed not to move at all, but grew larger and larger as Zepp watched. A minute later, he could make out the straining wings, the fat belly, the look of terror on the face of the halfling that flew towards him and Snomisch.

The poor creature was beating the hot air furiously with his wings, trying to get over the low hills where they had stopped. As it passed overhead, almost directly above the electric cart, it released the heavy load of explosives. The bomb went off only a few meters away with a horrible, bone-jarring, "KA-BOOM!!"

Zepp yelped, and Snomisch jumped as rocks and dirt rained down all around them, littering the inside of car and bouncing off Zepp's head. The halfling flew away towards the sea.

Zepp quickly scanned the skies to see if any of the flier's companions were following in his path. It looked clear.

"Come on," he said. "Let's get out of here."

Snomisch just blinked as he started up the car and raced over the top of the hill and away from the city.

The attack by the halflings was not unusual for Suridash's uneasy neighbors. Considering the number of different breeds, cultures, taboos, and tribes, it was not surprising that open conflict broke out often between them. The surprise was that so many different kinds of chamalian beast were able to live together in a single city at all.

As they drove on down the far side of the hill, Zepp's nerves still jangled and his ears still rang from the explosion.

He had just received the latest installment of a lesson that all the creatures of his world began at an early age: first, that life on Chamal was filled with countless hazards, and second, that any one of them could be aimed at him.

CHAPTER TWO

Elger Carlonzia, the Rikabarian trade counsel, sat alone in his office awaiting the agent from Suridash. The office was a metal shed unbroken by inner walls, its windows taped up with cardboard. It was illuminated by a dim fluorescent strip along the rear wall. It was hardly brighter than moonlight, but it was light enough for the nocturnal bureaucrat to clean his pistol.

His thick, gray fur fluffed out beneath a sky-blue, short-sleeved uniform and a bushy, ringed tail poked out the back of his shorts. A mask of dark fur covered large eyes in a face marked by sharp, triangular ears and a sharp angular snout.

Carlonzia did not like this post. The dry air made his fur stiff and brittle and his skin itch and flake. But he was a loyal Vegetarian and this was a political assignment — the kind of job you couldn't refuse. At least it was better than his last station, deep in the torrid rainforest south of his home in Rikabar. And in the service of his ambition, he was willing to put aside any longing for the dark shadows of the cool, thick forests of his homeland.

A refrigeration unit behind the desk, among the crates and boxes and clutter, made life almost bearable. If it were only more reliable. But every few minutes, the compressor motor would strain to turn over, emitting a loud hum until a reset switch turned it off. Then it would start up again, repeating the process until he kicked it to get it going.

He had pilfered it from a food ship that had called on the Tradetown a few months ago. In fact, he had stolen or misappropriated almost the entire contents of the shed. When he arrived at the settlement, all Carlonzia possessed was a bag full of uniforms and a political appointment. Everything else he scavenged during forays in the night — from the packing crate he used for a desk up to the shed itself.

It was only proper. The Rikabarians were the world's greatest thieves. For generations their vessels had raided the long southern littoral of the chamalian ocean, plundering and looting without challenge. In more recent years their larceny had extended to the conquest of the vast, fertile grain lands behind that shoreline by potent mechanized armies. It was only natural that the trade counsel be a master thief himself.

Rikabar sat at the opposite end of the ocean from Suridash. It was a land of low hills, thick forests, and shallow bays. Its great cities had grown up along the shoreline as fishermen became sailors and sailors became raiders and raiders became traders. Now it was the world's greatest — and only — ocean-going power on Chamal's one landlocked ocean.

The impulse to empire had come only in the last twenty years, when the Vegetarian Party came to power in the homelands and began implementing its radical social policies.

Carlonzia's life and career had been linked to them almost from his birth. The Vegetarians — otherwise known as the Royal Onion Party — had a simple, straightforward goal for Rikabarian society. They wanted to eliminate all predatory traits from the gene-pool. When Carlonzia was just a pup, the inspections began.

By the time he'd grown into a halfling, the party had begun to neuter all the young who showed evidence of predatory or carnivorous tendencies. He passed his own tests, but just barely, and in turn, he became a zealous member of the Onion Youth and began to watch his younger cousins and neighbors for unhealthy, un-Vegetarian activities. Just after he reached adulthood, he blew the whistle on a ring of local meatleggers, making a grand impression on the local party apparatus and launching his tenure as a full-time party official.

But Rikabar was not as successful as its sons. The party program was an effective one, but the problem was that it was too effective.

After only a few years the percentage of predators in the population had declined, but the population itself had doubled. Without the predators, all the gentler breeds of the Rikabarian woodlands could breed without limit. And breed they did. It soon became impossible to process the growing hordes of young pups and the Vegetarians resorted to a simpler tactic — outright elimination of the offending creatures. It was distasteful, but necessary, the party leaders insisted, if a new age was to be forged.

Carlonzia was not quick to rush to the front of this new wave of Vegetarianism, but he did his part, organizing inspection teams in the crowded villages of rural Rikabar. This new program proved to be even more efficient and effective than the original one. Within a few more years, the population had quadrupled.

Conditions worsened. As the cities exploded with hungry, wailing mouths, the demand for food rose sharply. Bargaining with the rich grain lands to the east did not work out well. The Rikabarians were too desperate and the rulers of the grain-producing lands, typical chamalians all, had no interest in the welfare of their neighbors.

But the Vegetarians were not discouraged. What they could not purchase, they stole. For five years now, their armored and mechanized armies had swept the coastal breadbasket, invading from the desert to the south, devastating the cities and shipping the grain back home to the voracious masses.

Carlonzia, exercising the better part of valor, took up a post in the foreign ministry that put him far from the fighting.

The propaganda magazines that littered his desk were full of bright color photographs of the triumphant armies marching through conquered cities, loyal Vegetarians waving from their tanks, and ungrateful foreigners receiving their proper rewards. That was the closest he wanted to get to war.

Carlonzia was no fool. Despite his loyalty to the party and to Vegetarian principles, he knew that things could not go on like this much longer. He was beginning to realize what the Seedkeepers could have told him immediately — the chamalian gene-strain never forgets a trait.

That was the secret of its survival. Eliminating a trait was impossible. Chamalians were more resilient than that. It would continue, hidden in the inner depths of the seed, returning each year, never to be eradicated. The sheer numbers of newly born litters made the weeding-out process more and more difficult each year. It wouldn't be long before the whole mess came crashing down around the heads of the Vegetarians.

Until then, Carlonzia was going to carry out his duties here beyond the empire, staying as far from the homelands as possible to avoid the crash when it came.

He finished cleaning his pistol, slipped the clip of bullets back into the grip and set it on the table.

Where was that barbarian?

It was bad enough that he had to rise early to accommodate the fools from Suridash who were frightened by their own shadows and by the equally foolish curfew his nervous cohorts imposed on the natives from the city.

Now their agent was late on top of it.

And why were the Suridash Elders so reluctant to reveal the topic of the meeting? They obviously weren't peddling radishes. That meant something sensitive — either to Rikabar or to Suridash. Probably something impossible, which would make this all a waste of time.

Perhaps the empire would last long enough to send its armies this far east, conquering Suridash and sending Carlonzia on another posting. He couldn't see what value this desiccated old city would be to Rikabar, but it was a comforting thought.

* * *

Zepp could see the Tradetown from several leagues away and the brackish blue sea beyond it. The sight of such a wide expanse of water gave Zepp an uncomfortable feeling, as if he might slide off the road into it if they didn't keep careful control of the car.

A Rikabarian steamship was anchored in the harbor and another was just slipping over the horizon. A cloud of dust and smoke hung over the settlement.

The long, narrow sea that led out to the ocean had shielded Suridash from Rikabar's sea raiders for untold ages. It was too far across storm-tossed waters to interest sailors in square-riggers. But when steam was put to powering ships strong enough to weather the storms, the traders preceded the raiders to Suridash.

For eight years they had been coming, building and trading, and the settlement had been growing steadily. And for eight years, the

Seedkeepers had been eyeing the gene-strains from the west covetously, waiting for the proper time to bargain.

The Rikabarians were a secretive lot. Little was known about them in Suridash — aside from their ambitious eugenics policies and their voracious foreign adventures. And swapping genes was a sensitive subject anywhere on Chamal. Or so Tedrak had told Zepp when preparing him for his mission.

As a result, Tedrak told him, the Seedkeepers, in concert with Council of Elders, were approaching the Rikabarians in a cautious and time-honored manner. They were sending a young and inconsequential envoy to broach the subject — namely Zepp.

This method lowered the risks for the city considerably. The Rikabarians would hardly take offense at the entire city of Suridash for the suggestions of a single, ill-advised youth. At worst, Suridash could lose its envoy, but the delicate relations between the city and the empire would not be damaged.

This was not at all reassuring to Zepp.

"That is why we are sending a bodyguard along with you," Tedrak had told. "Remember the words of Jobe, 'Expect the unexpected, you won't be disappointed.'"

Tedrak had given him much advice. "Be polite. Don't press your case. We just want to know how they feel about the idea. Even if they refuse to talk about it, you have accomplished something. If you come back at all, it's a good sign."

Zepp almost choked at that last comment.

"And in order to make the most of this opportunity there is something else you must do," Tedrak told him.

Zepp trembled as he prepared to receive the orders.

"We know little about the Rikabarians. Anything you can see or uncover or pick up will be helpful to us. If you get the chance you must bring us anything that could be useful to us. Messages, shipping lists, notices, records, books, any important papers — anything you can easily get your hands on. Do you understand?"

"Yes, sir," Zepp croaked.

"Good, good. Don't forget this. What you bring back may worth much more than trading for a few foreign halflings. That is the only reason we are letting the Seedkeepers send you. You aren't frightened, are you?"

Zepp shook his head, unable to lie to the elder out loud. "Good. No need to be. The Rikabarians respect a good thief. It's always good to put one over on them. They deserve it," Tedrak said with obvious good spirits. "Just don't get caught."

"Why me?" Zepp asked himself as they approached the edge of the settlement. It must have had something to do with that strange inspection when Tedrak looked at everyone's teeth, but Zepp had no idea what that had been for and no one had bothered to tell him.

He soon found out.

The Tradetown was surrounded by a thick ring of hedgewire, a tangled mass of jagged metal eight hands high and eight hands deep — thick enough to discourage the bravest desert bandits. The road led to a sharp break in the fence manned by lazy-looking guards in a wooden shack and protected by a steel gate and an abundance of automatic weapons, which poked their snouts out of earthen bunkers.

Snomisch stopped the cart in front of the shack, and Zepp prepared the entry visas Tedrak's assistant had given him.

A highly unofficial-looking official came out of the shack and walked up to them. A straw hat shaded his head from the sun, and he wore a pair of ragged shorts with shoulder straps. His face was broad and flat with a fringe of yellow beard at the chin. Two horns poked through the hat and curled sway from his head, and his legs were covered with thick, curly fur and ended in black, cloven hooves.

"Out of the car," he ordered as he took Zepp's paperwork.

Zepp and Snomisch climbed out of the cart and stood nervously in the hot sun. The official inspected the visas, then he began inspecting Zepp and Snomisch.

He spread Zepp's fingers, twisted his hand roughly around, then produced a small ruler, which he used to measure Zepp's fingernails.

"Open your mouth," he said.

Zepp hesitated, then did as he was told. The goatish inspector tipped his head from side to side as he stared at Zepp's eyeteeth. Then he stuck his dirty fingers into Zepp's mouth and prodded the bicuspids. He pushed up on Zepp's lips and pulled out his small ruler again.

He repeated the process with Snomisch.

"What was all that about, anyway?" Zepp asked timidly.

"Predator check," the goat replied. "Were civilized over here, you know. Can't let just anybody into town."

Zepp was suddenly glad that he had resisted the temptation to bite down hard on the official's fingers when he had the chance.

He finished with Snomisch, wrote something on their forms, and returned to the shack. A moment later, he returned, a grubby, unwashed halfling at his side.

"Go ahead," he told them. "Here's your guide. You can find your own way back to the gate. Don't stick your nose where you don't belong."

The gate opened, and Snomisch rolled the cart into the town.

The goat-faced official called to them as they drove off, "And remember, your visa expires at sunset — if you're still in town after dark, it'll be ba-a-ad news."

* * *

Zepp waited outside the Rikabarian trade counsel's shed, trying to steel his nerves for the meeting. Unfortunately, the longer he waited, the more anxious he got.

After five minutes of sitting in the dusty street, watching oversized trucks loaded with Rikabarian merchandise roll by, Snomisch broke the silence. "Aren't we going in?" he asked innocently.

Zepp broke out of his self-interested fog. "Huh? Oh yeah, we're going in. In a minute."

But another five minutes passed before Zepp finally got up the courage to climb out of the cart and approach the door. He stepped into the building, Snomisch following him closely. A strong spring slammed it shut behind them, plunging the interior into darkness and startling Zepp. He panicked at first, his hearts squeezed tightly and breathing became difficult, but nothing happened to him and after a moment he became aware of the cool air circulating around the room — an unexpected relief from the afternoon heat.

As his eyes adjusted to the darkness, he could make out the luminous green bar across the back of the room — and a large shadow moving in front of it. A machine of some kind was humming in the corner. Zepp addressed the shadow with a tentative voice: "Hello?"

Suddenly a light came on — a bare, round bulb that shined harshly in Zepp's eyes while a metal shade shielded the figure behind it. The shadow disappeared, but a voice issued from behind the light where Zepp had seen it last.

"One of you must be the agent from Suridash — which one?"

"I am, sir," Zepp replied. "This is my bodyguard — for the ride across the desert."

The Rikabarian harrumphed incredulously.

"So you trust us as much as we trust you. Well, let's get down to business. I do not enjoy negotiating at this hour of the day, and I would rather not waste words. Tell me what your city wants from us, and I'll tell you if we can make a bargain."

Zepp was not used to directness like this and it took him a while to collect his thoughts. "Actually it's not the city of Suridash," he said, "but the Seedkeepers who have sent me here. It's a very delicate matter, sir — not so much for us, but maybe for you — so please understand why it's difficult for me to explain. Do you have any knowledge of the Seedkeepers or their mission?"

"I don't have the time or the interest to explore barbarian superstitions, but it appears you are about to enlighten me, so be quick about it."

Zepp's mouth was dry and his tail twitched nervously about. There was no place to sit so he remained standing and tried to relax. He held up his hand to shield his eyes from the light and saw the dim shape of the Rikabarian seated behind his desk.

"You see, sir, the Seedkeepers were charged many generations ago with gathering the seed of the gods together. In order to do this, they have culled the seed from the halflings, steplings and pups that less-advanced races have discarded and banished in the past. Our great Hall of the Seedkeepers is filled with many of these lesser breeds, which we study carefully to be sure they have not missed a single strain of God's Seed."

"I understand," the Rikabarian interrupted. "A breeding program. What has this got to do with us?"

"Well, sir, the seed of the gods has been scattered far and wide. We have gone to great lengths to bring together strains from many parts of the world. But we regret the lack of the fruits of Rikabar. The Seedkeepers would be grateful if you could help them to repair that lack. Perhaps even with that surplus of predators that you find inconvenient. In return, they offer the use of their stock to help you with your own design for the Rikabarian races."

Zepp was unsure at first if the Rikabarian realized he was finished. He looked over the counsel's desk, recalling now that his mission was twofold. Whet was there to pilfer and return to Tedrak? And how could he do it? In the darkness, with the light in his eyes, he couldn't see much of anything in front of him.

Then he noticed trade counsel's breathing, forced and heavy, like a fighter working up to a rage.

"You want us to take part in your breeding program?" he demanded in a frighteningly loud voice.

"Yes, sir," Zepp responded meekly.

"Do you realize what you are suggesting?" he asked. "Do you realize that it is inferior races like yours who submit to our program, and not the other way around?"

Zepp could sense that he had risen to his feet, though it hardly seemed to make him any taller.

"Do you really think we would allow you to cart off our predatory scum to breed as spies and assassins against us? Do you really believe we would accept your tainted beasts as Rikabarian breeding stock?" His voice grew louder with each question, and Zepp realized he was not expected answer.

He also realized that the first part of his mission had failed.

"Out, little diplomat!" Carlonzia ordered angrily. "Get out now, and be glad you are taking your life with you. The Rikabarian Empire does not take insults such as this lightly. Tell your masters that the next envoy who suggests this abomination to us will not be so lucky as you."

Zepp squirmed where he stood, afraid to move. Snomisch took the cue to depart, however, and pulled open the spring-loaded door. The room filled with bright sunlight and a blast of hot air brushed past Zepp's fur.

He was about to turn and go himself when he recalled once more the second part of his mission. In his fear, he had almost left without fulfilling it. A double failure would be too much to bear. He looked back at the trade counsel's desk.

The trade counsel was still behind it, but his arms were up across his face, shielding his eyes from the bright daylight. Across the desk Zepp saw a scattered pile of papers, some colorful magazines, and an automatic pistol.

While Snomisch held the door open, Zepp rushed forward, grabbed the loot — pistol included — and ran. The door slammed shut behind them and they jumped into the cart. Snomisch switched it on and hurried to the gate. They narrowly missed running down five halflings and a slow-moving Rikabarian mechanic on the way out of town, but there was no pursuit.

* * *

Carlonzia settled down after giving his air conditioner another kick to get it started. It was a few minutes before he noticed the thievery of the pup from Suridash. At first he was angry. He considered telephoning the main gate – as if the tradetown had such equipment. But the settlement was too primitive an outpost with too little need to communicate to bother with phones.

Instead, he went to one of the crates behind his desk, pried off the top, reached inside and pulled out another pistol, identical to the first — the crate was full of them. As he began to strip and clean it a wry smile broke across his face, a toothy grin usually kept hidden from party cohorts.

If there wasn't honor among thieves on Chamal, at least there was an uneasy truce.

* * *

Snomisch didn't slow down until the Rikabarian settlement was out of sight behind him. Zepp's hearts squeezed furiously and his arms and legs tingled from the bouncing and jouncing of the cart on the road.

They finally slowed to a stop and watched the thick clouds of dust drift away behind them. Zepp stood on the seat, peering into the distance, looking for pursuers. Only when he was sure there were none did he examine his loot.

The pistol was heavy and gray with a plastic handgrip and a full clip of bullets. He aimed it at a rock on the side of the road and squeezed the trigger. The pistol cracked and bucked, and a puff of dust appeared eighty-eight hands east of the rock where the bullet fell. He shrugged at Snomisch, apologizing for his poor marksmanship, and slipped the weapon into his vest.

The papers were government forms and letters, written in intricate Rikabarian script that held no meaning for Zepp. He would leave it up to the experts of the Council of Elders to interpret them.

The propaganda magazines held the greatest interest for him. While the words were indecipherable, the color photographs fascinated Zepp — he had never seen anything like them in Suridash. He leafed through them slowly, inspecting the close-up shots of the armored fighting vehicles with their grinning crews, the long vistas of desert horizons overshadowed by towering clouds of black smoke, and the provocative photos of unclad females yielding to the conquering soldiers of Rikabar.

He lingered over one scene of carnage that struck a chord deep within him — a family of small, green apes huddled, eyes wide with fear, by the smoldering wreckage of their home.

After staring at the page for a while, he put the magazine aside. The sun was moving quickly towards the horizon. Twilight didn't last long in the desert and a drive through the night — even for the short time it would take to get home — was not an inviting prospect.

"Let's get going," he said to Snomisch.

The sky turned orange as they drove along, then quickly ran through red and violet into black. The stars came out, burning with harsh intensity. The dark did little to hold the desert heat and a chill wind began to nip at Zepp around the edge of the windshield.

They were still several leagues from Suridash when Snomisch startled Zepp by grabbing his arm.

"I have to stop the car," he said. "I think I see something out there."

"What is it? Bandits?" Zepp didn't want to stop for anything until whey were safely behind the walls of the city.

"Not bandits." Snomisch pulled back on the simple electric throttle and the cart hummed to a stop. The driving lights – mounted on posts on either side of the instrument panel – cut through the gloom before them, but night wrapped around them like a blanket everywhere else. Zepp grabbed one and swung it in an arc across the emptiness to either side of the road, but there was nothing to be seen.

Snomisch climbed out of the car and urged Zepp to follow him.

"Over here," he said.

Zepp followed reluctantly. "What's going on, Snomisch? What do you want."

They walked along the roadside in front of the car, just to the edge of the area illuminated by the driving lights. "Over there," Snomisch said, pointing a shaggy hand at the ditch beside the highway. "See?"

Zepp preceded his bodyguard cautiously, still bewildered by his strange behaviors "I still don't understand," he said.

Behind him, Zepp heard the slinking sound of metal on metal, but it took him a moment to identify it as the noise of a sword being drawn from its scabbard. A wave of fear swept over him.

He began to turn around as the horrible hiss of steel slashing through the air met his ears. He looked up in time to see Snomisch bring his sword down towards Zepp's shoulders. With a surprising burst of energy, he threw himself to the ground and the sword passed harmlessly over his head.

He wasted no time asking foolish questions. Snomisch was obviously trying to kill him.

He moved more quickly than he ever had in his life, running off the road and into the darkness. His body was twisted by an instinctual fear reaction — his lips pulled back to reveal his teeth, his shoulders hunched, his head ducked down, and his arms folded above it. He hadn't gone more than a few hands when Snomisch began shooting at him with his Red Monkey pistol. The bullets whizzed by him in the dark and ricocheted loudly in the distance.

Suddenly a dark shape loomed out of the desert before him — a rock outcrop a eight hands high. He clambered up the steep slope and scrambled right over the top without slowing down as Snomisch's bullets struck the ground at his heels.

There was a moment of silence broken only by the peeping of fur-coated frogs out on the salt flats near the sea,

"Hey, Zepp," Snomisch called. "Come on out. I have to kill you now."

Zepp peeked around the edge of the rock and saw Snomisch standing in the light in front of the car.

"But why? What for? What did I do?"

"You ain't done nothing," Snomisch replied. "I just have to kill you. It ain't your fault. The general told me to do it."

"Sheverek?"

"That's right. He's afraid of you, Zepp. He don't like you at all. So he told me to kill you on the way back to Suridash. Why don't you come out so I can kill you and we can get back to the city?"

Fear gripped Zepp like a wire-snare. What was he going to do? He couldn't stay there all night. The shooting was bound to attract bandits quickly and the cold night air sapped the warmth from his body. His hearts squeezed tightly, his lungs labored heavily, and his vest bumped against his ribs.

But there was more than the vest bumping his ribcage. He thrust his hand into his pocket and came out with the trade counsel's pistol.

"Snomisch!" he yelled. "You can't kill me tonight."

"Why not?" he asked.

"Because I still have the Rikabarian's gun."

That gave Snomisch something to think about — and since thinking was not his strongest strait, he was stymied.

"I don't know. Sheverek won't be happy about it."

"Come on, Snomisch. I don't want to shoot you. Put your weapons down in the road in front of the car and step back from them."

"Are you sure you got the gun?"

Zepp fired once into the air as proof and Snomisch complied with the orders slowly. He stood there docilely as Zepp picked his way back to the road, gathered up Snomisch's arsenal, and dumped it in the back of the cart. He slid into the cart, then ordered Snomisch in beside him.

"Don't try anything, Sno. I still don't want to hurt you."

"It's all right, Zepp. I won't," he said. "But the general's going to be mad at me."

"I'm sorry, but there's not much I can do about that."

"And I'll bet he tells me to try it again."

Zepp thought about that for a moment as he switched the cart on and started it rolling along the gravel road.

"What are you going to do about it?" Snomisch asked.

"I don't know, Sno," Zepp said unhappily. "But I guess I'm going to have to do something."

CHAPTER THREE

Master Tedrak, representative on the Council of Elders of Suridash for the tribe of Jobe, waited alone in his chambers for the arrival of his assistant, Whirlpitt, and contemplated the end of the world.

It was a practice in which he frequently indulged — the contemplation, not the waiting —having long ago taken upon himself the responsibility for the fate of his city. It was a powerful position and a frightening responsibility and Tedrak hardly looked capable of the task.

He was short and rotund, with shoulders that merged with his head without the benefit of a neck — sure evidence of eating well for many years. From the chamalian genetic grab-bag, he had drawn the form of a burrowing creature with short, stubby arms, curved claws, and a bad case of myopia, which the spectacles perched on his broad muzzle only partially relieved.

He kept his chambers in a modest, subterranean vault with an arching ceiling and tiny windows high overhead to let in a smidgen of daylight. His desk was cluttered with documents of state, reports, unanswered dispatches, and a brass incense burner smeared with gray charcoal. The walls were jammed with maps of Suridash's neighbors, and a copper plate with the likeness of Jobe hung behind his desk. A bookcase jammed with scrolls and handbound volumes filled the curving wall between two doorways at opposite ends of the room.

If this were almost anywhere else but Suridash it would be a dank, damp place to do business — at least he was spared that. The climate made the office pleasantly cool, a refuge from the sun-baked streets above. It was also quiet, offering no distractions from the weighty reflections pursued by Tedrak this afternoon.

In the past, when wondering over the possibility of world apocalypse, Tedrak was concerned by a number of dangerous trends in chamalian civilization. In his lifetime, he had seen his world grow smaller and smaller as technology made contact between its disparate races easier and easier. And at the same time he had seen the world grow increasingly dangerous as weapons of war and destruction became more and more powerful.

It grew worse each year as chamalian science progressed with its usual fits and leaps of inspiration and insight. Every day some young genius blew himself apart tampering with new and more dangerous chemistries.

This technological progress was a perilous new ingredient in the old concoction of Chamal's world politics. The social order on Tedrak's world had never been very sturdy or resilient. No society can be better than its people and the people of Chamal suffered from moral burdens beyond all reasonability. From the very smallest social unit up to the very largest, Chamal was cursed. There could be little family stability among a race where the offspring had only half a chance of resembling their parents and where a dominant form could vanish in a few generations. There could be few great, persistent dynasties on such a world — the Red Monkeys notwithstanding. Great states could not endure the onslaught of internal disorder and external hostility for long.

The social history of Chamal resembled nothing so much as the natural history of the swamps and bogs from which life on the planet had evolved — but with one fatal difference. Nature had nothing in it like the self-destructive fury of a race tortured by its own perverse biology. There was present in chamalian society a nihilistic force that had its roots in the sufferings of wisdom that could never sever itself from its ties to the wild and that was forever being submerged in its primitive, feral beginnings.

Added to that was the unyielding competition between different social norms — mutually opposed, mutually exclusive, and mutually destructive social norms — erected by all the self-important and self-deluded breeds of Chamal. Put simply, Chamal was not an easy place to live.

The constellation of great powers surrounding Suridash presented the immediate threat — a potent one for the small city. Although it was isolated by the desert to the south and southwest, the sea to the northwest, and the volcanic uplands to the east, Tedrak's city was situated in the midst of Chamal's most powerful societies.

The Empire of the Royal Onion, Rikabar, had made surprising gains in territory as its armies swept across the deserts to the west — and Tedrak was worried that before long their armored fighting vehicles and warships would be converging on Suridash itself.

Far away to the south, the trading cities of Meshkar, situated in the mountains ringing the high inland sea, tightened its mercantile grip on the kingdoms below, spreading its rule slowly but inexorably throughout the tropical belt.

Off to the northwest, in the Great Rift Valley, the Blue Monkeys were busy consolidating their rule over the other rifters. They still bore resentment towards Suridash for harboring the last of the Red Monkeys, who had once been masters of the entire rift. They also lived in fear that the Red Monkeys would return to the rift and depose the usurpers.

And to the east, Shipar, the land of towering volcanoes thirty leagues high, traded missiles with their rival highlanders from Kwikorak — whose volcanic ridge straddled the equator further east — and from time to time one would overshoot its target and land near Suridash, eliciting loud complaints from the citizenry.

The prospects for the future were not good. The arsenals of each of these great powers were growing daily and in recent years more and more terrible weapons had been developed — deathrays, energy beams, bigger and bigger rockets.

Several of these great states had even achieved space flight.

Now their weapons could be deployed in orbit around the planet to rain down destruction anywhere on the surface they desired.

It was true that chamalians had learned to live together here in Suridash — but that was the result of centuries of adaptation and accommodation. Tedrak had no illusions about the ability of the other races of his world to develop the necessary social skills, diplomatic tact, and will to compromise that preserved a modicum of order in Suridash. Not before it was too late. The natural greed, intolerance, paranoia, and ambition of chamalians wedded to the awful technologies of destruction they were cultivating could only lead to disaster.

But within the last few days, something had happened that set Tedrak's mind spinning, taking him from the depths of despair to higher and higher plateaus of hope and optimism about the fate of his world. Something had happened that had the potential for world-shattering change, diverting Chamal from its headlong plunge towards armageddon and forcing it to come to terms with itself at last.

The angels were coming ...

42

He had heard the truth for himself yesterday, after climbing the stairs with Whirlpitt to a misshapen tower adjoining the Hall of the Seedkeepers to meet with one who knew.

On the outside, the tower was a tilting pile of sun-bleached stone with an odd peak at the top and a few narrow, barred windows to let in light and air. On the inside, it was a sweltering ordeal for Master Tedrak. His legs were not well-built for climbing stairways and his bulk made any such effort a true labor. He usually enjoyed traveling about the city, seeing things firsthand — but this was taking things to extremes.

"Tell me once more — huff, huff — why must visit him —huff, huff — and not the other way around?" Tedrak asked as they rounded the landing.

Whirlpitt hissed and paused to let his master catch his breath. Hissing was the closest Tedrak's assistant ever came to laughter. He was a humorless sort, lacking any kind of sentiment — quite unchamalian in his way. Whirlpitt possessed a long, slender body, coated with sleek, black fur. His head perched atop a long, sinuous neck, his mouth was wide, his lips narrow, and his eyes normally rested half-shut in feigned disinterest.

Unlike his master, who was a pedigreed member of the tribe of Jobe, Whirlpitt had been spawned in the rubble of the tumbledown ruins of Suridash's interstitial slums. The relentless wisdom that burned in his brain had been slumbering in some matriarchal line of the scavengers who dwelled there, competing with halflings for food and living space. That wisdom had carried him far, always in search of power, power to manipulate and control.

Tedrak trusted him, but not without limits. He suspected that Whirlpitt's ambition was to make a place for himself on the Council of Elders or to someday travel to the commercial cities of Meshkar, where his manipulations could result in much greater rewards. Tedrak hoped it was the latter. It would make for fewer ill feelings between them when the time of decision came round. Whirlpitt was a valuable asset — one Tedrak didn't want to lose.

"He thinks it is out of deference, but it is for our own good," Whirlpitt said. "It is not safe for us to let him out of his cage. We would lose him too easily. He has no spies — he needs none, of course — but his agents are absolutely loyal."

"You would be, too," Tedrak said with a laugh, "if someone knew all your secrets. Blackmail is the oldest profession, you know."

Whirlpitt hissed again and nodded knowingly. Overhead was the home of one of Chamal's wild sports, a creature who claimed he had psychic powers, that he was a clairvoyant who still retained a measure of sanity in spite of his strange talent. He had long been a prisoner and a servant of the Council of Elders, often playing off one member against another, but usually employed in affairs of state, a master spy over all of Chamal.

He was another asset too valuable to lose.

Whirlpitt explained the procedure as they passed through a double set of locked doors, each with its own jailers. "He can always get a string on the guards beyond these doors. But the lower set of jailers is beyond his reach. They stagger the watch, so the two sets never mix. And of course, there are all those below here," he added, glancing towards the massive complex of the Seedkeepers and the smaller civic buildings of Suridash where guards, soldiers, and armsmen lingered in abundance.

Tedrak was always surprised by the luxury that greeted him within the tower chambers. Plush carpets covered the floor, bright tapestries hung from the walls, a mechanical fan swung overhead, creating a comforting draft, and soft, well-stuffed leather chairs faced a fireplace where cold ashes lay.

Seated in one of the chairs, a glossy photograph in one hand, was the wild one himself, Tezar the Psychic, snoring loudly through an open mouth. Tedrak laughed heartily at the sight.

Tezar snorted and his eyes blinked open in surprise. "Oh yes," he said. "It's you. I was expecting you, of course. I must have nodded off."

"Don't try to fool us, Tezar," Whirlpitt countered. "We caught you by surprise. We know you have no vision of the future. Your powers lie elsewhere."

"While it's true I cannot foresee the future, it doesn't take a soothsayer to realize that you two would he up here in my little castle before too long."

Tezar was an elderly beast: his large curling ears and long pointed snout revealed a mongrel ancestry. His chin whiskers were turning white at the roots, and wide, dark pupils gleamed out of yellowing eyes at the two visitors.

"You look comfortable enough," Tedrak said. "Most of those who dwell behind bars in the city center do not live as well as this."

"Most are not as potent a force as I am," Tezar said. "I prefer to think of you as my protectors, not my jailers. And judging from this –" he waved the photograph at them, "— I need protecting."

Whirlpitt snatched the photo away from him. "You mean it's true?" he snapped.

"Most assuredly," Tezar answered. "This is a picture of the alien vessel itself. You've seen the chemical rockets of the rift and the highlanders? Well, this rocket burns with the fire of the sun, like a star burning out there in space. It is an omen of great changes."

Tedrak smacked a fist into the palm of his hand. "Then the telepaths weren't just swapping nightmares?"

"No , Master Tedrak. This truly is the coming of the angels."

"Spare us your fables, you superstitious old faker," Whirlpitt said. "What are these creatures? Where are they from? What are they doing here? We need answers to important questions. Facts and information. If we want more ravings we'll go back to the telepaths."

"You will not. They're all fakes and most of them are mad and you know it. You'll never get a straight answer out of any of them. You'll hear it all from me and wish you hadn't. This could mean the end of the world — for all of us."

Whirlpitt and Tedrak were silenced by that. They sat down in front of the cold hearth facing Tezar and waited for him to reveal what he knew.

Tezar sank back wearily into his chair, rubbed his bleary eyes, flipped back a loose ear in order to listen more closely to questions and let the whole frightening story spill out.

"This is a picture of a high-energy radiation source taken by an observatory on a volcano in Shipar. It is two weeks old, delivered into our hands by methods which we all know well.

"At the same time as this print was being made, telepaths around the globe began to grow agitated, raving in their pens, disturbed by some source of alien wisdom that they all described as the angels. At first it was feared that some form of common madness had infected the lot of them, but upon further questioning we learned that the angels were approaching from that part of the sky known as the Tarpit."

"Which was the precise location of the strange radiation source, of course," Whirlpitt interjected. "We already know that, old one."

Tezar glared at the sleek-furred beast but pressed on with his report. "I have used the photo to focus my talents on this visitation. It is indeed a spacecraft — a vessel much like those used by the Rifters or Rikabar, but much larger — more on the order of a seagoing vessel. And it is just under a billion leagues away, just as the highland astronomers claim — that is how they knew it could not be a star.

"But what is frightening to me — and to all who know the awful truth — is the nature of the beast that drives this spaceship," Tezar said with a shudder.

"Their power is so far beyond ours that we all look like savage halflings in comparison. Do you know where these creatures were before they appeared in our sky two weeks ago?" he asked.

Tedrak and Whirlpitt had no reply save their blank, questioning faces.

"They were in the sky of their own world an unimaginable distance away — off among the stars somewhere. They have the power to leap the huge gaps between the stars in the blinking of the eye. It would take another generation of Red Monkeys for us to match that kind of science. And they have weapons and defenses whose nature I cannot even begin to explain."

Whirlpitt snorted. "Someone with a club can kill someone with a musket if the conditions are right," he said. "And this vessel has come alone."

"But the most frightening thing about them is not a material possession," Tezar responded. "It is not their science, nor their machinery that we must fear. No, my cousins, the greatest threat to us comes from within these angels — from their seed!"

"Their seed?" Tedrak asked, squinting at the aged psychic.

"That's what I said. Their seed! The reason the telepaths think they are angels is because they are – they are purebred!"

That image gripped Tedrak in his guts and brought a tingle to his skin. "Are you certain?"

Tezar' s eyes were on fire. "Yes, yes. I do not lie. These creatures are as alike as beans in a pod. I'd be surprised if they can tell each other apart. I wonder if they even think of themselves as individuals — that's something I'll have to look at further.

"But I know for sure that they've held the same form for countless generations. There are no others aboard their vessel who carry the seed of the gods within them. Nothing but a few creatures too small for eating in cages and a few running loose as servants or something — too small for much work, though. I think they're aboard for entertainment."

"Faith of Jobe," Tedrak muttered. "What a strange miracle!"

"Faith of Jobe, indeed," Tezar replied. "This is the original seed of the gods — the unspoiled germ."

Whirlpitt snorted, he would have none of this and he showed it. "I believe in neither miracles nor angels. This strange breed of creature may have unusual powers, but I cannot believe it has no weaknesses. Nor selfish interests."

"True enough. They once suffered in a world of pain and terror much like ours. But that was generations ago. I get the impression that their machines drove them crazy."

"Their machines?" Tedrak asked, looking up at the lazily spinning fan overhead.

"Even so, compared to us, they are indeed angels. And that is how our cousins around the world see them. As avenging angels, come to mete out the wrath of the gods. We know ourselves well, cousins. It is our curse to comprehend the depravation we all must suffer. This is why we hate one another so deeply and because of such trivial differences. Should the angels be any less discriminating? Surely, once they see us in all our moral perversion, they will want to eliminate us from the sight of the gods, won't they?"

"Perhaps," Whirlpitt said. "But only if they are as pure and without sin as you portray them to be."

"This is not how I portray them, but how our counterparts in Rikabar, Meshkar, Shipar, and Kwikorak portray them.

"At this very moment, they are preparing to meet the threat. The highlanders are re-targeting their missiles — away from each other and towards the invaders. In the rift, plans are being drafted for rocket-propelled fighters to attack them in space. Arms merchants in Meshkar are jacking up their prices on heavy weapons. And Rikabar has changed the name of the space cruiser whose keel is now in orbit to *Deragathon — The Angel Killer*. I believe they are taking the threat from the angels to be quite serious."

"Should we also take that threat seriously?" Whirlpitt asked. "Is that the mission of the angels? Have they really come all this great distance in order to annihilate a grubby race of sex perverts?"

Tezar chuckled. "No, sir, they have not. This is no race of bloody butchers or conquering warriors. Nor are they avengers concerned with our moral character. They pose no overt threat to our world. This is a vessel full of scientists and scholars."

Whirlpitt hissed at Tezar in disbelief. "Scientists? Scholars?"

"They have come to take our pictures, measure the length of our fangs, the thickness of our blood, to map our histories, and to record our philosophies. Does that surprise you?"

"No, Tezar, it angers me," Whirlpitt said. "I cannot believe this is an expedition of pedants, and I think you must be lying to me." There was a sudden tension in the space between the two strong-willed creatures.

"No lie. This is also the truth. Perhaps you do not accept it because you have never taken pleasure in knowledge for its own sake. You have never felt the joy of casting your net out into the great world simply to marvel at the treasures it brings in. Or of overlooking the city in the dark of night, knowing all the little details of life that lurk behind sputtering candles in distant windows."

"To what end? Knowledge without purpose is a waste of time. Tell me, strange one — to what purpose will these angels put their knowledge? Assuming they ever get the chance to gather any."

Tezar looked sad. "As you suspect, there is a danger in their knowledge-gathering — and it is the kernel of truth in the fears of our foreign friends. It is within their power to bring an end to life on this world — if they perceive within us sufficient danger to the peace of their universe. They would do this reluctantly, and for their own self-protection, but not out of malice."

"Malicious or not, we would still be dead," Tedrak noted.

"So will we all be one day," Tezar said. "People pass away, races, breeds, tribes — nothing is permanent in this world. Why would you expect anything else? The world will end for each of us eventually, why not for all at once?"

"Because we are not all as old as you are, Tezar," Tedrak said quietly, casting cold gaze in the direction of the psychic. "We do not surrender to our fates gracefully as you seem eager to do. And we are not all so selfish that we do not wish life to continue after we are gone. Tell me, though, how could they accomplish such a thing?"

"I am not sure," Tezar said sheepishly. "But their powers are tremendous indeed. The flame that appears in the photograph is eighty-eight leagues long. If it passed over our city even once, it would leave utter devastation behind."

"They must get here, first," Whirlpitt said defiantly. But his master was not so quick to argue.

"I must think about this," he said abruptly as he rose to his feet, bringing the meeting to a close. "Send for a messenger if you discover anything new."

They left the tower apartment and began the much easier trek down the long, twisting staircase in silence. At the foot of the stairs, Tedrak stopped and faced his assistant.

"Angels!" he said. "It boggles the mind. Tell me, Whirlpitt, can you imagine a race of creatures that would be alien to us."

The subordinate shook his dark head and said, "No, sir. I confess that I cannot."

Since then, Tedrak had spent a long sleepless night, pacing the floor of his bedchamber, pondering the awesome news he had received from Tezar. At first he was struck dumb with a gnawing, mindless fear that he resented most sternly — he was not accustomed to fear and would never admit to experiencing it, even to Whirlpitt.

But towards dawn, as the pink hues of an imminent sunrise colored the eastern sky, an inspiration came upon him. When Whirlpitt entered the office of his master, he found Tedrak in amazingly high spirits — the last thing anyone would have expected.

Tedrak's smile broadened and he laughed as Whirlpitt seated himself before the desk and removed the thick wad of official-looking reports from his pouch. "Why so glum today, Whirly?" Tedrak boomed.

Whirlpitt retained his cool detachment. "The seriousness of the situation that faces us is hardly cause for joy, sir. Especially when you consider the possible consequences if we fail to act in a prudent and timely manner."

"Consequences?" Tedrak said, shaking his head disappointedly. "Tell me, Whirly, what are the consequences — even if we do nothing? What will happen to this world six months from now when the angels arrive if none of us on this whole grimy planet does a damned thing?"

"If we do nothing, in all likelihood, the angels will indeed judge us as too dangerous to be allowed to live. And upon that judgment, they will probably make a serious effort to destroy us — either piecemeal or all at once," Whirlpitt said in a cold, unfeeling voice.

Tedrak nodded, thought for a moment, then said, "And what if the angels were not coming? What then? We both know the answer to that question, don't we.?"

Whirlpitt looked confused for a moment, then replied uncertainly, "Yes, master, we both know the answer to that. Sometime in the next generation or so, we will accomplish the same result by ourselves. As long as the Meshkarian merchants continue to arm the warring rainforest kingdoms and as long as we continue to develop newer and deadlier technologies, we increase the chances of a worldwide armageddon. At the moment, the timing all depends on the fate of the Rikabarian Empire. If it remains intact for the next eight years then we will face such a crisis within sixteen years. If it collapses in the next three years as predicted, the crisis will be postponed for another sixteen years. But no matter how we figure it, a vast, genocidal war — much like the one that deposed the Red Monkeys from control of the rift, but on a larger scale — will sweep the planet. And despite all our machinations and subversions, there is little we can do to prevent this from happening."

"A pretty grim picture," Tedrak said. "But still, it is not a certainty, is it? This is all speculation, of course. Well-educated speculation, but not a certainty, correct?"

"Yes, sir," Whirlpitt admitted reluctantly. "But given the absence of any restraining impulse, the natural destructiveness of our race and the ingeniousness of our wisdom can produce no other result. Barring unforeseen events, of course. But even so, this fact cannot be hidden from the angels and that makes their threat to us even more serious."

"Unforeseen events!" Tedrak bellowed as he slammed a fat hand down on the desk. "What do you think this is?"

Whirlpitt did not reply and was not expected to.

"Couldn't these angels throw this tropical cat our world is riding off its course? Couldn't it change things in some unpredictable way?"

"Certainly," Whirlpitt said. "By accelerating events — by acting for us, destroying our world before we have the chance to."

"Couldn't it go the other way, though? Couldn't we use the angels to our advantage, to change the course we are on, to upset the fruit cart before we are all crushed by it? Can't you imagine anything we can do to avoid either of the terrible fates you have set out for us? Can't you?"

Whirlpitt was speechless. His machinelike brain raced to counter Tedrak's questions, but the contradictions were too immense to handle quickly and even Whirlpitt was unable to reply with anything but a weak-voiced, "Perhaps."

Tedrak sank back in his overstuffed chair, his brows creased above his nearly opaque bifocals. He stared at his assistant for a long, tense moment. Finally he spoke in a softer voice, with a touch of compassion.

"I'm being unfair with you, Whirlpitt," he said. "I'm sorry, it is your place to analyze, it is mine to be creative. I shouldn't expect you to anticipate my thoughts or read my mind. Let me make myself clear to you.

"What I am proposing is just a possibility right now, but we can make it a probability and, gods willing, a certainty. It is an almost inconceivable notion, I admit, but it is not impossible.

"We are facing a crisis unlike any our world has ever seen and it requires action unlike any we have ever taken. Unified action, Whirly. Not the endless antagonisms that will doom us to extinction, but cooperative, organized effort. Look at what's happening today, as we speak. Every race, every state, every tribe is going off on it own to meet the angels and save Chamal. What chance do each of these individual efforts have for success?"

"Very little," Whirlpitt said, his composure returning. "Attacking piecemeal means scattering our forces and dispersing our energies. To be effective we must concentrate all our power at once, as you are saying. But —"

"But unified action is unprecedented on our planet, isn't it? Impossible, unheard of, madness to even suggest it."

Whirlpitt began to speak, then hesitated. He let Tedrak make his point instead.

"Madness everywhere but in Suridash! Look around, here is a miracle unparalleled throughout the world. All the divergent races of our planet living together in close proximity — and they aren't even destroying each other. Oh, they try every so often, like the Ravina thing last week, but we have peace nevertheless. Do you know why? Not because of anything in our Seed — but by wisdom. By habit of thought. Through planning and organization and tolerance.

"And if we can do it, why can't the rest of this godforsaken planet try it? Considering the incentive the angels have provided, it's worth the chance. Tell me, Whirlpitt, do you think the threat from the angels is sufficient to bring all the tribes of Chamal together?"

Whirlpitt turned the question over and over in his mind, studying the angles, considering the politics involved, the obstacles and the pressures required to overcome them. After a long time, he spoke.

"I believe what you are suggesting is possible. It would mean combining all the separate efforts of Rikabar, Kwikorak, the rift and the others into a single force. We would have to bribe and blackmail and coerce half the planet. We would have to set to work today and expend every last bit of political capital Suridash has amassed over the years. And still it will probably fail. But yes, master, I believe it could be done — if the rest of the world is as frightened by these angels as we are, it could."

Tedrak smiled. "I believe so, too," he said. "And I believe we must do it."

"In that case, I am afraid I have a lot of work to do. If you will excuse me, master, I must be going," he said as he rose from his seat, then hesitated. "I have one question that is not pressing at the moment, but that will require some thought."

"Ask it."

"What happens afterward — once we have eliminated the angels? How long will our unity last after we have overcome the threat?"

Tedrak frowned at his assistant, then smiled. "What makes you so certain that we <u>can</u> overcome these creatures? Or that we should even if we could?"

CHAPTER FOUR

In **the beginning, the** fable went, the gods created the beasts of the wild and put them in the rainforest that wrapped the world. But when one of them went down to Chamal to see his work, they turned on him. He was seduced, assaulted, and raped. They spilled his seed, mixed it with their own, and spread it through swamp and bog with wicked abandon.

When he escaped, he punished them. Instead of casting them out of the garden, he condemned all chamalians to remain in their tropical Eden forever as it grew soggy and rotten with decay. And as an added curse, he gave them wisdom, so they could know how perverse and depraved they were.

There were as many fables as there were tribes of Chamal, but almost everyone knew the story of the original sin of their world and the reason for their suffering. Many even believed in it. Zepp wasn't sure.

In any event, the chamalian gods were not comforting figures who dispensed salvation, but absentee slumlords of an impure and imperfect world. And Zepp was left with no one to turn to in his despair.

Wisdom had become his curse.

For days now, Zepp had suffered almost unbearable terror, waiting for the blow to strike or the gun to fire, ending his stay in the world forever. He never went anywhere in the Hall of Seedkeepers alone and he was always looking over his shoulder at noises and shadows, alert to every potential assassin.

Now he knew how Sheverek must feel with his feverish suspicions stirring his already addled mind.

After work, Zepp trod the dusty streets of the inner city silently – keeping to the shadows lest he offer too good a target in the gathering gloom. It was a long walk from the hall to the tribe's enclave, and Zepp died a thousand deaths each night on his way home, alone, without even his gods to protect him.

By the time he passed through the enclave gates, the sun had finally slipped around the tight curve of the planet, its light fading from even the uppermost layers of Chamal's deep atmosphere. He relaxed as he followed the gravel path between the tribe's sprawling households – one- and two-story brick buildings that had grown over the years as additions and extensions were built by each generation. With a sigh of relief, he turned at the top of the hill and hurried on to his own kitchen door.

Despite his worried apprehension, the assault took him by surprise.

There were three of them – high-speed streaks of colored fur launching themselves out of the darkness in the bushes and off the rooftop. A purple one wrapped himself around Zepp's legs, a red one came down on top of his head and locked his arms across Zepp's eyes, while the third one – bluish-green from the brief glimpse Zepp had of him – caromed off Zepp's belly, knocking the struggling mass of flesh and fur to the ground.

Zepp felt his arms being pinioned by the small but irresistible creatures and before he could stop them, they were going through the pockets of his vest. He felt his coin-purse shoot out of its place and suddenly they were off him and running away.

His blind panic had passed, but now the hot blood of fear surging through his small body energized even the tips of his fur. He was swept by rage at being frightened so completely.

As the trio of thieves fled into the household, Zepp recognized them as three of his cousins – Lang, Todd, and Kam – half-grown imps who wouldn't be up for sorting until next spring.

He was on his feet in an instant and after them in hot pursuit. This was not the first time this had happened, and he knew where to find the little muggers. Sure enough, they were all in the kitchen, barely out of breath, seated at a long wooden table with their short legs dangling from the bench. They were trying hard to ignore their older cousin and pretend nothing had happened.

It didn't work.

"Hear me now," Zepp announced. "I'm too tired to fool around tonight. Which one of you has it?"

"Has what?" Todd quipped.

"What?" his brothers echoed.

Zepp reached out quickly and grabbed Lang by the loose skin at the back of his neck – he chose him only because he was closest – then he plucked him from the bench and held him at arm's length while cranking the hand pump at the kitchen sink behind him.

"Who has my purse?" he asked as the water splashed into the deep porcelain basin. He held his cousin over the sink where he could see the water gushing out of the spout in a steady stream.

Lang squealed and twisted and scratched at Zepp's arms, but he made no sign of confessing. Zepp lowered him into the sink and let the water run over his head until his blue fur was plastered to his small, round skull. He sputtered and pointed across the kitchen.

"Todd has it," he said.

Todd and Kam made a rush for the doorway into the rest of the household – there were enough cubbyholes and hiding places in there to keep Zepp hunting for weeks.

But they came up short at the last second as the doorway was suddenly blocked by Zepp's three sisters – Tarina, Filomie, and Sree. Their only escape route cut off, the pair reversed direction only to run straight into the arms of Zepp – who carried them over to the sink as they yowled in protest.

Just as he was about to dump them into the sink to suffer the same fate as Lang, Todd screamed out: "In the salt-box!"

Zepp handed his cousins to his sisters – whose non-stop, high-speed, traveling conversation had been interrupted by the crisis in the kitchen – and went to the pantry where he recovered his purse and checked its contents – three gold coins, two silvers, and a brass.

"You can let them go," he told his sisters. "It's all here."

The girls let the children go and they vanished into the household before anyone could say a word to chide or chastise them.

It was just as well, as far as Zepp was concerned. In another year they would have to face sorting and the odds were that only one of them would pass, while the other two would be consigned to somewhat less than normal lives – even by Chamal's standards.

Because of that, he could hold no grudge against them, giving them instead his tolerance and his sympathy.

"Poor Zepp," Tarina cooed. "Is the terrible trio bothering you tonight?"

"Hey, Zepp, you want some supper?" Filomie asked. "There's still some soup left over."

Sree just smiled wistfully and slipped in behind her older sisters.

Zepp sat down at the table, brushing the salt from his leather purse while the girls fluttered about the kitchen. They were a typical group of chamalian females in that they resembled neither each other nor their brother. Tarina, the oldest, was a forest-cat with gray-green fur and large, oval eyes whose vertical pupils could catch and reflect the light from lamps around the room. Filomie was Zepp's litter-mate. Her brown fur was curled and wiry, and her large ears flopped down the side of her head – somewhere in her genetic history were hunting dogs who guarded ancestral fire pits on the wide northern prairies. Sree was the youngest of the group and the smallest – even shorter than Zepp – a delicate blue lamb with straight white teeth and a shy, withdrawn disposition.

Filomie went to the stove and began to heat up the vegetable stew left from supper, while Tarina and Sree joined their brother at the table. Tarina produced two combs made of carved seashell and began working the tangles out of his long fur while Sree sat across from them, gazing in an awe-filled, almost worshipful manner at her big brother. Soon the soup was ready and Filomie joined Tarina in grooming Zepp while he ate.

Females held an ambivalent position in Zepp's tribe. Jobe had taught them that the female passed on the mysterious, unknown heritage of the inner circle of the chamalian seed. From that hidden ring all manner of unpredictable beasts could emerge. Males could only replicate themselves, no better, Jobe said. But females were a wellspring of new forms and ancient traits.

Jealous of their mystical power, the males kept the females at home, away from commerce and politics, delegating to them only the responsibility for hearth and household.

It was not so everywhere or always – there were no absolute rules to chamalian life. In the early days of the race, when wisdom was still new and unused to the world, before historical times and the rise of the cities and great political states, females had ruled. And in the underworld of the south, primitive tribes prayed to the Great Mother and matriarchs made decisions for the tribe. In those places and times, the females controlled the economy – planting, growing, keeping time with nature. Here and now it was the males – the makers and users – who controlled things, but the females did not forget the old days.

The males of Chamal treated their mates and their daughters with awe and respect, frightened by what they couldn't understand, indulging them to a much granter degree than they would each other, granting them a freedom that Zepp and his male cousins did not enjoy.

In turn, the females played the role of devoted servants, catering to the whims of the males, even as they connived and manipulated them. Husbands, fathers, and brothers were catered to, waited on, and doted upon by wives, daughters, and sisters. And behind their backs, they were insulted, plotted against, set up, knocked down, despised and betrayed.

Zepp's family was no exception, so he was accustomed to this kind of treatment from his sisters. He accepted it, but did not take advantage of it – he had been taught that it was his responsibility to allow them to carry on like this, no matter what he thought of it.

"You know who came to visit us today, brother?" Tarina asked as she struggled with a knot in Zepp's green coat. She went on without waiting for a response. "Nimeninokus from the Chorai – I adore those cute little wings, don't you? He and his four wives came for a visit with Grandfather Kobi."

"They all visited him?" Zepp asked.

"Well, just the prince. But his wives came downstairs and talked with us for hours. You should have seen the way they were dressed."

"They had silk veils all the way from the Great Rift Valley," Filomie said.

"And pearls from Meshkar," added Tarina.

"And gems from Shipar," Sree piped up. "Oh, Zepp, they were beautiful."

"I'm sure they were," Zepp replied with exaggerated interest.

"Did you know that Nimeninokus' wives are his sisters?" Tarina asked in a harsh whisper. "All four of them!"

"That's pretty kinky," squealed Filomie.

"Not for them," Zepp said. "Jobe's taboos don't apply to outsiders. The Chorai are starting to lose their gene-pool – not enough winged ones in the lest few generations. And they won't listen to the warnings of the Seedmasters about the problems inbreeding can lead to, either, so they're going ahead with abominations like the prince's harem. You'll see, though. In a few years their enclave will be crawling with halflings and the Chorai will be in worse shape than ever. I'll bet they all turn to winged halflings and fly off to Arkaria."

"Oh, brother, don't be such a storm cloud," Tarina said. "You know too much for your own good."

"I still think it's kinky," Filomie said.

"How would you like to try it?" Tarina asked her sister. "It would be just like in the fables. Like 'The Princess of Parishandra.' Haven't you ever thought about wedding your brother the way she did? Just imagine – no more taboos, no more laws, no more brass belts, free to do as you please. You'd never have to leave him and he'd never have to leave you. What about it, Zepp? Wouldn't you like to be our husband instead of our baby brother?"

She stroked his arm gently to tease him, but he pulled away.

He said nothing to his sister, but grumbled into his soup as he scraped the bottom of the bowl. He cursed the fables, even though he knew that they taught valuable lessons about the chamalian seed.

In his short time at the Hall of the Seedkeepers, Zepp had learned that the sexual taboos of the tribe of Jobe were not primitive, superstitious rituals designed to intimidate and control the members of the tribe, nor were they the irrational compulsions of an aging patriarch imposed upon his descendants by the inertia of repetition.

On the contrary, they were an integral part of a highly-developed system of genetic screening that had evolved over many centuries in many different societies. They were the results of painful lessons taught by chamalian nature over the generations. And they had as their goal the conservation of wisdom itself.

In their natural, uncivilized state, all the many breeds of Chamal had once practiced – and in many places continued to practice – full interbreeding of all the subspecies of the chamalian genus. There were problems with this practice, however, problems that threatened the stability of the breeding population. The greatest of these were the overall curses of chamalian genetics – the spread of wisdom throughout the ecology, the degradation of the original life-forms into more and more wild and primitive subspecies, and the breakdown of the social group as internal tensions were magnified by the changing composition of the population.

Historically, the first response to these problems had been the segregation of those fully possessed of wisdom from the less-developed forms – a response that coincided with the emergence of larger social groupings such as the extended clan. Interbreeding with lesser animals was prohibited and interbreeding between families was encouraged.

But this only served as a partial solution.

It, too, had its problems, not least of which was the migration of the qualities of wisdom – the gift of speech and hands that could make and use tools – out of the breeding population in the form of halflings carrying hidden traits. This accelerated the degradation of the gene-pool instead of slowing it, which had been the original point of the practice. And in addition, the custom led to the growth of new populations of wise breeds outside the original group – tribes growing up in the forests and valleys with a whole new set of dominant traits inherited from the wild. More often than not, the outsiders were hardier and more aggressive than their forebears and conflicts inevitably arose over control of resources and living space.

Chamalians had come up with several solutions to this development – all radical, drastic measures in keeping with the chamalian character. At first, the halflings born to full adults were simply executed when they failed to mature. But this was a terrible waste of life and many cultures chose the less drastic option of castrating the little beasts – leaving them to be bought and sold in the slave market. These solutions were usually associated with more advanced city-states and larger societies where the institutions of social and political control existed to impose these practices upon the population.

But there was a more creative solution to the problems segregation produced – and one addressing the problem of gene-pool degradation that segregation only aggravated.

That solution was inbreeding.

Initially, inbreeding seemed like a good idea. Chamalian siblings were not close genetically. Usually half of the first generation of offspring from chamalian inbreeding duplicated each parent gene for gene, solving the problem of family unity and keeping the gene-pool intact.

But it wasn't safe to fool with nature – especially on Chamal. Successive generations of incestuous offspring were not as productive as the first. Some inner counter in the seed kept track of the sins of the fathers and mothers, and as things proceeded, the number of full-grown wise adults in each generation drooped off dramatically.

After three or four generations, the halflings and steplings outnumbered their more developed cousins eighty-eight to one. Aside from defeating the original goal of the breeding practice, inbreeding created another problem: what to do with the excess halflings that were soon cramming the cities and towns and forests and valleys.

It wasn't just coincidence that the development of incest accompanied the decay and downfall of the city-states and empires that originated the idea.

The survivors of these catastrophes generally reacted by imposing the harsh taboos against incest and bestiality that the tribe of Jobe practiced, and letting the gene-pools take care of themselves. Halflings ran away from home and formed imitation empires where they stole junk from the towns and cities and abused each other, while changelings – wild offspring who grew into their wisdom away from the centers of civilization – were adopted by their wise cousins.

But Jobe had taken this one step further.

Like the more civilized societies of the planet, he had instituted a policy of conservation. By founding the Seedkeepers, he began the careful, painstaking monitoring of breeding patterns. By segregating the non-adults from the adult population and culling their seed systematically, the degradation of the gene-pool overall was brought to an end. By preventing incest, the added strains imposed by meddling with nature were removed. And by encouraging the interbreeding of disparate breeds – an easy task in the polyglot population of Suridash – he hoped to arrive at a higher breed of chamalian.

This was the ultimate goal of the Seedkeepers, to bring together the spilled seed of the gods and to end once and for all the insane mixing of traits end forms, species and subspecies, adults, halflings, and steplings. To finally and completely separate the wise from the wild. It was a noble cause for such an ignoble race. And from time to time, heretics in the tribe had voiced an unspeakable suspicion in whispers along the dark galleries of the Hall of the Seedkeepers: that it had no chance of ever succeeding.

In the meantime, the members of the tribe of Jobe were consigned their taboos – the wearing of the brass chastity belts, the harsh punishments for violations and the relentless, intrusive inspection of every creature born to the tribe.

It was only natural, therefore, for Zepp to be troubled by his sister's fanciful suggestion that they adopt the manner of the Chorai and intermarry. It was almost embarrassing when she went on in elaborate detail with her fantasy, including her two sisters in the tale. Sree blushed at the bold talk.

"We could go off to the far side of the enclave and start our own household, just the four of us. And all our children would be just like us. Wouldn't that he nice?"

Zepp shuddered, and without warning or anticipation, lashed out at the blasphemy Tarina was proposing – even if in jest. He didn't like being teased like this and his tolerance had limits.

"Yes, it would be lovely! And all our grandchildren would be half-wits and halflings, grubbing in the streets for their food. Is that what you want?" he demanded with a snarl.

Tarina reached out to touch her brother, to ease his anger, but Zepp backed off. He was not so quick to calm down. Part of his anxiety was fueled from within – not so much by the fears of the past few days, but by an inner guilt.

The thing most disturbing to him was that ideas such as these were never far from the mind of any member of his tribe. Always, of course, with a sense of terrible guilt that struck at the hearts, and only, of course, because the tribe had such an obsession with preventing it, and mainly, of course, when they were younger and still naive. But even Zepp had thought about it just the same, and now his trouble with Sheverek seemed to be a long-delayed punishment for his sins.

He looked down at the table to avoid his sister's eyes and saw that the soup bowl was empty. He dropped his spoon into it and rose from the table, almost fleeing from Tarina. "I'm through," he said. "I'm going upstairs, now. I'll see you tomorrow."

His sisters had barely time to speak before he was gone, leaving them to laugh at him behind his back.

* * *

Zepp did not go straight to bed. For too many nights now, he had lain awake, tortured by visions of Sheverek's assassins finding him alone after dark, cutting his hearts out, leaving him to bleed on the streets. He didn't want to suffer another night like that, so this evening he paused in the incense room before shuffling off to his bedchamber.

He was not accustomed to relaxing before the hearth in the round, smoky chamber – it had only been a year since he had reached the age where he was allowed its pleasurable atmosphere and he was still not used to the intoxicating drug. It was the smoke that really bothered him, not the effect of the incense – that he rather enjoyed.

The room was empty except for grandfather Kobi, asleep before the fire – he always seemed to be there. Zepp was pleased – he wanted to be alone tonight, to face his fears in solitary silence.

He pulled a splinter from the woodpile and lit the end, then he carried the flame to the brass incense pan and the lit the gummy stuff beneath the conical chimney. When the smoke began to pour out, he snuffed his match out and inhaled deeply, letting the fumes spill up past his nostrils. He filled his lungs three times, then covered the pan to extinguish the incense.

The drug took effect before he reached the cushions strewn about the floor in front of the fireplace. It relaxed him, eased his tension, removed the weight of the day from his back. His arms and legs felt weightless, his face lost its tightness, and his tail stopped its otherwise ceaseless twitching. And for a moment he forgot the threat which had harried him without mercy for the past two days.

He stretched back on the warm, soft, leather pillows and let his thoughts drift, recalling younger days, before he grew up and all the burdens of manhood made themselves known. Then his mind seized upon another memory, not so pleasant and idyllic – a memory of how those happy days of childhood had come to an abrupt and decisive end.

This was not the first time in his life that Zepp had faced great danger.

* * *

The sorting ritual was a perilous time in the life of every small boy in the Tribe of Jobs. It was a time when mothers eyed their children fearfully and fathers sharpened their knives.

It was a trial especially designed for the chamalian male, designed to address an age-old problem – how to prevent inferior seed from permeating the gene-pool.

The solution chosen by Jobe and his descendants was short and simple. Only the truly wise were permitted to breed within the tribe. The rejects – halflings, near-wise, and the like – were sorted out at the end of puberty, when the differences among them began to emerge. The lucky few were initiated into the tribe and fitted for brass belts. The rest were swiftly put before the knife and had no need of the belts at all.

But when it came time for Zepp to undergo this terrifying judgment, things were just a little more complicated. The striking resemblance between Zepp and his Uncle Tapp was no asset among the jealous, squabbling factions of the tribe. Tapp, an arbiter of disputes and a powerful leader, had accumulated many enemies in his lifetime – many of them within the tribe and a few even within his own household. While it was difficult to get at Tapp directly – he was too wily and cunning for his antagonists – the indirect approach seemed very inviting.

It had driven Zepp's mother frantic with worry. "It's all your fault," she had screamed at her brother. "They'd never think twice about Zepp if it weren't for you."

Zepp had been his mother's favorite – the runt of the litter and the only male, as well as a dead ringer for her brother. It was not considered healthy for a mother to grow too attached to her sons – especially before sorting time – but now that she had, Zepp's mother was not about to allow her son to he harmed by her brother's enemies.

Zepp's father – bound by ritual to strict and formal relations with his son – was not a close or loving figure in Zepp's life, but his uncle, unfettered by family duties and obligations, took that place, teaching him what he had to know to become a full member of the tribe.

For a long time before the sorting, Tapp and his nephew had worked together, rehearsing the complex recitations and rites that Zepp would have to go through before the assembled tribe when the time came. Zepp was not the best student in the world and it was a slow and difficult task. As the last few days before the ritual slipped by, tensions within every household reached and even passed the breaking point.

Zepp's mother was so fearful for her son's fate that she turned on him and his uncle the night before the ceremony. "Why can't you teach him what he needs to know?" she demanded. "You're the big family hero – do something!"

Then she turned on her son. "And you, you little half-wit – why don't you learn faster? What's wrong with you? Are they right? Are you just a sport, a bad seed? If you don't smarten up, they are going to take you away from me, you know that. They're going to put you in the Hall of the Seedkeepers or worse – and you don't even care. Why did I ever bother to love you or care for you, you ungrateful little imp?"

Tapp and Zepp labored into the night, as Zepp slowly mastered the most critical parts of the ritual. The worst of his mother's fears vanished the next day when Zepp took his place among the dozens of younglings in the circle at the center of the tribal enclave, surrounded by the older, mated males, the fathers and uncles and cousins of those to be judged.

He recited the passages from the Word of Jobe carefully and without error – his elders scrutinizing his performance, awaiting the tiniest flaw. But there was none, and when half the pack was led away, he remained behind to continue the process. The recitations served to weed out the clearly deficient youths, but the next tests were more demanding and more difficult to pass.

He was poked and prodded, his body twisted and abused, his head and hands measured, his tail pulled, and a dozen other indignities were inflicted upon him as the older males inspected him closely, searching for some imperfection. He grew weary, knowing that his uncle's enemies were ready to seize upon any excuse to reject him – and some were ready to send him down without an excuse.

But he passed this and was sent on with sixteen of his cousins to face the two concluding tests – tests that would determine finally if he was to join the tribe as an adult or be cast out forever.

The first of these was another recital – this time before a formal judge, dressed in a white tunic and carrying a huge, wide sword of polished silver. Zepp watched as his companions approached the judge, gave their readings, and were evaluated. The role of the judge was to interpret the response of the hooting, jeering crowd surrounding the boys. Zepp's morale was dealt a serious blow as he watched his cousins precede him and fail – those who had reached this point in the process were visibly upset when they were removed from the circle.

Then it was his turn. He quivered with a wretched fear as Uncle Tapp's enemies shouted derisive words at him even before he began his reading, but he went on, knowing what would happen if he failed.

Unlike the earlier recitations, this reading was not prescribed by ritual. Instead, it was chosen by each boy – actually by his family, who knew more about these things – and was delivered alone.

Usually, the reading consisted of worthless platitudes, essays on thrift, and complicated ditties to show off verbal acumen. Not Zepp's, though.

Tapp had carefully considered which of the Words of Jobe Zepp would speak before the judge, and then he had coached Zepp with diligence until he had everything just right.

This was the moment of truth.

Zepp's voice cracked as he began, but he quickly gained control of it. "Hear now the Word of Jobe," he said.

His voice was soft and high-pitched, but it carried a note of authority that brought a hush to the crowd – and that only made him more nervous,

"'I have walked the world and seen the squandering of the seed of the gods. It has spread to the meanest and the lowest of animals and has become infested with their spoor even to the wisest and noblest born. The gods, in their revenge, have allowed their households, their tribes, and their empires to fall, teaching a lesson to those who came after. Do not forget that lesson, my children, or their fate will be yours.

"'Let no seed pass amongst you which has not been tested for the spirit of the gods. Be harsh and demanding in your tests, for the seed of the gods was meant to endure all. But take care, my children, that you do not cast the seed of the gods out of the tribe in your zeal. For that is a greater sin than spilling his seed amongst the beasts of the forest and field. And whosoever offends the gods by disposing of their seed lightly – even in the smallest of his creatures – shall be visited by their wrath, even unto the final generation of his kind.'"

His words drew a startled buzz from the crowd. With anyone else but the nephew of Tapp, the passage would have been resented as arrogant and impertinent, but today, for Zepp, it worked. The message had not been lost on Tapp's enemies – who restrained their accusing cries under the glaring eyes of Zepp's uncle. Even the most unrepentant of his foes held back after that reading, aimed so directly at their hearts.

It wasn't over yet, however. There was still the last test, and if Zepp failed that, Tapp's enemies would have succeeded.

The hardest part of the sorting ritual still faced Zepp. This was where many of his cousins had failed before him and this was where his courage almost fled from him.

All their lives, Zepp and his cousins had been tutored in obedience – obey the Word of Jobe, obey the taboos, and most important of all, obey the dictates of the older males of the tribe. It was appropriately chamalian, therefore, to make the passage into manhood with an act of disobedience.

Now that his reading was finished, Zepp was required to face the judge and do something disrespectful – to spit in the devil's eye. Or in Zepp's case, to twist the devil's tail ...

He almost failed, that heavy sword looming over his head was a strong deterrent to action, but in the end he did not. The judge's tail was longer and thicker then his own, but it was no harder to grasp. And when Zepp moved, it was with a swiftness born of fear, surprising everyone, including the judge, who lost his balance and went down with a loud thud on the ground as Zepp ran to his mother's arms.

Zepp had passed the tests. His mother and his uncle were overjoyed, hugging him tightly until he couldn't breath. Later he was fitted for the belt that he wore to this day. And later still, less than a year after the sorting, his uncle succumbed to the Blue Plague, ending forever what little joy there had been in Zepp's life.

And now he faced a threat even more serious – and this time without his uncles help. What could he do? What would Tapp have done?

He wouldn't have quit, surrendering to his fate, Zepp realized as the fog of the incense wore off. He would have fought back.

He would have found a way out. He would have faced Sheverek down single-handed and in open combat if it came to that.

Zepp couldn't take that route – he was too small, too inexperienced, and Sheverek was still a deadly fighter, an old war-bull.

But there was something he could do, Zepp realized with a start.

If what he'd been told was true ...

Suddenly the decision to act had been made, almost without Zepp realizing it. And now, for the first time in a week, he felt at ease. Sheverek might still hasten his departure from this life, but Zepp was ready to depart fighting.

CHAPTER FIVE

"Know thy neighbor," Jobe had said – the words were gold set in marble above the library's entrance.

In the center of its skylit rotunda was a globe eight hands in diameter with a surface of intricate mosaic, depicting the landforms of Chamal and the journey of Jobe traced in silver and gold.

Zepp was always amazed at the work that must have gone into the globe and wondered what mad artisan had devoted his life to the project. This afternoon was no exception. He paused as he entered the echoing chamber to gaze at it once more.

But his awe-filled admiration was interrupted as a handful of busy scribes – four identical rodents with buck teeth, puffy cheeks, and russet fur – scurried past him. Then he noticed with surprise that the whole library was alive with activity.

He wasn't the only one using the noon-sleep for something it was not properly meant to be.

The entire staff must have been busy. That was strange, hardly anyone worked through the hottest part of the day – even here inside cool stone buildings – unless something important was up. Zepp wondered what it was.

He decided to keep to the shadows and avoid notice. Like all of his tribesmen, he had learned at an early age not to get involved in the important business of his more powerful cousins.

He was tiptoeing around the outer edge of the rotunda when a creaky old voice spoke up behind him, scaring the wits out of him. "This is an odd hour for you to be here, nephew."

Zepp spun around, his arms over his head and his lips curling away from his teeth. It was his great-uncle, Griz, a wrinkling old scribe with white hairs spreading throughout his fur and a pair of bifocals clipped to his long, canine nose. Griz was a senior bookmaster at the library. He had taught Zepp and his cousins the fables of Chamal, the Word of Jobe, the story of his journey. And his post at the library meant that he knew the location of much of the information stored within its halls.

The one big problem with the library was its casual organization. It was run in a typically chamalian manner. The records of state, dispatches from diplomats, reports from pilgrims along the Way of Jobe, commercial bulletins, military chronicles, all were taken in by the library, read and sorted by the bookmasters, and then dumped haphazardly into rooms containing all the other information from the same part of the world. There was no method – the arrangement of the rooms, no relation of one to another, no cross-referencing or card catalog. That information belonged only to the bookmasters and to those who used a room once and remembered where it was.

Zepp was neither, but he had hoped to run into one of his kinsmen, like Griz, who could help him find the way to the information he needed.

"I've come to do research," Zepp said, avoiding deception by restraining his explanation. "Where can I learn about the kingdoms of the tropical belt?"

A distant expression fell over the old hound's face, and Zepp could imagine him reflecting on every scrap of paper in every room in the library.

"Follow me," he said, and he led Zepp down long corridors bustling with hard-working scribes who all seemed loaded down with books, scrolls and sheaves of unbound files. Eventually they arrived at a small chamber, and Griz switched on a dim light in the ceiling.

"Here is the room, nephew," he told Zepp. "I am sorry, but I don't have the time today to help you any further. You know your own way around a records hall, don't you?"

Before Zepp could speak, the old one was gone. He looked around at the crates and shelves and files and papers. A thin film of red dust had accumulated over the years, building up at a gradual but steady rate. It was easy to find the proper era in time by checking the amount of dust on a given pile of records. The dry air of Suridash preserved the paper well and some of the older documents rested under almost a digit of dust.

It took an hour for Zepp to find what he wanted.

Despite his experience with the chamalian art of data retrieval, he had no easy time of it. The room his great-uncle had led him to contained material on sixteen tropical kingdoms in the same general area of the equatorial belt – all of them far from the Way of Jobe and lacking the more complete reports made by pilgrims from Suridash. But finally, he pieced together the story of General Sheverek, the Scourge of Rudabet.

Rudabet was a typical kingdom from the deeper parts of Chamal's equatorial mire. It occupied the high ground in an area surrounded by undrained swamps and it was dominated by a short-lived dynasty of aggressive war-bulls – Sheverek among them – who practiced strict expulsion of creatures with inferior traits. As a result, the traits for wisdom migrated out of the dominant population, transforming the angry and jealous wild breeds surrounding them into wiser and wiser strains and spurring them to emerge from the bogs to assault their cousins on the high ground.

The wars dragged on for years until the war-bulls were defeated, debased, and dispersed. The high ground, with its refuge from the ruthless struggle among the violent breeds of the wetlands, was occupied by the victors – who called the new land Flammaria. Soon they would begin to squabble among themselves and start a new round of warfare, but for the time being things were quiet there.

Included among the latest dispatches in the pile on Rudabet and Flammaria was the item he needed most – the location of the Flammarian embassy in Suridash.

He let out a whoop of joy when he found it. Scribbled it down on a scrap of parchment covered with foreign writing, jammed it into his vest pocket, and nearly flew down the corridor.

He slowed down as he entered the rotunda and caught the wary eyes of suspicious scribes, but he gained back some of his speed as he orbited closely around the towering mosaic globe in the center of the chamber.

He was just entering the hallway that led to the front door when a dark figure emerged without warning from a side room. Zepp could not avoid him and the two collided, knocking each other down.

Zepp was mortified when he discovered the victim of his undue haste was none other than Tedrak's assistant, Whirlpitt.

Zepp could barely speak, he was so frightened, but Whirlpitt wasn't angry at all.

"Our work is pressing, youngling, but we must still take care not to get in each other's way," he said as he regained his feet. He even gave Zepp a hand in rising, studying the small green ape with a careful eye.

Zepp wished he were invisible, but he stood silently waiting for whatever rebuke was to come

"I know you – you're the young spy we sent to the Tradetown this week. What are you doing here? I thought you worked for Sheverek over at the Seedkeepers."

"Yes, sir," Zepp said nervously. "I do, sir. I mean I'm here for research, sir. For Sheverek." He sweated out the uncertain gaze of the administrator, knowing he had not yet told any lies.

"I see," Whirlpitt said. "Well, then, you'd better get about your business. Someone in as big a hurry as you must have something important to do."

Zepp nodded and backed away slowly, turning at last and rushing breathlessly for the door.

He worked his way across town as rapidly as he could. The merciless yellow sun sucked the breath out of him, but it did not dry him out as it did many of the city's residents – his family's seed had migrated across two deserts already and his green fur helped insulate his skin. The worst part was the hot pavement that burned his feet through his sandals. That and the awful feeling that his time was running out.

He reached the Flammarian embassy – or what passed for it – with only a few minutes to spare before he had to return to work. The building was flat and long with a high fence surrounding both it and the yard in back. Zepp could see thick vegetation behind the building and he heard the regular chugging of an irrigation well in operation.

He rang the brass bell at the gate, wondering why it hadn't been stolen by now. An alien head poked lazily out of the window.

"Go away!" it yelled.

"I have to talk to the ambassador" he replied.

There was silence. Zepp rang the bell a second time, producing the strange face in the window again. It had the normal round shape of a chamalian face, but horns and barbs protruded all over – on the cheeks, the ears, the muzzle, and the brow.

"Come back later!" the face yelled.

"I can't," Zepp called back. "It's important."

The ugly face emerged slowly from the building atop an equally ugly body – sharp ridges and spikes at the joints end shoulders threatened painful injury to an unwary wrestler. He wore a loincloth, wrapped carefully around the sharp projections. Rough scales grew over his eyelids, knuckles and fingertips. This was what the swamps of the rainforest belt did to the mutable genes of Zepp's race. He recognized the signs quickly.

"What could he so important that a little monkey like you stirs someone like me from my sleep'?" the Flammarian asked as he approached, stopping at the fence.

"Are you the ambassador or the gatekeeper?" Zepp snapped back.

The creature scowled, scratched one of the two largest horns on his forehead, then laughed. "What are you peddling, son?"

Zepp looked around conspiratorially, then said in a loud whisper, "Vengeance."

"Oh?" the tropical-beast said, his dark, gloomy eyes widening. "Vengeance on whom?"

"The general of the armies that opposed you in the conquest of Rudabet – Sheverek."

The Flammarian turned his stiff head sideways, looked carefully at Zepp, then laughed loudly in his face.

Zepp began to worry. His plan was not proceeding as he had expected. "You mean you aren't seeking him out to pay for his crimes from the war?"

"His crimes are infamous, but they were not against us."

"But ... but – why not? I thought ... " Zepp's heart sank, his hopes smashed.

"The war was long and we fought many battles. Each time Sheverek would defeat us, but each time, the old lunatic would send a messenger across the lines to our generals berating them for their poor tactics, criticizing their conduct on the battlefield, telling them why they had lost. As the war went on, our generals began to learn from the messages until they finally outwitted him with his own advice."

Zepp just stared in disbelief. What was he going to do now?

"No, we're not the ones who want him. It's his own people who have a death squad on his trail. We'd make a hero out of him, like as not," the swamp beast mused.

"His own people?" Zepp's head turned with a snap. "Where? When? Are they here in Suridash?"

"Of course. Where else would refugees go? The vermin infest a block on the far side of the city – at least they did a few months ago. That's the last time I heard anything about them. I believe even the well-tempered citizens of this city do not favor them as neighbors, so they may have moved on since then."

"Do you know exactly where?" Zepp asked hopefully.

"Near the vineyards ... past the Red Monkeys. I'm not sure precisely where, but you'll recognize it."

Zepp cursed. There wasn't time enough to get there during noon-sleep. He'd have to wait until after work. That meant another afternoon watching out for Sheverek. He turned to the gatekeeper-ambassador and said, "Thank you, sir. Good day."

"Good luck, lad," he replied as Zepp took off down the street towards the Hall of the Seedkeepers. "You'll need that brass belt of yours where you're going," he said with a chuckle that Zepp never heard.

* * *

The afternoon dragged on forever. Zepp could barely sit still. His nerves were buzzing like the high-voltage transformers outside the Red Monkey enclave. Kirbum kept rushing around, lingering in Sheverek's office now and then, making Zepp ever more fearful for his life.

The day finally came to an end, and Zepp hurried down the hall and out into the streets. There was still plenty of daylight when he found the run-down neighborhood where the Rudabet refugees made their home,

The streets were littered with the debris of falling buildings, discarded tools and broken machinery. Small creatures scampered about the jumbled blocks of masonry in an empty lot. Zepp walked slowly and cautiously down the broad avenue, searching for the most prominent house. That would be the most likely place to find a large band of refugees.

He found his goal, a large cubical structure three stories tall with a flat roof, mud walls, glassless window-holes and a barren gravel lot for a front yard. It was past the city vineyards and the smokestacks of a Red Monkey mill loomed over the block.

A pair of tough-looking young males with long brown-and-red fur followed Zepp and flanked him closely as he entered the building. They gripped his arms and twisted them sharply, making him yelp in pain.

They hurried him upstairs, his feet knocking helplessly against the steps as he was lifted roughly into the air, then tossed headfirst onto the floor at the head of the stairwell. He rolled about four hands and came to a stop in front of a heavy wooden table.

Behind the table sat three hairy, fanged old chiefs with dark, sunken eyes that studied him closely. They jabbered together in a foreign language that reminded Zepp of the curses old Sheverek spouted daily.

The one on the end spoke to him in the Suridash tongue. He had a weak voice and his round head bobbed as he talked.

"Why do you intrude on the Rudabet? Answer quickly or your life will end here and now."

Zepp choked and sputtered, trying to get the words out of his mouth before it was too late. "I wish to speak with the elders of your tribe," he said.

Zepp was shocked by his own boldness. He could just picture himself trying a similar approach with the elders of his own tribe.

"On what business?" the oldster snapped back at him with unexpected speed.

Zepp hesitated, then said, "Vengeance for your people against a great war criminal."

The oldster looked at him thoughtfully, then conversed with his fellows.

Zepp gazed around the large, open loft that stretched out behind the table. It was filled with creatures moving slowly in the dim, dust-filled room. They crowded the floor and the attics, collecting themselves into small groups of a half dozen or so, each surrounding a small pile of possessions.

The old ones suddenly let out a yell and the soft buzz of activity burst into a confused uproar with cries and shouts echoing throughout the hall. Adults flowed towards Zepp and the front table, quickly jamming the space around him. They pushed and squirmed, their faces twisting with erratic emotion. A few hung upside down from the rafters overhead, howling wildly, while others dropped to the floor with a lunatic screams and began clawing the walls. A pair of winged halflings flapped across the empty space in the center of the loft.

After a moment, quiet returned, but it was a pregnant, violence-ridden quiet that threatened to break out into chaos at the least provocation.

The old ones stared down at Zepp again, along with nearly eighty-eight of their clansmen.

"Quickly, young one. Give me details. My family is hungry now for blood and we will satisfy them one way or another."

Zepp stood up tall and outlined his plan. At the mention of the general's name, the whole loft became excited. It made what had gone on before seem like a tribal mass. The noise was almost more than Zepp could stand. It began with whispers echoing around the room, "Sheverek ... Sheverek," then shouts repeating the name: "Sheverek! Sheverek!"

"Can this be done?" the old man asked Zepp.

"Two days from now, we will be passing through the outer city with a wagonload of halflings for delivery to the Baratu enclave. Our route will take us into an abandoned neighborhood. You can attack him there. I will guarantee your success. The general will be yours," Zepp said, feeling a twinge of guilt, if only a small one.

"Why do you do this thing for us?" the elder asked suspiciously.

"He wants to kill me. I have no choice." Zepp replied honestly.

The old one smiled, then laughed. As he repeated Zepp's intentions to his relatives, they lost all control.

Younglings pulled out their knives and guns, small pups wailed with fear, and angry braves beat their chests and bellowed.

Zepp was swept off his feet by five small females who ripped the loincloth off his thighs. They scratched and clawed at his brass chastity belt for several minutes, pulling at his fur and scraping his skin. He struggled against them, but with as much effect as their efforts to liberate him from his family chains. The old one at the table bellowed an order and the girls dropped Zepp on the floor, then fled into the growing riot.

"Go," the old one told him.

Zepp found his clothes and his dignity and bolted down the stairs. He paused in the front yard to refit his loincloth, then he hurried away from the loft and the jubilation. The sound of the Rudabet filled the air for blocks and sent chills out to the end of Zepp's tail.

But now he felt much better. He had set the wheels in motion, and it was just a matter of surviving the next two days.

Sheverek's fate was sealed ...

... but so was his own.

CHAPTER SIX

It **was not** a pleasant morning in Suridash.

A blanket of fog had drifted in from the sea during the night, trapping beneath it the sulfurous fumes from the factories and refineries of the Red Monkey district. As the sun burned down through Chamal's deep atmosphere it turned the mixture into an eye-stinging smog – the kind that could hang over the city for days.

Beneath the murky morning skies, thousands of miserable chamalians began their miserable day. Many did nothing but emerge from the rear of their property to the shops and markets in the front. Others struggled to resume operation of the machinery and apparatus that formed their prisons. Some, among them Zepp, plodded wearily down the crowded streets to the center of the city, in a rush to get to their jobs ahead of their bosses.

Most of them had no inkling of the terrible fate that was burning its way across the sky towards them, just as General Sheverek had no inkling of the terrible fate that awaited him on the streets of Suridash that day.

That was the thought uppermost in Zepp's mind as he climbed the broad steps up to the main entrance of the Hall of the Seedkeepers.

He was as nervous as a halfling at sorting tine. He'd had little sleep the night before.

He passed through his morning duties like someone in a trance, unable to concentrate. He was frequently distracted, losing his place in the record book as he transcribed the barely legible notes of an anonymous seedmaster.

Sheverek was like a simmering volcano that could erupt at any moment and without warning. Zepp was a reluctant geologist perched on the rim of the crater, waiting for the volcano to erupt. He tried to ignore Sheverek, but every time the old general snarled from his office, the fur rose along Zepp's shoulders and the back of his neck and his tail began to twitch.

The morning dragged on and on, providing a subtle and excruciating torture for Zepp. But finally, to the green ape's relief, noon-sleep arrived and he was able to escape for a short time and review his plan. His pessimistic imagination conjured up an endless list of disasters – the Rudabet death squad would back out, Sheverek would back out, the Rudabets would blame Zepp, Sheverek would find out about the plot, someone else would find out about the plot, the death squad would succeed, but he would he killed in the crossfire. He wished he could call it off now, but it was much too late.

When noon-sleep ended, Zepp made his way through the labyrinths of the Hall of the Seedkeepers to the stables, where he had to prepare a team of draft animals for hauling the load of halflings to the Baratu enclave.

Deliveries of that kind were made regularly by the Seedkeepers. Their interest in the seed of the gods was not entirely academic. They managed a great deal of trade in small, capable servants – halflings without important genetic assets, but with high commercial value. They also operated a rudimentary gene-exchange. The interbreeding of different trait-groups produced unusual results and many of the enclaves had genetic experimentation programs of their own.

Among these were the Baratu, who were trying to revive a flagging gene-pool by breeding a new king and founding a new dynasty. The current heir to the throne was a long-eared stepling who spent his time munching on orange-roots.

The program was not producing spectacular results, but that was to be expected – the main line of effort was to interbreed a number of low-level steplings all at once to create a spontaneous quantum leap to intelligent, self-conscious offspring. But the Seedkeepers carefully culled the stock they put on the market, and the Baratu were not interjecting any of their own seed into the project, so the chances of success were extremely low.

They kept good records, however, and that was what mattered most to the Seedmasters. As a result, a record keeper had to make each delivery of new stock to the enclave in order to collect and inspect their genetic almanacs for the Seedmasters.

Today that record keeper was Sheverek.

The air in the stables was thick with the acetone smell of silage and manure – a welcome relief from the smog that cloyed at Zepp's nose all morning. The wooden building was lit by a string of fluorescent lights across the rafters.

The red-faced stable boy – a halfling with puffy cheeks and a round belly – led Zepp to the far end of the stalls and pointed out the tackle and the two draft-animals that would be pulling Sheverek's wagon. The bridles, harness, and reins were hanging from the wall, and the two drays were busy in their stalls with a bale of hay and a couple buckets of grain. The stable boy was gone before Zepp could ask for help, so he went on alone into the stall of the first beast, a bridle in his hand.

"Come on, big fellow," he said in a soothing voice – just as he had been taught by Uncle Tapp years ago in the tribe's stables. "Let's get this thing on you."

"Come on, yourself," a deep voice said, "Lunch isn't over yet."

Zepp leapt against the side of the stall in fright, then rushed back out into the center of the stables. Towards the entrance he could see the stable boy peeking around the edge of a stall and snickering.

Was this a trick of some kind? Or was the voice that of a new assassin sent to eliminate him? The small ape looked around cautiously, his eyes straining for evidence of any threat.

Then another voice made itself heard, this time from the adjoining stall. "Hey, Pik, what's the cargo today?"

Zepp spun in the direction of the new voice, then charged to the edge of the stall. "Who said that?" he demanded.

"Not me," said the first voice, originating from the first stall. "Must have been him. I think we're getting the load of blue stripers sitting across the yard."

There was a resounding bellow from the second stall, followed by more of the voice. "That's what I was afraid of. They look like a well-fed lot, too. Plenty of weight. Hey, Greenie, how far do we have to haul this load?"

Zepp was frightened and confused. He looked at the two stalls, which contained nothing but a pair of wide-bottomed, four-legged, hay-munching beasts of burden and no assassins. Then he noticed that the one on the left was staring at him – waiting for an answer to his question.

"The Baratu enclave," Zepp said as he watched the large, brown eyes and the wide, tooth-filled mouth of the beast.

The mouth twisted and a huge tongue licked its lips. It opened wide and bellowed again. "Oh, my aching hack," the animal said. "That's on the other side of the city."

"Quit your belly-aching. Be glad it's not you they're delivering.

"Ah, Forg, you've got it too easy. I've seen a lot more summers than you have, you know. It won't be long before they send me off to the glue factory."

"You're talking!" Zepp exclaimed suddenly, finally overcoming his surprise.

"You're listening!" replied the beast who called himself Pik.

These two were not simple animals, but near-men, creatures touched by the seed of the gods, but bound forever by the limits imposed on them by their powerful bodies. Zepp had never encountered this breed before – not at first hand. There were no such animals in the tribe of Jobe's stock, and he'd had little previous occasion to converse with the draft-animals who filled the streets of Suridash.

Forg turned himself around in his stall slowly, then stuck a large, bony head out over the edge to peer at Zepp.

"Hey, Pik," he said. "Look at this, the kid's a brass belt. No wonder he was surprised. Hey, kid, sorry if we scared you. Almost everyone around here knows us. You ain't going to get weird on us, are you?"

"Who, me?" Zepp asked. "What for?"

"Considering your family chains...." Forg said. "You wouldn't be the first. I understand you've got some strong taboos against the likes of us."

"Not actually. In fact, we're supposed to watch out for your kind."

"But Pik and I are in this state because some herdsman went around salting his stock ages ago."

"That's a fable. We do have taboos against that sort of thing – but only against the act, not its fruit."

"Fruit?" Forg asked.

"I mean you're okay with me. I've got nothing against you," Zepp said. "By the way, my name is Zepp."

"Pleased to make your acquaintance," Pik replied. "Im Pik and this is Forg. Experts at hauling and shipping."

"I am surprised to find you two in the Hall of the Seedkeepers. Wouldn't they rather have you working here in another department?"

"Shhhhhh!" Forg said in a loud spray. "Speak too loudly and that's exactly what we'll be doing. No, my boy, we're not the property of the Seedkeepers. We belong to Agmet the teamster, who supplies all the stock here in the stables."

"That's the key to our privacy, Zepp. We haven't got a bad life – if you don't mind sleeping on your feet. And before the glue works, we get a few good years as breeding stock – a final reward for faithful service. It's better than slaving away in a Red Monkey factory, ain't it?"

"I have to agree with you on that," Zepp said. "But I don't have time to stand here talking with you all day. We have a delivery to make."

"Don't remind us," Pik said sadly.

Zepp realized with a start that for a few minutes he had actually forgotten the plot with which he had bean obsessed for days. The urgency of the moment now came back to him with full force. The hour was almost upon him and there was still much to be done.

Pik and Forg cooperated as Zepp dressed them in the yoke and harnesses. It didn't take long – with their direction it took only a few minutes to connect the team to the cart with its cage full of squealing halflings.

"By the way, fellows," Zepp said as he tightened the bolts at the front of the cart, "don't be surprised at what might happen today."

"What do you mean?" Pik asked.

"Nothing," Zepp answered. "Just keep cool if something unusual pops up. Okay?"

They nodded their heads in agreement.

* * *

Half an hour later, Sheverek came down to the yard, huffing and puffing and wheezing as he plodded across the cobblestones. Behind him came Kirbum, his nose high in the air and a pair of leather-covered record cases under his arms, and Snomisch, armed to the teeth, but with a dazed look on his face and his eyes half open.

The general and his entourage, Zepp observed silently with odd humor. He wondered if Kirbum found his way around by scent instead of sight.

Keeping a safe distance from the trio, Zepp climbed onto the cart, passing from the driver's seat to the roof of the cage. The halflings below grew still at the sight of Snomisch, except for one that took a grab at Zepp's tail just as it twitched out of reach.

"We are ready, you think?" Sheverek said, looking up warily at Zepp. "First we must inspect. Give me my case."

He turned abruptly and Kirbum stumbled into him, dropping the cases onto the cobblestones. He apologized, caught a swipe of Sheverek hand across the brow, and recovered the cases. It was not the one Sheverek wanted and he traded it for the correct one and another swipe – one that missed. Sheverek examined the bill of lading for the halflings, and then looked at the cargo itself.

He mumbled under his breath and tried to count them, pointing at them one by one and muttering under his breath. But after a few attempts he gave up – the way they huddled together and their identical coloring made an accurate count nearly impossible. Was this old bull truly the same Sheverek who had once commanded armies?

He paused to look Pik and Forg over carefully, checking the straps and harnesses for tightness. He stared at up at Zepp and sneered.

"You are not careful with the harness. This is loose. You want to make me lose the team? I catch you this time," Sheverek told him.

In fact, the strap was loose because Pik had asked Zepp to set it that way so it wouldn't chafe. But Zepp said nothing to Sheverek for fear that his voice would betray his intentions.

Finally, Snomisch clambered up onto the top of the cart with Zepp, Sheverek and Kirbum took the reins, and the expedition was under way.

The rugged streets of Suridash and the crude leaf-spring suspension on the axles of the cart combined to give Zepp an eventful ride, which he managed only by keeping a white-knuckle grip on the handrails provided for passengers like himself.

From where he sat, Zepp could almost see over the walls of the wards and free-holdings in the heart of the city, and as they crossed over into higher ground he could look down into the cloistered maze of buildings inside the Chorai enclave where trees and gardens and pools and fountains sprouted randomly from the stone and brick.

Farther out, in the unclaimed land between major enclaves, the Red Monkeys had built tall factories of yellow, sun-baked brick with towering smokestacks. Zepp could hear the throbbing machinery inside, smell the sawdust, the lint from the mills, the chemicals and solvents. He could see into the dark, dusty workshops crowded with refugees from the tropical lowlands and from the coastal littoral of the west, producing manufactured goods for the Red Monkeys in return for food for the day and a warm place sleep at night. The fate of those poor souls was better only than that of the creatures who lived within the walls of the Red Monkey enclave itself, but only barely. According to the stories Zepp had heard, workers in the enclave spent their lives tied to the machines, eating, sleeping, working and eliminating at the end of eight hands of chain.

Zepp was well aware of just how lucky he was to born into the tribe of Jobe,

Beyond the tropical neighborhoods was the no-man's land of what had once been Baratu territory, now open to all comers as the enclave shrank in size. The streets here were strewn with the rubble of crumbling buildings. Empty lots choked with weeds lined the avenue.

Once this had been home for hundreds of Baratu refugees from Meshkar – their commercial empire had been swindled away from them many generations ago and they had come here out of shame.

Even here, the citizens of Suridash found a home. Zepp could tell where many of them had come from just by the common traits they bore – recalling the teachings of the Seedmasters. The squatters on the corner were forest-dwellers – the gray-and-brown fur and the wide, dark eyes showed that. The loafers on the steps to a solitary apartment hall were desert-creatures with leathery skin and thick brows covering tiny eyes. The group rolling dice in an abandoned warehouse probably came from the eastern highlands, sweating under shaggy white coats of fur.

Zero was sweating heavily himself by now – and not just from the bright afternoon sun. He had felt a strange calm as the wagon rumbled through the city, as if nothing anyone could do would stop his deadly plan from proceeding.

But now they were approaching the area Zepp had identified to the Rudabet as the spot for the ambush. His fears resurfaced. Would it work or not? What would go wrong?

They had gone barely a block when Zepp noticed that the street was suddenly crowded with pedestrians and loiterers bearing an unusual family resemblance to the Rudabet. His first fear was that the general would notice it too, but Sheverek seemed to be dozing quietly despite the rough ride.

The first sign of trouble came from an unexpected quarter.

The loud rumble of the cart's iron-rimmed wheels stopped abruptly as the draft team came to an unplanned halt. Forg's deep voice called out: "Hey, Pik, something's going on here."

Zepp looked up quickly at the team. He couldn't believe his ears. Forg had just given everything away.

Sheverek was just as alert. "What's that?" he asked as Zepp's hearts leaped into his throat.

Sheverek's head twisted around on his thick neck, his eyes opened wide, a puzzled, fearful look crossed his face. Zepp was afraid all was lost. Then a heart-wrenching scream split the still, thick air, the rubble erupted with red-and-brown-furred furies, and Kirbum shouted: "Death squad!"

The cry echoed up and down the street. Beasts of every stripe and color – the legitimate street-lingerers – headed for cover, ducking into doorways, alleys, and gaping, paneless windows. Snomisch drew his sword and pistol as the members of the revenge squad burst out of their hiding places.

Zepp saw gunmen on the rooftops taking aim and suddenly felt small and vulnerable. Storm drains opened up and red-and-brown halflings poured forth onto the street, dodging the heavy hooves of

Pik and Forg. A team of gunmen rushed around the corner of the nearest building and charged at them.

The assassins were shouting and screaming as they surrounded the wagon. Snomisch waved his sword in the air above his head and pointed his pistol to and fro without firing. Zepp jumped down to the ground and scrambled under the cart. Overhead, the halflings squealed and massed together at the front of the cage.

Sheverek stepped up onto his seat and tried to grab the reins away from Kirbum, but he was too old, too slow, and too worn-out to make an escape. A dozen guns popped and cracked and banged away at once. The Rudabet were all excellent shots. The bullets all ripped into Sheverek's bloated body at the same time and he fell to the pavement.

Zepp looked out from his hiding place and found himself staring straight across four hands of hot, dusty cobblestones into the old soldier's face. Sheverek squirmed weakly where he lay. One arm was pinned under his chest and his bloody cheek was jammed against the street. He sneered through the pain and fixed his jaundiced eyes on Zepp.

"You," he croaked. "You did this." He reached towards Zepp with his free arm.

Zepp shuddered with terror and backed away, crawling further under the cart to escape the dying clutch of this incarnate evil, crawled out of the swamps of Chamal to snatch the life away from him.

Sheverek's face turned dark as thick blood ran from his wounds and stained the paving stones. Then, with a gurgling moan and a sigh, the Scourge of Rudabet, the Grand Marshall of the Ivy Horde, the Wielder of the Golden Lash, who had consigned so many souls to extinction, was claimed at last by death.

Kirbum drooped to the street beside Sheverek and threw himself onto the general's body, weeping uncontrollably.

The revenge squad approached cautiously, encircling the fallen traitor. The leader of the group pushed Kirbum out of the way, yanked the ring of keys from Sheverek's belt, and opened the rear of the wagon. The cargo of halflings spilled out the open door and rushed off in twenty directions, laughing giddily and hooting in a foreign tongue.

The rest of the squad then converged on Sheverek's corpse. Kirbum rushed about behind their backs, beating his small fists against their legs until one of them kicked him aside.

From his vantage point, Zepp could see them working on the corpse and his stomach churned with disgust. Then they finally backed off, the old general's head was gone. It had become a trophy to testify to the horrible assassination when the avengers returned to their home.

Then, almost as swiftly as they had appeared, the squad was gone.

Kirbum was wild with grief. He hugged the battered body of his master once again. Zepp crawled out of hiding and Snomisch climbed down from his post atop the cart.

"Is it over yet?" asked Forg from the front of the wagon – his eyes were shut tightly.

Kirbum looked up at Zepp as he approached. "You did this, didn't you? He was afraid of you. He knew you were plotting against him. Don't deny it. It's the truth, isn't it?"

Zepp shrugged. "I didn't want to. I just didn't have any choice. Ask Snomisch – it was him or me. And he started it."

Kirbum began to growl and foam appeared at the corners of his mouth. Then, without warning, he launched himself at Zepp, wrapping his legs around Zepp's waist and gripping his neck with powerful fingers.

Zepp struggled, pulling at Kirbum's hands as the pup choked off his air. The edges of his vision began to turn red and a rushing sound filled his ears.

Then Snomisch, whose performance as a bodyguard so far had left much to be desired, came to the rescue. He batted Kirbum across the head with the butt of his sword, leaving him staggering across the street.

"He almost had you there," Pik remarked.

"Good show," Forg said. "Thought for a moment we were all done for."

Zepp rubbed his throat where Kirbum's thumbs had pressed painfully against his windpipe. He surveyed the carnage that he had so cleverly engineered: the empty cart, the blood-stained street, the motionless corpse, Kirbum holding his head in his hands on the curb.

His emotions were still in turmoil. The threat to his life was over. By all rights, he should have felt relief. The downfall of Sheverek was an accomplishment that would have been envied by many a soldier in Rudabet and Flammaria. They would have told Zepp that he had every reason in the world to feel proud of himself for besting such a potent adversary.

So why did he still feel so anxious now that the danger had passed? Had it truly passed? That was what worried Zepp now. Suridash was like a still and stagnant pond, crowded with hungry, suspicious bullfrogs. When a little tadpole like Zepp made a splash as big as this one, it disturbed the bulls. It attracted their attention.

And the last thing an intelligent youngling wanted was attention.

That was best saved until full maturity, when the subject had the power to defend himself from the curiosity of his elders.

The brief moment of relief was over before Zepp could savor it. Now his thoughts turned to tomorrow and the inquisition that was sure to follow Sheverek's death.

Not for the first time, Zepp wondered if he would have been better off if he had never passed the sorting long ago, or escaped Snomisch's sword that night in the desert, or been rescued from Kirbum's choking grip.

* * *

Zepp had a lot of explaining to do.

He stood in Tedrak's subterranean chambers, his face downcast, his tail curled tightly around one leg, trying to keep his lips from curling back from his teeth in fear. Tedrak sat behind his desk in his overstuffed chair, his spectacles perched on the end of his wide snout, reading over the report from the Seedkeepers on the slaying of Sheverek. Whirlpitt stood behind Zepp, out of sight, but not out of mind as he paced slowly hack and forth, awaiting his attention.

Zepp was prepared to maintain his innocence in the attack, describing only what he had seen yesterday afternoon. Unfortunately, he was never given the chance.

Tedrak harrumphed loudly, and looked at Whirlpitt. "So they finally got Sheverek. It's about time. Maybe those squealing beasts from Rudabet will leave town at last."

"That is unlikely, sir," Whirlpitt said.

"But what does this one have to do with it?" he asked, indicating Zepp.

"This one and I collided in the library shortly before the assassination. When I inquired around, I discovered he had been researching the tropical area between Rudabet and Flammaria. It is logical to assume that the two events were connected – though I find it hard to believe that this young creature was responsible for the downfall of the great General Sheverek."

Zepp's stomach twisted around and his knees grew week. They knew. He was undone.

"Do not be surprised at anything this youngling may do. He is the nephew of Tapp, remember. You are much like your uncle," Tedrak said, addressing Zepp for the first time since Whirlpitt had brought him into the office. "Your uncle was clever and bold. You are obviously clever – it remains to be seen how bold you are. Tapp would have denied nothing. In fact, he would have boasted loudly about his part in the plot. What about you?"

Zepp had faced death twice in as many weeks. His fear could not be increased, and he had little to lose by confessing his crime to Tedrak now. The thought of asking for mercy never entered his mind.

"I had no choice, sir," he said.

"Oh?" Tedrak raised his eyebrows in surprise.

"Tell us more."

"He was trying to have me killed."

Bit by bit, Tedrak and Whirlpitt worked the story out of him – the night in the desert, the meeting with the Rudabet revenge squad, the bloody murder in the street. When he was through, Zepp waited for Tedrak to make a judgment and seal his fate. He was astonished that the judgment did not come.

And he was shocked when he realized that Tedrak and Whirlpitt were amused by the entire incident.

"Imagine the old general done in by an apprentice clerk," Tedrak said with a billowing laugh. "Such irony. Such humiliation."

Zepp felt himself blushing with embarrassment.

"Relax, youngster. Sheverek was a scoundrel. He was of little value to Suridash or to the Seedkeepers, and we bear no grudge against you for eliminating him. Indeed, I fear the greater loss would have been you. We can use someone with your spirit – especially now. The only ones who will mourn the loss of the Scourge of Rudabet will be a few loyal officers who escaped the retribution of Flammaria – and all they shall ever know is that a revenge squad of their former countrymen was responsible for his death."

Tedrak sank back in his chair and his gaze wandered into the distance. Zepp still felt uneasy. What was in store for him now?

"Yes, youngling, you showed a great deal of initiative – much like your uncle. These are exceedingly difficult times for Suridash and for Chamal. We need more of your kind if we are to survive the next few months. There are a number of things we have in mind for you. A number of things ..."

Zepp chilled at that suggestion. As far as he was concerned, nothing Tedrak had in mind for him could possibly have any appeal. He came very close at that moment to cursing the memory of his uncle.

Tedrak sat up suddenly and turned his attention to his cluttered desk. "You may return to the Hall of the Seedkeepers now. Keep yourself in readiness for our call. When we need you, I will send Whirlpitt to summon you."

Zepp looked over his shoulder at the expressionless face of Tedrak's lieutenant who snorted in surprise at that last instruction.

Zepp could hardly believe it himself. Tedrak would send his seniormost assistant just to fetch him. Then he was gripped with dread as he considered what kind of task Tedrak might have ready for him if Whirlpitt himself had to present him with his orders – obviously it would be nothing menial or slight,

"Now go with the luck of Jobe. You are dismissed."

Zepp hurried out of the apartment and up the stairs into the daylight. His head was still spinning – probably from forgetting to breathe while standing before Tedrak. He didn't even notice that Whirlpitt had followed him out of the office and into the courtyard. He nearly jumped a hand off the ground when he heard the sibilant voice behind him.

"Remember, small one, do not hesitate when the order is given to appear before Tedrak. It is no hard task to inform Sheverek's followers who was responsible for the death of their leader."

Zepp shivered and scowled. Threats and blackmail, that was the chamalian way. Would there ever be a moment in his life when he could be free of fear?

* * *

Whirlpitt slinked off into the bowels of City Hall, leaving Zepp to quiver in the shadows of the courtyard. Zepp returned to the Hall of the Seedkeepers as quickly as he could. He wanted to return to work, to bury himself in the musty, yellowing pages of the heavy genealogical records of generations past, to forget the weighty events of the nest few days.

But that wasn't to be.

When he reached the chamber where he had worked faithfully for months, he was met by one of the seedmasters who bore unwanted news – he was being reassigned. There were no explanations and he was allowed no questions. He was simply led through the maze of the hall, descending to the lower levels where more distasteful duties were performed by the less qualified and less fortunate of Zepp's cousins. Finally, they arrived at a large garage near the motor pool and the stables.

So that was it, he realized when he recognized their location. He was being assigned to the rat patrol.

Jobe's commandment to gather the seed of the gods was absolute and knew no exceptions. Some societies suffered the infestation of lesser breeds in their cities – allowing an unregulated mingling of wild and domesticated seed – and others expelled them or exterminated them as vermin. Suridash, however, sent out the Seedkeepers to collect the discarded breeds that roamed the city. Occasionally, they even brought in a gem of genetic potential. It was another of the hallmarks of Suridash's civilization – a sanitary environment, untainted by the sour fruit of the wilderness.

Before departing, the seedmaster gave Zepp the only reason he was to get for his new job. It was because the Rudabet had released the halflings from the cart after killing Sheverek. "You lost them," the tall, robed figure said solemnly. "You find them."

Zepp turned to his new task with silent resignation.

CHAPTER SEVEN

Tedrak knew that if you wanted to conquer the world, you needed a good map – and he had plenty. Some were intricately inked by hand by explorers who had traveled the ground. Others were the newest photographic products of Chamal's spacefaring civilizations. They spread across his desk like runaway flatweeds, layer after layer, with only glimpses of their edges to give them identities. Some were marked by candle wax, others by splattered drops of tea, and Tedrak's notes were scribbled across the margins.

Jobe had been a mapmaker – though only briefly. He had learned the craft in Shipar atop the volcanic peak Parishandra before escaping his apprenticeship aboard a cartographers' balloon, which brought him to the Rift of the Red Monkeys, but that was another story.

Less than eighty-eight years after the patriarch's return, pilgrims following the Way of Jobe had presented themselves as mapmakers. At first, the charade was a convenient way to protect their freedom of travel in a world where predator and prey were not limited to the wild. But over time, the pilgrims infiltrated their way around the world and became what they had pretended at. While their maps, once sold, never lost their value, they lacked what the Pilgrims of Jobe could continue to provide – up-to-date knowledge of what was taking place across the world that the maps only hinted at.

In the course of doing so, the pilgrims had become the nerves of chamalian wisdom, linking the senses together in a great world-straddling web.

But Tedrak would be the first to see if these nerves also found their way into the muscle and sinew of Chamal. He would learn if the mind could lift the body from its slumber.

And so he pored over his maps, long into the night ...

* * *

The belt of thick tropical rainforest that wrapped around the middle of Chamal began in the eastern foothills of the volcanic uplands of Kwikorak and ended in the western foothills – or vice versa, depending on which direction one was traveling.

But Tedrak knew from the wisest of the wise that it was not an unbroken expanse of foul swamps, thick, overhanging foliage and rotting vegetation. It was, instead, subdivided into hundreds of smaller cells. The landscape of Chamal was marked by the remnants of the last stages of planet-building, when giant meteorites peppered the surface of Chamal leaving layer after layer of deco impact craters. The craters had filled in with sediment, the walls had eroded, the central peaks had been worn down by the weather, but the lack of continental drift and the absence of a planet-wide ocean had preserved the outlines of the antediluvian cataclysm. A series of overlapping rings that formed low hilly ridges covered most of the planet – excepting only the lava flows from the volcanic ridges, the Great Rift Valley and the windblown deserts.

The low hills that broke the rainforests into basins, hollows and bowls, were no great obstacle to determined or energetic travelers, but they did form an effective barrier to the flow of the omnipresent ground water. It was in these soggy dales that the myriad breeds of Chamal had evolved. Each cell had its own ecostructure, its own peculiar organization of life-forms and genetic strains. Evolutionary pressures within the cells brought forth more advanced species, the hardiest of which finally broke over the threshold of ancient crater walls where they either displaced or were absorbed by the new neighbors they found there.

The pattern repeated itself again and again for ages. The first contenders for world domination in Chamal's natural history was a species a hardy little amphibians with strong jumping legs. They shared the wild genetics that cursed Tedrak and his kin, but never achieved anything approaching wisdom. When the ice ages came, the frogs developed fur and evolved rapidly into warm-blooded omnivores, losing their connection to their wet, cold-blooded roots, but carrying on the incessant competition for dominance.

The natural history of the tropical belt was mimicked centuries later by its political history. The region today was a patchwork of warring states, each self-contained and isolated and involved with its own social structure and sexual taboos. Where differing breeds co-existed within a single cell, the stronger dominated, oppressed, exploited, and abused the weaker. The tensions between and within these ingrown societies were inflamed by the natural decay of gene-strains, and while the overall conditions within the belt had remained the same for thousands of years, there was a constant flux in the names and the roles of the major players.

War, rebellion, conquest, the rise and fall of petty empires – this was the constant state of affairs in the tropical belt. It was mirrored in the pseudo-societies of outcast halflings who built empires out of junk, hoarding worthless rubbish and kicking each other around.

And in the midst of this chaos rose the mountainous rim of the inland sea of Meshkar, like a blister on the face of Chamal.

Jobe had a saying: "Water and power run in opposite directions."

And it was immanently true that the most advanced and powerful races on Chamal had grown up in the areas with good drainage – for it was only there that life could rise above the constant struggle with itself and become something more than untamed conflict.

It was only natural, therefore, that the creatures who had found a new life by migrating from the swamps to the central highlands surrounding the Meshkar Sea should return to their ancestral homelands and show them what conquest was really all about.

The first Mehkarians to go forth were the prospectors, searching for gold, silver and the other precious metals in the shallow rifts, the crumbling rimwalls and the stinking swamps below their cloudy perch. After them came the soldiers, imposing direct rule over the closest of the kingdoms so their untapped wealth could be exploited without opposition. And finally the arms merchants descended on the more distant tribes, fueling the fires of war, peddling momentary advantages to one side then the other, allowing the gold-diggers and the fortune-hunters to pillage the land where the army would have stretched itself too thin if it had come in one its own.

Over the years, the great riches of the tropical belt had been excavated methodically and carried back to the great cities of Meshkar. Wealth beyond imagining had been piled up in the vaults of those cities. Powerful banks burrowed deeper and deeper each year to accommodate the fortunes accumulated by the merchants of Meshkar. Ostentatious luxury, gross extravagance, and unabashed prodigality were the rule on the shores of the great circular sea.

While the Red Monkeys were the most technologically advanced race on Chamal, and the winged devils of Arkaria the most arrogant, the bankers of Meshkar were by far the wealthiest. Others were certainly jealous of such wealth, but the citizens of Meshkar were secure from external threat. There might he squabbles among themselves over who controlled the amassed capital of the ages, but there was never any danger of it falling into the hands of anyone beyond the sacred circle of Meshkar's rocky ramparts.

Until now.

In the face of the new threat from the skies, even Meshkar was impotent and afraid. It lacked even the simplest of weapons to defend itself from the invaders from outer space. Missiles and rocket ships had always been the toys of lesser races, frivolous luxuries to the conservative bankers and businessmen who never invested in anything that would not show an immediate profit. And for this reason, it was Meshkar that Tedrak approached first in his lunatic scheme to unite the planet in opposition to the alien invaders.

He could hardly have started in Rikabar, even if it were the more attractive and well-prepared of the two.

Rikabar was not the only great power on Chamal to overpower gravity and launch itself into space – or even the first. The Blue Monkeys, building on the legacy of their crimson forebears, had an efficient space transportation system. The highlanders of Shipar had sent missiles into orbit, only to have them shot down by Kwikorak. And the snowmen of Kwikorak had conquered space years ago without leaving the planet – establishing temples in the craters of the highest volcanoes, where the air thinned into insubstantial vapors..

But the Vegetarians had made the most progress in space. Starting with simple satellites to assist in navigation and communication, it had progressed in a few years to manned spacecraft, small orbiting platforms, and even a cursory exploration of Chamal's tiny moons. Their most ambitious project to date was a giant space-cruiser whose keel had been completed in orbit. The intent of the Vegetarians was to transfer their maritime experience into the cold vacuum of space, thereby extending their control of the sea into control of space – an instrument of power that would be applied anywhere on the planet.

With the arrival of the alien survey ship, the Royal Onion Party had begun scrambling madly about to find the resources to finish the project before the day of the confrontation arrived.

So far, all they had accomplished was to change the vessel's name.

Tedrak would have liked nothing more than to exert his subtle pressures on Rikabar, manipulating the opinions of its leaders, blackmailing influential parties, making discreet suggestions in confidential dispatches. But Rikabar was a closed society, its seat of power nearly halfway around the planet from Suridash. It had risen to its imperial heights too rapidly for the Pilgrims of Jobe to have infiltrated their spies into the Vegetarian Party ranks. They had never acquired the scandalous data necessary to move chamalian statesmen.

Meshkar, however, was another story.

The Pilgrims had sway there. He could set voices buzzing, attract the interest of powerful groups, launch conspiracies and ply factions. And it had the added advantage of being nearby – in close communication with its trading partners in the city of Jobe.

It only took a few days for Tedrak to start things rolling with Meshkar, to make the proper suggestions and to persuade the shakers and movers of the merchant cities that his plan was really one of their own making. Fortunately for Tedrak, ideas spread on Chamal much the way gene-strains did – with overpowering velocity.

Meshkar, in turn, had some influence with Rikabar. The tendrils of power that snaked westward through the tropical belt mirrored the conquering armies of Rikabar racing eastward over the ocean.

And most important of all, each of them had something the other lacked.

Meshkar had no means of projecting its power into space and was growing anxious at the prospect of suffering helplessly at the hands of the angels. Rikabar had some resources, but fell far short of what was needed to complete even the most modest of designs for their orbiting cruiser in the time that remained to them. Space operations were an expensive hobby, and an empire bent on subjugating its neighbors and looting their agriculture could hardly afford the drain of capital needed to counter this strange new threat.

The negotiations were brief and direct. The chamalian character was swift to recognize the obvious and discard petty prejudices when threatened with extinction. Although obstinate, it was not immobile.

Rikabar's fanatical vegetarians swallowed their principles and agreed to the financial support of Meshkar. Meshkar's wary bankers abandoned their conservative fiscal attitudes and granted the Empire of the Royal Onion unlimited credit towards the purchase of the hardware needed to make the *Deragathon* the most formidable weapon Chamal had ever seen.

The ready denial of their own deepest natures was unusual, but not beyond the limits of chamalian temperament. On Chamal, as elsewhere, greed, fear, and the lust for power could overcome almost any obstacle.

But success with Meshkar and Rikabar created a new problem for Tedrak – he was worried that he might have been too clever in planting the seeds in the minds of the Meshkarians that this was their plot and not his. It soon became clear that Meshkar wanted to run the show itself, leaving Suridash out on the street.

Tedrak had a solution to that problem, however. Suridash was not the only interested party afraid of being left behind.

Chamal sported two great volcanic massifs. Shipar, close at hand to the east of Suridash, rose from the desert sands, a towering ridge of red rock and windblasted stone, climbing skywards to the pinnacle of Parishandra, ancient home of astronomers, numerologists, and cartographers. Kwikorak, on the other hand, lifted itself up out of the fetid swamps of the equatorial belt. The circulation of wet tropical air brought heavy rains to its foothills and snow to its broad shoulders. Glaciers clung to its sides, high clouds shrouded its summits – which stood above the atmosphere itself.

Shipar's history was long and tattered, colored by the tyranny of wisdom for wisdom's sake, the oppression of a merciless, relentless pursuit of knowledge. Kwikorak's peaks, on the other hand, were home to lofty philosophers, teachers of the mystic ways of the spirit, explorers of wisdom's own vision of itself. The two traditions resembled one another closely, but their differences were irreconcilable. Their mutual self-discovery had launched a great rivalry, which had extended over the years.

Now in Shipar and Kwikorak, tempers flared, threats flew about, angry dispatches were sent. But not to one another, as they had for ages, but towards Meshkar and Rikabar.

With help from Tedrak, rumors began to circulate that highland missiles were being targeted on the banks of Meshkar and that the feuding mountaineers were suspending their age-old disputes in order to turn their attention elsewhere.

Tedrak spent several sleepless nights at the Pilgrimage House across the square from the Hall of the Seedkeepers, pestering the radio operators there for news, passing on whatever misinformation he could, until the situation neared a crisis. Then, with dramatic flair, he had the radio crew send his offer to arbitrate, or at least help negotiate, between the groups.

They agreed, as did Meshkar and Rikabar. And Tedrak had secured more than an agreement among the world's great powers, he had secured a place for Suridash at the center of the agreement.

Within a few days, gold began to flow from the coffers of Meshkar to the mountain strongholds of Shipar and Kwikorak. And in return, missile engineers from the two highland powers began designing the weapons systems that would be installed aboard *Deragathon*.

The Rifters, both the Blue Monkeys and the cave-apes from the upper valley, while less contentious, were no less interested in the fate of their world. Tedrak brought them into the negotiations quietly but quickly. The Way of Jobe ran the length of the Great Rift Valley, and Pilgrims had much influence there. The Blue Monkeys were especially important since they possessed a space shuttle system that surpassed that of Rikabar. Without them, the logistics of the operation would have been complicated almost beyond the limits of practicality – a point Tedrak stressed as he asked the other powers to invite them in.

Far to the south, the vast bowl of Arkaria, carved deep into the face of the planet, was the home of several tribes of winged warriors, who managed to insinuate themselves into the project on their own. Combining with the Blue Monkeys, they offered a system to utilize the small, one-man space fighters the Rifters had designed – with Arkarians handling fighter-direction. The system was so attractive the others leaped at the chance to include it in their plans in spite of the natural suspicion with which groundlings everywhere regarded the winged devils.

Tedrak was still congratulating himself on these triumphs when a new snag appeared that threatened to wreck the entire scheme.

The giant feline predators of the steppes of Birhat – a dry, unappealing land northeast of the rift and west of the Rikabarian Empire – demanded that they be included in the crew of *Deragathon*. Always a thorn in the side of Rikabar, the panthers were now the only technological power on Chamal that had not become part of the project.

Rikabar balked at their inclusion. Swallowing principles was one thing. Being swallowed by the planet's most notorious predators was something else. They threatened to pull out, canceling all agreements.

The rest of the parties were not so particular about their shipmates. After all, Shipar and Kwikorak had set aside their disputes for the duration, why couldn't Rikabar do the same?

The obstinacy of the chamalian spirit began to show itself again, threatening to wreck everything that Tedrak had so skillfully built up in less than a month. He paced the floor of his office at night, hoping beyond hope that the crisis would resolve itself, there were three attempts on his life in one day – a sniper, a bomb, and a bottle of poisoned wine.

Birhat finally laid down an ultimatum. If it was not included in the project, it would declare war on Rikabar and do everything possible to sabotage and delay the work done by the others.

Tedrak was thrown into a deep gloom. Things hadn't seemed this dark since the night he first found out about the angels. He couldn't sleep, he couldn't eat. The worst thing of all was the awful sense of powerlessness. He felt as though there were nothing he could do to influence the calamitous rush of events as he relayed messages from one member of the shaky alliance to another.

The world waited with tense terror for Rikabar to make some response, but no word came from the Vegetarians.

The other partners burned up the airwaves with radio dispatches, far too many of which went unmonitored by the Pilgrims of the Way. If only his information were better, Tedrak raged, he wouldn't feel so helpless.

But after two and a half days of this torture, a break came in the stale atmosphere of Tedrak's chambers and in the foul stench of armageddon that cloaked Chamal. The other members of the alliance had discussed the alternatives, eliminated options, and arrived at a course of action – something even Tedrak would have thought impossible only a year ago.

They issued their own ultimatum to Rikabar.

If the Vegetarians did not give in and allow the Birhat cats aboard *Deragathon*. Then the others would seize the spaceship by force, take over the project themselves and leave Rikabar out.

* * *

The next day, Tedrak had his fur carefully groomed, his spectacles polished, his nails manicured, and his finest official cloak cleaned.

Shortly after sunset, he donned the cloak, drank a small glass of fruit brandy and walked the long corridor from his rooms to the chamber of the Council of Elders of Suridash.

The chamber was the cynosure of civic government for the city. Jobe himself had established both the government and council on the pattern of Red Monkey municipal administration – although in practice the bureaucracy never came close to the simian ideal.

The civic departments managed the inner city – its health and sanitation, the rudimentary police force – while the council handled broad policy and affairs of state. The two never had much to do with each other and nobody had any authority over the enclaves but their owners.

The Council Chamber was a large, round room, divided by heavy iron grillwork into thirteen separate cells, each large enough to accommodate a member of the council and his entourage. The front of each cell opened on the common center. The drop from the front lip of each cell was a good eight hands and iron spikes decorated the lip, making it unattractive to high-jumping assassins. The opening could be blocked by a bamboo screen for privacy and by a bulletproof steel deadfall that could come crashing down at the touch of a switch for protection.

Interracial discussions were valuable, of course, but actual trust had sharp limits. After all, there was no way to pick and choose members of the council – any treacherous lowlife who was lucky enough to overrun an aging enclave could gain access to the chamber.

Every enclave was entitled to take part in the council discussions, even if its interests weren't always taken into consideration. Members arrived at their separate cells by secret tunnels that could only be entered from inconspicuous buildings in the inner city – a precaution against ambushes. When newcomers displaced the owners of an enclave, the location of the tunnel entrance was one of the valuable items that were extracted from the older tenants by any means possible.

The council was not exactly a representative democracy. Members continued to act unilaterally despite council decisions. The more powerful usually got their way by bullying the others. The less powerful almost never cooperated against their common opponents. But nothing like it existed anywhere else an the planet,

The address to the council was long-winded – as were most of

Tedrak's speeches – but that didn't matter to Tedrak.

He went on anyway, the words spilling from his mouth effortlessly as he improvised on his prepared text freely, extending it by long digressions.

The news in the speech was several hours old – and that meant that every member of the council already knew what he had to say – but that didn't matter to Tedrak.

He told his story, full of embellishment, building to a climax, as though the ending would be a surprise only he knew was coming. He told of the last-minute demands of Birhat, the Rikabarian reluctance, the ultimatum, the brink of world war, his sleepless nights.

"But my worries evaporated," he droned on, "this afternoon, when a dispatch reached my office from the bankers in Meshkar. Last night, the Royal Onion Party of Rikabar met in secret caucus. The meeting lasted long into the night, as the members studied our final proposal. By the time the dawn painted the sky above their capitol with pale pink hues, the party had lost a quarter of its membership and the dispute was ended.

"Birhat is to be included in the great plan for the survival of Chamal."

There was no spontaneous outburst of applause, no wild cheers, no hoots of joy, not even any howls of protest. Not a sound greeted Tedrak's announcement – save for the echo of his own voice from the rafters.

The council chamber was almost deserted. No one had come to hear Tedrak boast. They all knew what he was going to say. Three of the cells had been empty and deserted for years. Six others were dark and screened by bamboo. The only soul in Tedrak's view was a Red Monkey scribe in the cell opposite his, furiously scribbling Tedrak's speech down on yellowed paper. In the Ravina cell a pair of puplings with long, thin tails fought over a melon rind.

But that didn't matter to Tedrak. He went right on with his speech. There was seldom an audience when he spoke before the council and he seldom cared.

"In a short time," he said, "rockets will begin lifting off from Rikabar and the rift, loaded with cargo for *Deragathon*. Even now, the shops of our own Red Monkeys are assembling materials for spacesuits and life-support equipment that will be needed for the work ahead. All across the planet, preparations are being made for that fateful day, less than six months from now, when our race will be tested in combat and our future determined.

"My fellow citizens, construction of the last hope of Chamal – and of Suridash – has begun in earnest."

That last comment brought a rise from the Red Monkey scribe, who stuffed his quill pen under one arm and clapped energetically. His record of the speech – with commentary – would be in the hands of every member of the council by morning.

Tedrak bowed sharply once, drew the bamboo screen and left the council chamber.

Behind him, in the Ravina cell, the larger of the two pups hit the smaller one with the melon rind and ran off with it.

* * *

Three weeks on the rat patrol had given Zepp time for thoughtful reflection. It was tedious work, relieved from time to time by the excitement of the chase, but in the quiet times he had considered the implications of Tedrak's warning to be ready for a special assignment.

It filled him with a sense of deep foreboding as he tried to imagine what Whirlpitt and his master could be planning.

There was something going on in the city, that much he could tell.

Important figures were coming and going from the civic buildings at the center of the city with surprising frequency – accompanied by large and noisy entourages not even the dullest halfling could miss. And there was the brooding silence of several of his household's senior members and the unusual activity at the Library of Jobe during noon-sleep that Zepp had witnessed and that continued even now. Finally, the great metal spires of the Pilgrimage House buzzed and sang throughout the night, sending messages across the planet, while smoke poured from the Red Monkey power plants.

Rumors flew about the city like winged halflings in spring migration to Arkaria. Stories of a vast project involving the Rifters and Meshkar circulated regularly. Trade missions of the neighboring powers were crowded with foreigners. Some were saying war would soon sweep the world, others repeated tales of mad telepaths raving about angels and demons in the sky.

And even Zepp saw a strange sight one evening on his way home from work – the dark shape of an Arkarian flier circling in the sky above the Hall of the Seedkeepers.

The thought of becoming involved in these inexplicable events was not at all exciting to Zepp. His cousins might be interested in strange new adventures, but having experienced such things himself he considered the quiet life of the household much more preferable.

This job wasn't as bad as his cousins made it out to he. He spent his days touring the abandoned blocks of the city, driving an electric cart, learning to use the oversized nets that his cousins employed to catch the scavenging pups and halflings who homesteaded the rubble and debris of the slums.

This morning they had been working in the northern section of the city near a dry wash that drained the hills when it rained. As the cart wheeled into the courtyard on their return Zepp spotted the unwelcome figure of Whirlpitt standing near the stables. He wanted to run and hide, but it was too late. Whirlpitt had seen him too.

Zepp approached him anxiously, fearful of what might be waiting for him.

"Come with me," Whirlpitt said with a hiss. He walked quickly out of the yard and across the city square in the direction of the low building that held Tedrak's office, Zepp following obediently.

"Can you tell me what you want with me?" Zepp asked with a cautious voice, ready for a blow that never came.

Whirlpitt looked over his shoulder at Zepp, studying him briefly with a penetrating glare.

"Not now. There will be orders, but first there are things you must be told. Great events are occurring around us and neither your life nor mine are worth much in the face of them. The fate of our world hangs in the balance and only by total obedience can we avoid disaster. You are young, but you are not foolish. If you wish to grow old, you had best use all the wisdom your young mind can muster. And do not ask questions."

Zepp felt sufficiently cowed that he promised himself he would never again speak in the presence of Whirlpitt unless questioned directly.

But he did not wonder what he had done to deserve this – he knew.

A few minutes later he was ushered into the presence of Tedrak, who sat behind his desk studying a pile of documents and reports that had spilled onto the floor.

"Zepp! Welcome back!" he said cheerily. Zepp was set back by the obvious good humor of the elder after the serious words of his assistant. The contradiction was too much for him to fathom.

"The time has come, young one, for us to explain a few things, and you are among the first to be told. Don't look so shocked, you are not as unimportant as you believe, my kinsman. In fact, you are at the center of my plans, valuable in a way that even Whirlpitt does not yet understand."

Zepp stood stiffly in the center of the room. Tedrak had not calmed him at all.

"What I am about to tell you is the most momentous thing you will ever hear in your entire life. All else you have ever known will pale into nothingness compared to it. You are very lucky to be alive at such an exciting time in the history of our race, Zepp. You are even more fortunate to be involved so closely in the great events that are unfolding about us. I cannot yet reveal just what part you will play in those affairs, but there are certain things that I can tell you.

"But I must warn you, what I am about to impart to you is shocking news, capable of unseating even the most stable intellect. Weather it well, and you will be of great value to me, to Suridash, and to your entire race. Fall to pieces under its impact, and even I cannot guarantee your safety."

Zepp began to sweat despite the cool air of the basement chamber. He was like an empty vessel, ready to be filled,

"Are you ready to hear what I have to tell you?" Tedrak asked.

Zepp's voice cracked in his dry throat and he nodded vigorously.

"Very well," Tedrak began. "Listen carefully and do not doubt that it is the truth ..."

Slowly, steadily, and without pause, Tedrak told Zepp of the alien starship that was rushing toward them from the outer reaches of the solar system, of the great project to complete the *Deragathon* in time to meet the threat, and of the central role Tedrak and Suridash had played in organizing the immense task.

When he was finished, Zepp was ready to collapse. He had stood too long in one position, the blood pooling in his legs, and he had again neglected to breathe deeply enough to feed his oxygen-starved brain. Tedrak saw the discomfort that struck the small ape's face and responded.

"Have some water, boy, and be seated before you fall over. Your face is absolutely white."

Zepp grasped the cup awkwardly and moved towards the chair offered him by Whirlpitt as if he were in a dream. He was speechless, in shock. This couldn't all be true.

But if the threat by Snomisch, the death of Sheverek, and all the other tragedies of his life were true, why not this? In his daze, Zepp believed for a moment that he had brought this catastrophe down on the world himself. It was punishment for the murder of Sheverek, for his impure thoughts about his sisters, his disrespect towards his elders, his lagging in his lessons, and a thousand other transgressions that he had committed in his short life.

It was Judgment Day, to be suffered because of the sins of an evil and depraved world, and he was just as evil and depraved as the worst of his cousins across Chamal.

This was why he had been spared death from Snomisch's blade and the bullets of the Rudabet death squad. He was to be subjected to a much greater suffering – the destruction of his world. It was not enough for him to be snuffed out of existence painlessly and swiftly.

He must first witness the extinction of his family and friends, his sisters, his mother, and his cousins, the tribe of Jobe and Suridash, all that was familiar and pleasant.

Tears welled up in his eyes and rolled down his cheek. Were his sins so terrible as to deserve this?

"Are you all right?" a distant voice asked, bringing him back to his senses. It was Tedrak, still seated behind his desk. Whirlpitt was standing nearby, a cup of water in his hand.

Zepp composed himself quickly, remembering the warning words of Tedrak before the terrible news was told. He wiped his eyes on his arm, matting the thick green fur. His throat burned, but he swallowed hard, taking the cup of water from Whirlpitt and drinking it down quickly.

"Yes, sir," he said in a weak but steady voice.

"Good!" Tedrak boomed. "I knew you'd be able to handle the truth. Now I want you to return to work, think carefully about what I have told you today, and be ready when Whirlpitt calls you again. Remember, we are not powerless in the face of this threat. There are things that we can do, and that we are doing. We expect nothing from you that you cannot accomplish, so you have no need to fear failure. Take care and be well. Go with the luck of Jobe."

Zepp was escorted from the room by Whirlpitt, who led him to the stairs and sent him on his way without further comment.

CHAPTER EIGHT

It **would have made** things a lot easier for everyone if the rest of the population of Chamal had accepted the news of the coming of the men from Earth as gracefully as Zepp.

They did not.

It would have been better for all concerned if the word of the imminent invasion were never allowed to circulate.

But it was.

Keeping a secret on Chamal was as hard as trying to keep a pure gene-strain and for much the same reason. As more and more creatures became involved in the project and as word spread, the panic grew.

It started in Suridash. The city of Jobe had the most open society on Chamal, and secrets there seldom lasted overnight. It was remarkable that this one had remained below the surface for as long as it had.

On the heels of the terrible news came stories of lesser catastrophes throughout the city – and then throughout the world. In some enclaves there were mass suicides, blood coloring the shallow river that ran through the city center. In others came news of rebellions and revolutions. The Baratu were overwhelmed by their slaves, the Chorai put down an uprising at the cost of a tenth of their number, and the Red Monkeys were forced to place extra overmasters in all their shops.

From Rikabar came word of riots in the homelands and a wave of guerrilla warfare in the conquered lands. Food shortages aggravated the situation, and the membership of the Royal Onion Party shrank again from sudden midnight purges.

Flocks of Arkarians blackened the sky above their craggy roosts in the mountains around the dusty basin they called home. The Blue Monkeys raised an army to suppress rebellions up and down the rift. A small handful of astrologers in Shipar predicted disaster for the *Deragathon* and were swiftly put to death. The outlands of Birhat were struck by insurrection as the boldest of the tribes that served as prey for the big cats tried to escape their tragic destiny. The tropical belt under the thumb of Meshkar writhed with its continual turmoil and the change was hard to detect, but even there tensions increased and violence flared.

And four more attempts were made on Tedrak's life.

The tribe of Jobe had neither the time nor the inclination for madness. In Suridash, much of the burden of coordinating the building and outfitting of the *Deragathon* fell on them. Members of the tribe had a part in all the important missions, the Pilgrims of the Way were all members of the tribe, as were many of the technical liaisons between the disparate races of Chamal. They were too busy to lose their minds over the impending doom – as was Zepp himself.

Thanks to the disorder, the rat patrol was busier than ever. Halflings and puplings escaped in great masses from the troubled enclaves, taxing Zepp and his cousins to the limits of their endurance. The days were long and the work endless with Zepp arriving home late night after night to dine on cold soup and suffer the gently taunting attention of his sisters.

The most surprising thing to Zepp was that life continued on around him as if unaffected by the approaching tragedy. He still grew hungry, the morning air still stank from Red Monkey smokestacks, escaping halflings still made abusive gestures at him, and Grandfather Kobi still had little to do but lie in front of the fire in the incense room and snore,

How could things be so ordinary, Zepp wondered, under such extraordinary circumstances? He expected more of a reaction from his cousins and uncles – at least from the females of the tribe. But the followers of Jobe were too stolid for that, as he should have expected from his own subdued response.

A few days after he found out about the alien invaders, the emotional impact had worn off. The knowledge had become an abstract bit of knowledge that had little relevance to everyday life until, from time to time, he would remember it with a sudden jolt of panic.

The world was coming to an end – but not for months yet.

It wasn't fair. Certainly he was no innocent himself, but there were others in the city, like Pik and Forg, or his sisters Sree and Filomie – he had doubts about Tarina – who did not deserve to die. There had to be others like them on Chamal. Was it right for them to suffer because of the sins of their cousins?

There were many societies on the planet that would have said yes, but those societies also advocated blood feuds, hate campaigns, and brutal retribution for petty crimes. That was a warped form of justice in Zepp's view. Jobe had taught that individuals were largely responsible for themselves, and that the innocent were exempt from punishment for the crimes of their relatives – radical ideas on Zepp's world.

Zepp took these precepts for granted, although as he grew more aware of the different practices of his neighbors in Suridash, he began to appreciate them more and more.

The more he thought about it, the more he realized that his initial belief that the aliens had come as avenging angels – one he knew was shared by most of the inhabitants of his planet – was wrong. If they were truly angels, or even an advanced race similar to his own, they must also accept the same principles of justice as the tribe of Jobe. After all, as he had been taught from the time he was born, the members of the tribe were the most morally advanced and enlightened creatures on Chamal.

Could the angels be any less advanced or enlightened?

He began to look at these creatures with a new understanding. He remembered what he had heard from his cousins – that these were members of a pure breed, perhaps even the true seed of the gods, noble and unspoiled. A breed like that would not destroy his race indiscriminately – would it? And if it would, it couldn't be the agent of an angry and vengeful god. Gods probably had little to do with these angels, Zepp realized. They were just another strange breed of animal, like so many others on Chamal.

And if that were true, Zepp thought, then perhaps they could be prevented from exterminating Chamal, as Tedrak believed.

That actually made Zepp feel better. And in a strange way, it helped resolve the conflicting feelings that still lingered after Sheverek's murder.

After all these weeks, Zepp was beginning to understand why eliminating the general hadn't made him feel better.

The fear was gone, but there was no sense of conquest – something he had expected, to hear his uncles talk of their less terminal victories. The guilt that plagued him had a source that he couldn't get at until he had time to think and reflect.

Now he saw his problem: he had only been acting out of self-preservation, saving his own skin. That was certainly a worthy objective, but in the tribe of Jobe it was only what was expected of him. No praise came from avoiding death, that was too personal a matter, of no interest to the tribe. Tapp would have been pleased with his nephew, but not proud of him.

No, the tribe of Jobe was pitched towards higher principals than that. First and foremost came the survival of the tribe itself, and sacrifice of the individual towards that end was expected almost without saying. After that came the survival of the seed of the gods, the race of intelligent chamalians as a whole, regardless of their shape or form.

The tribe had been recruited from the variegated refugee population of Suridash, open to any breed who could pass the sorting. Jobe had impressed upon them the importance of the precious seed of wisdom that they all carried within them and that had to be nurtured if the gods were ever to show favor on Chamal again.

When Zepp began to question with a new maturity just what his place was in the world, that teaching came to mind. He had done nothing special in eliminating Sheverek, only what was necessary. He should never have expected to feel triumphant – and he should never have felt guilty. As a member of the tribe of Jobe, he should have accepted the assassination as a normal consequence of the violent, hostile world in which he lived, and not a selfish act deserving of praise or punishment. When he realized that, the guilt finally began to ease. He recognized that there were higher duties in life than self-preservation – one of which he was being called upon by Tedrak to fulfill.

He looked now with a sense of disapproval on his boasting uncles who had never had to take another life – directly or indirectly. And he looked with a new sense of anticipation at the mysterious task that Tedrak was to set before him.

He was just beginning to recognize that, like it or not, he was destined for important deeds. To be able to serve the tribe and the seed of the gods was something he almost looked forward to gladly, despite the unknown terrors that awaited him.

It was far superior, he thought, to awaiting the likely end of the world with passive indifference. He had already been faced with that choice once, and having made his decision, there was no turning back.

But if he had had any idea then of what he would be called upon to do, he wouldn't have been nearly so eager.

* * *

Tedrak's ears still rang with the aftermath of the latest bomb.

The explosives had gone off in the middle of the city square. A grain cart had been packed with them, and the blast had sent burning particles everywhere. The streets still smelled like a bakery.

He sat at his desk examining the places where his fur had been singed by cinders. The tiny burns on the skin below itched more than they hurt.

By Jobe, that one had been close.

As far as Tedrak was concerned the upheavals that wracked his world were an expected and unavoidable nuisance. So far none of them threatened to impair the scheme to defend Chamal from the coming of the Angels that worried most of the less stable creatures. From his basement stronghold he monitored the developments around the globe. Each day Whirlpitt brought him fresh news of the disturbances that plagued their allies, each day he grew more excited as work on the *Deragathon* progressed.

And this day, Whirlpitt had come to his master with some doubts of his own.

The day was not an auspicious one. The sky was still dark to the west where fires from the Baratu enclave disgorged clouds of greasy black smoke, and word from Meshkar of renewed strife in the lowlands nearest the rim of the inland sea seemed to have put Whirlpitt in a dark mood.

"But that is not what concerns me most," his assistant said, setting his notes in his lap and narrowing his eyes. "The weaponry that *Deragathon* will carry is impressive. Everyone is bringing along their favorite toys. The highlanders have their missiles, Kwikorak has energy-beams and Birhat is supplying projectile streamers. The Blue Monkeys have their fighters, which will be directed by Arkaria's computers. And the boarding parties will be armed to the teeth with sabers, axes, handguns, and death rays. The possibilities generated by this as assemblage are endless."

He paused, shaking his head slowly, then said: "And the probabilities are frightening."

"Picture this arsenal over our heads. Once the threat from the outside is gone, no one on this planet will be safe. There is no doubt that a struggle will break out for control of *Deragathon* the instant the angels are defeated. That struggle will only be the prelude for a bigger battle for control of the entire planet. Everyone will be after the vessel. The situation will be highly unstable – fluid is hardly sufficient a word to describe it.

"Whoever controls *Deragathon* will be able to dictate his demands to the entire tenet. No place on Chamal will be beyond its reach. All of the deadly machinery aboard the ship will be turned against us. There are some among our allies who would destroy their rivals without warning, others who would simply blackmail the world into submission. Retaliation will be immediate and total. The armageddon that we are seeking to avoid will be upon us before we know it. Master, I fear for our chances in the face of such overwhelming odds."

For the first time in his experience with his dispassionate assistant, Tedrak believed Whirlpitt was actually dismayed. He studied him for a moment, then smiled.

"Do not lose faith, my friend. Things are not as hopeless as they seem. Your fears are not groundless, but I think there are things you have not taken into account."

"Such as?" he asked skeptically.

"First of all, what you have descried must certainly follow the defeat of the angels. Our neighbors and allies may be committed to the destruction of this menace, but I'm afraid you are right. Our world could not survive such a victory. For that very reason, it must be our ultimate goal to avoid that victory at any cost."

Whirlpitt's eyes widened in surprise.

"Are you suggesting that we leave the planet vulnerable to the judgment of the aliens? Do you believe we could survive such a defeat?" he asked sharply.

"I am not convinced that we have a choice. Nothing I have seen so far indicates that we have even the remotest chance of destroying these creatures. They are so far beyond us in power – both offensive end defensive – that I am afraid all of our efforts are pitifully insignificant in comparison."

"Then why make the effort at all? We've gone to extreme lengths for a project that's doomed to failure in advance. If we are sure to be destroyed by the angels, why not use our limited time to devise a means of escape?"

"Because while victory may be unattainable and defeat may be unsurvivable, the slim possibility exists that we may be able to induce a stalemate."

Whirlpitt was stunned into silence by that suggestion and it took him a moment to recover. "But master, that is infinitely more difficult to achieve. And by what means do you suggest we accomplish this?"

"There's the challenge, Whirly. It merely requires a measure of control over unstable events. Study the story of Jobe and you will find examples. Look at the history of the world and you will see that there are ways. In the midst of chaos, if you create the chaos yourself, a world of infinite possibilities presents itself."

He paused for a moment, reaching for the incense burner. He struck a match and lit the black gum in the brass pan and inhaled deeply, staring at the ceiling.

"Do you remember a certain pilgrim who passed through here more than a year ago?" he asked Whirlpitt, "When all the plumbing went foul? Ah, now you recall the one."

Whirlpitt poked his pointed pink tongue briefly out of his thin mouth in disgust. "How could I forget?"

"You must find him. He could not have traveled far in a year – he was no Jobe, after all."

"A year is a long time, sir. Would this one still be alive?"

"Oh yes, have no fear. I realize ours is a dangerous world, but don't worry, this one was certain to survive all that fell his way. If you recall his affliction you will see where my plans are heading."

As Tedrak looked off into the distance dreamily, a slender smile broke across Whirlpitt's face.

"Yes, master, I believe I am beginning to understand."

* * *

Several days later, Whirlpitt brought Tedrak the good news. "We have found the pilgrim," he declared. "He is living in a wall of the rift, in an abandoned Red Monkey fortress. We can put our hands on him within half a day, no more."

"Good, good. For now, he must remain where he is. He will not be needed until the end is near. Can you guarantee that he will not move?"

"It is an isolated location. As you know, his pilgrimage has been forced upon him by his neighbors – and he has a distinct lack of those in the rift wall. As an added precaution, I have put agents in the vicinity. The pilgrim cannot move without leaving a clear trail, as we both know well."

"Excellent. Now we must turn our attention to young Zepp. We must be sure of that one, he is too much like Tapp. He must be completely ours before we put him to use. What I have in mind will bind him to us totally. We shall have nothing to fear from him when the next step is completed. And through him, we shall have the pilgrim."

Tedrak grinned. "Now we must approach Zepp's sisters. They are more easily corruptible than honest Zepp. Like all the females of our tribe their morals are loose. There is less to threaten them with. You will make contact with them immediately, laying your arguments skillfully. I don't think they will need much persuasion for this plan.

"Zepp will take more convincing, I am afraid, but there are methods that will put him where we want him. Explain these to the girls. And then, when they are ready, you will confront Zepp."

* * *

Zepp was returning from a long day in the south end of the town, recapturing some of the refugees from the collapse of the Baratu enclave. He was a few blocks from the entrance to the tribal enclave when he spotted a familiar dark figure beneath a dirty yellow street lamp. It was Whirlpitt. Zepp approached him slowly, fearful suddenly that the hour of destiny was upon him. It was.

"The time has come for you to begin your mission," Whirlpitt told him. Zepp trembled in dreadful anticipation and his insides turned to water.

"There are two tasks. The first must be completed before we can reveal the nature of the second, and the first is highly unusual. There will be much danger involved in the second task. Your life will be in jeopardy. There is a chance you might not return. At the same time, Master Tedrak has been told that your seed is of great value to the seedmasters and to the tribe. We must think of the distant future because of what faces us today. We cannot afford to lose your strain even if we do lose you. It is wisest, therefore, to take drastic action to preserve your seed."

Zepp flushed with excitement. "You mean you've selected a mate for me?" he asked. The tribal leaders and the seedmasters usually waited until one had established himself in society before choosing his mate. Zepp normally gave little thought to such matters – both the brass belt that hung about his loins and the strict taboos of the tribe discouraged it. It was something that should have been years away for him – long, empty, frustrated years.

But now the wait was being cut short. Zepp was bewildered. Why was this happening now of all times? It just didn't seem appropriate.

"In a manner of speaking," Whirlpitt replied. "This is not a lifetime bonding. It is not even being sanctioned by the tribal elders. The situation that faces our planet is severe enough to urge drastic measures. We cannot afford to wait generations for your seed to re-emerge. You may not be aware of it, but green apes are not common. As a consequence, we have selected three breeding mates for you.

"Three?" Zepp asked, his heart beating faster.

"Yes, three. Your sisters – Tarina, Filomie and Sree."

Zepp reacted predictably. He screamed. He beat his head with his hands. He scratched his face with his feet. He jumped up and down. He ran back and forth.

Whirlpitt drew a knife from his cloak out of fear for his own safety.

But after a few minutes, Zepp calmed down.

"You're mad!" he cried.

"You look somewhat unsane yourself. Don't be so shocked, every youngling has considered it at some time in his life. That's what these are for." He pointed at Zepp's brass chastity belt with the tip of his knife. "We're just going to make it happen for you."

"It's against all law. It's against Jobe. It's against everything."

"The times are serious. The rules can be bent when they have to be. Even Jobe could not anticipate a crisis such as this."

"Well, I won't do it. You can't force me to."

"The revenge squad can be after you too, you know."

Zepp choked back a sob. There was nothing more he could say, so he ended the argument the only way he knew how. He ran away.

"It won't matter," Whirlpitt called after him. "You'll come around. The fate of the world demands this, and we will not be stopped by one stubborn little ape."

* * *

In the center of the tribal enclave rose a small hill nearly forty hands high, covered at the top with a grove of conifers and an unruly weed patch that supplied the females of the tribe with herbs, spices, and drugs. The intoxicating incense was made from the root of a flowering plant found up here, and a number of medicines could be processed from these weeds – indeed, there were few plants that didn't have some effect on the chamalian metabolism.

Zepp sat on the edge of the grove, watching the sky darken and the lights of the city appear – blue arcs from the center and from the Red Monkey enclave, sputtering yellow gaslights in the Chorai enclave, and dancing flames of torches and cookfires in the no-man's land.

He had come here with stealth and caution, slipping through the gates unseen, circling around behind the granaries and stables, climbing the back side of the hill to avoid notice. He'd been here many times before. When he was a child, it was his favorite refuge from the intense pressures of the household.

At least from here he could see trouble approaching – usually in the form of an angry uncle huffing and puffing up the steep hillside. But there was none of that tonight. No one had missed him down below, and no one would come looking for him. Angry uncles were the least of his worries.

How could Tedrak ask him to do such a thing?

Murder, blackmail, treachery, and betrayal were bad enough, but this was a primal sin. They were not just forcing him to commit a morally repugnant act, they were forcing him to reject the tribe itself.

It went against all he had ever believed. The leaders who were supposed to uphold the laws of Jobe and seek the good of the tribe and its members were now asking him to renounce the taboos, the heavy-handed conditioning, and the teaching he had been subjected to as a youth. They were asking him to spill the seed of the gods in a most perverse way. He knew as well as any seedmaster the results of such a union – decay and disintegration for unborn generations.

And he knew the consequences for anyone found committing such an act – the very thought of it made him squirm.

Would his sisters really go along with this suggestion? Whirlpitt seemed to think so. Certainly Tarina needed no prodding, but what about the other two? Would Filomie's gentle pragmatism countenance a massive violation of taboos? And how could he do this to innocent little Sree?

His head spun with the enormity of his predicament. All that was familiar and comfortable in his life had become ominous and treacherous. The more he thought about Whirlpitt's depraved proposition, the more confused he became.

It fascinated him like a flame fascinated a frog. Despite the revulsion and disgust it stirred up, there was something compelling about the image that burned in his mind of stripping the chains from his loins and losing himself in a wave of passion, surrendering to some deep, racial urge to plant his seed in familiar but forbidden ground.

Why, he asked himself. Why did they want him to engage in this vile sex that tore at the very fabric of the tribe they were duty-bound to protect?

The answer hit him like a solid blow. In an instant he saw through to the blackmail at the heart of this thing.

If he did as they wanted, they would own him forever. A word to his cousins and he would he better off dead, although such a relief would not be granted him. If he did this, there would be nothing they could not ask of him. With the end of the world looming, the threat of death would have little persuasive power, but this was something else entirely. Zepp would have to go along with everything that was demanded of him, and without question.

What in the world did they want him to do?

Having betrayed his tribe and all it stood for, would they then ask him to betray his world and his race, the very seed of the gods itself?

Could he deny them if they did?

All the noble aspirations of the past few days blew away like smoke. There was nothing selfless or virtuous here. He was not defending the tribe or the seed of the gods, but submitting to the selfish will of Tedrak and Whirlpitt and their convoluted schemes.

If only he had seen this coming.

He cursed himself three times a fool for not being more suspicious. Uncle Tapp would never have let himself be surprised by this. Zepp was not even close to being what his uncle had been, but he felt shamed nevertheless. Even the crudest of his cousins would have had more guile than he had. They would have known that Tedrak and Whirlpitt would want a more secure grip on him before they had him do their bidding. After all, blackmail was the oldest profession, the way almost everything on Chamal was accomplished.

Zepp realized he was at the top of a slippery slope – in more ways than one. If he stepped over the edge, he would start to slide down into the depths of whatever Tedrak had ready for him. One move in the direction laid out for him would impel him irresistibly towards that goal.

Just what choice did he have? His legs were beginning to cramp and his rump had grown cold as the heat of the day was drawn from the ground. If he were to flee the machinations that threatened him down below, he would have to leave immediately, casting himself loose into a world going mad with the fear of apocalypse. He was without food, water, or weapons – without a plan or direction to go.

The path they had left for him was narrow indeed and the time for decision short. He could only hope that his sisters would object to the obscene suggestions of Whirlpitt, or that he could find some way to escape the fate that had been prepared for him.

He rose slowly and made his way down the hillside.

CHAPTER NINE

He slipped into the kitchen unseen. There was a pot of cold soup on the stove, but he had no appetite. A single oil lamp lit the room, and the odd-shaped shadows of the hanging kitchen utensils danced on the high ceiling.

Zepp was about to make his way to his room when a bubble of light and noise burst through the doorway.

His three sisters appeared, Tarina, Filomie and Sree, carrying candles as they hurried into the kitchen.

Zepp stepped back away from them, too stunned to think. They were the last ones he wanted to meet tonight, but they were upon him before he could move.

"It's about time you got home, little brother," Tarina said.

"We were worried about you," Since said.

"What have you been doing out there?" asked Filomie.

They had him surrounded. As they approached, he tried to back away. Filomie stepped aside and he stumbled into the long bench in front of the table. He sat down with a thump.

"I'll bet he's been slipping out of his belt with the town-girls " Tarina said.

Zepp blushed at the suggestion and mumbled a quick denial. Filomie and Sree had their combs out and were currying his tangled fur.

"Have you found a way to pick your lock?" asked Filomie. "Or have you found a girlfriend to do it for you?"

Zepp said. "I don't have any girlfriends."

"Poor Zepp," said Sree.

"That's all right, brother," said Filomie. "We'll take care of you."

The long-toothed combs of his sisters scraped slowly down his back, sending chills and thrills up his spine. The girls seemed to be grooming him much more carefully than ever before, stroking his fur, caressing his arms and legs. Zepp felt his skin grow hot beneath his green fur, from his forehead all the way down to the tip of his tail.

It was more than he could stand.

He pushed his two younger sisters away and stood up. He ducked beneath Tarina's arms and scrambled for the hallway.

"What's the matter, Zepp?" she asked.

"Come back, brother," Filomie implored. "We haven't finished with you yet."

That was what Zepp was afraid of.

He hurried down the darkened hallways of the sprawling tribal residence. No light followed him, no telltale chatter and laughter, so he felt sane for the moment.

There was only one place where he would be secure, however, and that was the incense room. Not even his hold sisters would dare to violate this strictly male domain.

The incense chamber was deserted. Even Grandfather Kobi had gone off to bed. The remains of a fire glowed in the hearth end the square, leather cushions were scattered hodgepodge about the room.

Zepp took a long wooden match and lit it against the embers in the fireplace. Then he set the match against a black, gooey gob of incense in the brass bowl that hung from the ceiling.

He inhaled deeply, letting the rough, sweet smoke burn the inside of his nostrils until his eyes watered. The smoke had a strange taste to it tonight, something unfamiliar to Zepp, but it took effect quickly, clouding Zepp's mind, stifling his curiosity, and making him sleepy.

He breathed in some more of the thick intoxicant, then sat back on a cushion near the warm hearth and after a few moments he dozed off.

But before long, he was awake again. His hearts were squeezing, his skin buzzed, and his loins ached. He was disoriented and confused. Incense smoke had never done this to him before – why was it happening now?

He stumbled over to the bowl and inspected the lump of smoldering incense. A tendril of smoke crept out and tickled his nose. A fire was burning beneath his brass chastity belt, and a wave of anguish swept through him as he began to suspect what had happened to him.

Then the door swung open as his sisters entered the chamber, confirming his worst fears.

"Have you found our surprise yet, brother?" they asked. Zepp was speechless. The sight of the three girls brought unwanted visions to his mind and a strong sexual yearning to his small body.

"Ooh," cooed Tarina. "I think he has."

Zepp had been drugged by his sisters. It was obvious to him now. They had left a powerful aphrodisiac in the incense burner. They had probably taken the clippings of his fur from their nightly grooming to mix the stuff – making the concoction tailored specifically for Zepp. It was a love-potion with a kick that wouldn't work on anyone but him.

His sisters teased him mercilessly now.

"Poor Zepp,' said Tarina. "Do you want us now?"

"Can't we do something for you?" asked Filomie.

"Come on, Zepp. We won't hurt you. It'll he fun," said Sree.

"We talked to Whirlpitt and he said it would be all right. It's what they want you to do, isn't it?" Tarina said.

"We'll be just like the ladies in the fables," said Filomie.

Zepp was torn between desire and shame, between passion and guilt. He wanted nothing more than to rip the brass belts from himself and his sisters. But at the same time, he wanted to run and hide from them and from his own terrible desire.

His world had finally crumbled – the last of his faith was destroyed, even his sisters were turning against what he had always known as right. The drug was overwhelming. He could stand it no more,

"All right," he whispered. "Whatever you want. I can't help it. I can't stop it. Let's get it over with."

"Oh good!" his sisters cried. They clustered close around him, pressing up against his body, making his torture all the more intense.

"Wait a minute," he said, as a half dozen hands stroked his body. "What about the belts?"

Zepp stood in the middle of the room, stunned momentarily by the silence.

"You'll have to get the keys," Filomie said. "Or else we'll be caught tomorrow. And you know what that would mean."

"The keys are locked away in the bedchambers of Grandfather Kobi," Zepp said. "And you know who's sleeping soundly beneath the box, don't you?"

"Grandfather Kobi?" asked Sree.

"Did you drug him too?" Zepp asked his sisters

They admitted sadly that they had not, and Zepp exclaimed, "Why not?" There was no answer to that.

Zepp still burned with desire. He was ready to attempt the

impossible task of stealing the keys from Kobi's bedroom. A small voice in the back of his head babbled away, warning him of the dangers of such a course, but he paid it no heed. The drug had made him bold.

"Let's go," he said.

Tarina led the way, while Sree and Filomie brought up the rear, with Zepp in the middle. Sree clutched his tail tightly while Tanrina kept a firm grip on his hand.

"Stop giggling," Zepp warned them. "You'll wake the entire household."

They padded down the darkened hallways in their bare feet, up the wide staircase to the second floor, and along the balcony to the patriarchal suite.

"We'll keep watch out here while you go in and get the keys," Tarina said. "Be careful. You know what will happen if you're caught."

"Yes," said Zepp. "Nothing to you, everything to me."

His sister cautioned him as he pushed back the heavy wooden door and stepped into the heavy darkness of his grandfather's chambers.

He waited for his eyes to adjust. After a while, he could make out the starry night sky with a couple moons through a window in another room. Then walls and a doorway appeared in the shadows. The only time Zepp had ever been in here before was on birthdays with the entire household, honoring the patriarch with breakfast in bed.

He tiptoed across the room to the doorway on the far side. Beyond that was the bedchamber – Zepp could tell instantly by the rasping snore of the old bull himself. He peered into the darkness as his eyes grew more accustomed to the dim light.

He could see the bed. High and wide with an arching canopy, and he could see the large shape of Kobi moving as ha breathed.

And above the head of the bed, hanging on the wall, was a glint of light from the golden box that held keys to every brass lock on every brass chastity belt in Kobi's household.

Now Zepp began to hear the pleading of the small voice of his wiser self again – or perhaps it was the sound of his fears. He began to think about the punishments prescribed for breaking into the box. They were swift and simple and irreversible – and even Master Tedrak would be unable to prevent them from being carried out.

Zepp wondered what would happen to him if he were caught and began to worry.

Then he wondered what would happen to him if he were not caught. That worried him even more. But at the same time, it excited him and prodded him to action.

He stepped closer to the bed, holding his breath and listening carefully to the snoring of his grandfather, alert to the slightest change. He examined the canopy and the four posts that rose from the corners of the bed to support it.

He moved to the head of the bed and took hold of one post as high up as he could reach. He pulled his weight up slowly, testing to see how much he would disturb the bedstead – and, Jobe forbid, his grandfather. The canopy creaked, not loudly, but it sounded like the crack of doom to Zepp. When it was clear that Kobi had not been roused by the sound, he pulled himself up higher, off the floor, until he could grip the post with his feet.

Now he was within reach of the box. But it was too dark to see clearly. He reached out to open the tiny doors on the front, and then froze in place.

The snoring had stopped.

Grandfather Kobi stirred beneath him. Zepp froze. Kobi sat up in bed, swung his feet slowly over the side and stood up.

Zepp closed his eyes tightly and waited for the end to come. A moment later, light poured into the bedroom. When nothing else happened, he opened his eyes,

The light streamed out of the lavatory. Kobi was in there, making the customary noises.

It wasn't over yet. Zepp's head began to swim until he realized he was holding his breath. He inhaled deeply. He wanted to climb down from his perch and flee while he had the chance, but there was no way of telling how long Kobi would take.

There would be little difference in getting caught running across the room or hanging from the bedpost.

Then Kobi emerged from the lavatory and decided the matter for Zepp. And worse still, he had left the light on.

Zepp shinnied further up the post until he was hidden in the heavy cloth of the canopy as Kobi rounded the foot of the bed.

Kobi climbed back into bed and thumped himself face down into the pillow. He hadn't seen Zepp.

It seemed like an eternity before the snoring began again. Zepp slipped back down the post a bit until he was within reach of the gold box once more. Only now he could see by the bathroom light that the box full of keys was itself secured with a lock.

Of course, he realized. The key to the box was carried by Kobi on a chain around his neck. Zepp was stymied.

He could not imagine a way to get the chain away from the sleeping bull below him without waking him and revealing his perfidious crime. Now he had a way out of this madness. But now he wanted to get the keys more than ever. Guilt struggled briefly with desire and lost.

He inspected the box more carefully, but there was no hope there. He tried the little doors, but they were immovable. Then he locked down at Kobi's thick neck, covered with stubbly gray fur and folded over several times with rolling fat.

The chain wasn't there.

If it wasn't around his neck then where was it? His eyes darted around the room quickly. It couldn't be far away. Then he spied it hanging from a nail on the opposite side of the bed.

Zepp moved recklessly. He stepped across the head of the bed, his feet wrapping themselves confidently around the intricate carvings. He snatched the chain from the nail, swung the key up into his hand and opened the golden box.

Inside, on a dozen small pegs, were more than fifty brass keys, each with a small tag attached to it. Each tag was inscribed with a symbol identifying the lock it was meant for.

Once again, Zepp was at a loss. He couldn't tell whose key was whose. He didn't recognize the symbols and there was nowhere near enough light even to see if he could. There was no choice but to take them all and pray he didn't drop one into his grandfather's bed sheets.

He snatched them out quickly and stuffed them into the pockets of his vest. He slid off the bedpost, and scurried across the room, keeping low and out of the light.

He pushed open the door to the suite, peeked out and saw only his sisters. Only then did he break into a run.

"Follow me," he commanded in a hoarse whisper. They came after him in a short file, moving as swiftly and as silently as they knew how.

They returned to the empty incense room where Zepp locked the door and Tarina pushed a heavy couch up against it as added security.

When they were all gathered around Zepp in the middle of the room, he dumped the keys out of his pockets and into a pile on the floor.

"Which ones are ours," asked Tarina.

"I don't know," said Zepp. "We'll have to find them."

For the next eight minutes they ran around in confusion as they tried to read each other's locks and locate the keys to match. It was a hilarious dance because the locks were all located on the rear of the belts and that meant that every time one of the girls went to look at her sister's locks she turned her own away from them.

They chased each other around the room that way until finally only Zepp's belt remained unlocked.

When they found his key, Tarina and Filomie sat on the floor before him, while Sree, trembling with expectation, sprung the lock.

He stood for a moment with the belt, chains, and lock in his hands, looking down at himself with wonder.

Then his sisters tackled him.

The rest of the night passed in a frenzied passion that he would never forget. Zepp would look back on it with a mixture of guilt and joy forever, recalling how his sisters introduced him to the mysteries of chamalian reproduction again and again and again – and again and again and again.

PART TWO

CHAPTER TEN

When they told Zepp what they wanted him to do, he didn't believe it. Traveling two thousand leagues from Suridash to the Great Rift Valley to find a reclusive pilgrim living in a Red Monkey wall fortress seemed beyond all his capabilities.

Now, even though he stood at the foot of a great wall of rock on the south side of the rift, he still didn't believe it.

The first part of the journey had been the longest – accompanied by forty of his cousins and fellow citizens, Zepp had set sail in a Rikabarian steamship for the Broken Lands at the mouth of the rift. There the group transferred to a Blue Monkey riverboat for a weeklong trip up the Daughter of All Rivers to Ring Pang Do, the largest city in the rift, the Blue Monkey seat of power, where he started his training as a crewmember for the *Deragathon*.

Three months had passed since his arrival there – months filled with rigorous training at the hands of overbearing rifter drill instructors. The trainers were all twice Zepp's size, speaking in foreign tongues and wielding painful batons whenever his performance lagged. He had seen spent two weeks aboard the unfinished space-cruiser encountering all the unexpected contingencies of living and working in space.

But since then, he had returned to the Blue Monkey capital and been ordered on the final leg of his mission. Late last night, he had boarded the crowded railroad train that led south from Ring Pang Do to the riftwall. The train was jammed with refugees, fleeing to the hinterlands as the final days before the end slipped by, and packed with the soldiers dispatched to keep order in the potentially explosive refugee camps that were forming in the shadow of the riftwall.

His legs and back were stiff from the train ride when they reached the small station at the foot of the cliffs. Here the rail line entered one of the valley s numerous side branches.

He was dismayed when dozens of refugees disembarked along with him and began following him up the road to the Red Monkey fortress.

How could he find the pilgrim with this mob behind him? With his luck, they were bound for the same wall fortress he was, looking for a safe place to hide and weather the apocalypse.

He kept near the front of the horde, his eyes fixed on the awesome cliff face that towered over their heads and faded into the blue sky a league up. He could see the fortress easily from here, its orderly lines and shadows projecting from the wall a thousand feet above the treetops.

He worried about what he would do if he couldn't shake loose from his shadowers, but when they reached the edge of the stunted woods that grew in the permanent shadow of the wall, his problem was solved for him.

Halflings on wing and on foot burst from the trees, flapping and rushing about, screaming words of warning at the refugees. Zepp could only make out part of it, but he recognized one of the cries – it was Blue Monkey pidgin for "bad magic." Then he saw the refugees making hex signs at the cliffs with their hands as, one by one, they turned away, heading back towards the railroad station.

From what he had been told by Whirlpitt, he had come to the right place. The pilgrim he was after was certainly a creature with bad magic, and given a choice between him and the invaders, the Rifters had chosen the invaders.

Against his better judgment and his deepest fears, Zepp continued on towards the cliff.

It was late afternoon when Zepp reached the base of the cliffs. The sun never shined here, the cliffs were too high and the valley too far north. The air was damp, thick with the smell of decaying vegetation and chilling to Zepp's skin where his passing disturbed it. The trees were draped with a dark, stringy moss and heavy vines wrapped themselves snake-like around shafts of black basalt.

The cliff stretched off to the west as far Zepp could see, but to the east – on his left – a gap opened up where the side-branch joined the main valley.

High overhead, covering the approaches to the gap and the broad, shallow river that flowed out of it, were the battlements of the abandoned Red Monkey fortress.

Bubbles, blisters, and balconies projected from the wall. Towers rose up from ledges and setbacks in the cliff. Narrow staircases and long galleries were carved into the black rock.

Much of the structure was a crumbling ruin, scarred by shell-holes, landslides, subsidence of the cliff itself. Time had wrought more destruction than the most violent of attacks by the foes of the Red Monkeys.

Once it had been part of a massive defense network. Its big guns could shower destruction on enemies all the way to the center of the valley. The strongholds and redoubts that honeycombed the cliff wall once bristled with Red Monkey infantry defending the complex.

Now the big guns were spiked, rusting behind the shattered embrasures, and the infantry were twice eighty-eight years dead. It had taken eight years for the rebel forces of the rift, led by the Blue Monkeys, to reduce this fortress and root out the defenders one by one.

The history of the Red Monkeys was studded with sieges such as that, the confining limits of the rift walls intensified the usual conflicts of chamalian life.

The Red Monkeys were not a constant presence in the rift. Their gene-strain remained dormant for centuries as life went on without disruption in the forests and rice paddies of the valley. But every thousand years they would emerge. Appearing in a single season from one end of the rift to the other. They were without equal in intellect and ambition, and within a short time, they were running things throughout the valley. Empire-builders of the first order, they linked together the disparate groups among whom they had spawned into a powerful civilization almost overnight.

Six times they bloomed, six empires they had built, and six times their subjects had banded together to overthrow their rule. They were the originators on Chamal of cities, written language, complex machines, astronomy and mathematics, medicine, chemistry, military science and political compromise.

The only survivors of the last empire lived in Suridash, using the knowledge of the Seedmasters to prolong their gene-strain.

The silence of these old stones was eerie. In all his life Zepp had seldom been without noise – living in the hustle of Suridash only an occasional foggy night brought this kind of quiet. It was hard for him to believe he was really here.

It was the first time in many weeks that he had been alone with himself, with a chance to think about all that had happened to him since that dreadful night with his sisters.

Much had changed since then.

His muscles had grown firm and strong from his strenuous training and he had acquired a new self-confidence as he learned how many things he could do that he had never dreamed of before. The ruthless taskmasters who oversaw the training had instilled a small measure of esprit-de-corps in Zepp and his fellows, even if the corps itself was less than integrated.

He had even grown accustomed to the regimentation and the bureaucracy required by a global military organization. He was used to wearing a uniform and a plastic badge embossed with his very own identity number.

He was surprised by the extent of his new knowledge – he knew first aid for a dozen traumatic injuries, he knew what to do in case of leak or explosion in space, and he was even beginning to learn the languages of some of the many races who were to carry out the *Deragathon's* deadly mission.

He would have felt much better, however, if it weren't for the threat that still hung over his head at home.

The morning after Zepp and his sisters had abused the tribal commandments, word of a scandal had swept through the household, and then throughout the entire enclave. There had been no way for Zepp to get the keys back into the box above Grandfather Kobi's bed that night, so he had left them in the hallway outside the bedroom. The uproar when they were found the next morning was enough to wake Jobe himself,

Although their crime had been discovered, Zepp and his sisters remained safe – at least for a while.

Zepp was sent to the rift for his space training long before the more damning evidence began to emerge. But now the word from home, passed through his cousins, Fripp, Longo and Groz, was not at all reassuring. Tarina, Filomie and Sree had been identified as the culprits the night the keys were pilfered – their swelling bellies gave them away. But every time they were questioned about their partner in sin, they burst into tears and refused to reveal his identity.

They were suspicions, but no one was ready to make accusations. There would he time enough for that in a few more days, when the girls bore their litters. Then everyone would know for certain who had sired the pups – half of them would be green apes like him.

Once more an awful fear gnawed away at the back of Zepp's mind, sapping his confidence, poisoning the simple joy of accomplishment he had discovered as a member of the crew of a spaceship.

Hardly a day would go by without the memory of that night arising unbidden, like an unsleeping ghost. Each time his legs would grow weak, his stomach uneasy, and his skin hot. He was plagued by a horrible guilt that threatened to drive him mad, leaving him powerless and unmanned. That would be washed away as he recalled the passion and an equally horrible desire would sweep over him. His imagination was graphic in ways he couldn't believe. Nothing he could do would put the images out of his mind. Finally the guilt would return, leaving him a whimpering wreck, torn by despair.

He didn't know that would be worse, the end of the world brought on by the invading alien starship, or the terrible fate that awaited him when his sisters gave birth.

And then, when he was in the darkest depths of his depression, Whirlpitt had arrived in Ring Pang Do with the final instructions for Zepp and his mission.

At this moment, alone, away prom the confining training camp and the oppressive atmosphere of the tribal enclave, desertion took on a new appeal in Zepp's mind, if not in his heart. He considered the possibilities that lay before him.

He could run off and join the refugees, losing himself in one of the growing camps that were springing up everywhere, abandoning his family and fellows and his home. It could only be for a few days – and then the world would be brought to a swift and merciful end by the disapproving angels.

Or he could face the danger – and the fear of danger that was so much worse – and continue on with his assignment with the knowledge that he might actually help prevent that end.

The new experiences of the past months had challenged him, strengthening his resolve. Now he discovered that the strength to turn away from the fearful course set for him by Tedrak and Whirlpitt was also the strength to press on.

He began to climb a narrow staircase carved into the rock.

The steps were worn and smooth from the tread of countless armies and the wash of countless rains. A high parapet ran along the outer edge, punctuated by numerous loopholes for the defenders of the fortress.

Zepp pictured them at their posts, as filled with fear as he was. He expected to hear the war cries of their ghosts from within the dark tunnels as he passed.

The debris of battle was everywhere. Great heaps of pockmarked masonry, were piled wherever there was empty space. Tunnels were sealed with wreckage. Black scars remained from fiery rocket barrages. In some places the rock was blasted to a rough, cracked glass. And mixed in the wreckage here and there were what looked to Zepp like the bright remains of centuries-old skeletons.

As he rose higher and higher above the treetops, Zepp could see the broad panorama of the rift stretching out below him. Narrow canals divided the flatlands into a ragged checkerboard. Watergrain paddies alternated with fields of fiberroot interspersed with closely cropped stands of fruit trees. Villages and towns rose from the valley floor – seemingly at random, but in fact they were the visible nodes of trading paths, roads, and waterways and the silvery lines of electrical power cables. Zepp could even make out the ruins of a Red Monkey palace, a massive heap of overgrown stone down by the river.

In the distance, where the details become lost in a wash of blue, he could see the dirty gray sprawl of Ring Pang Do and the unhealthy brown air that hung over it.

He paused for a moment to absorb the view, then made the mistake of looking over the edge of the parapet. It was some time before his head stopped spinning.

About halfway to the main fortress where the pilgrim had his lair, the stairway came to an abrupt end at a wide crater where the rock had been blasted away from the cliff. It continued about thirty hands away, but to Zepp it looked like the far side of the rift.

He looked around for a way to bypass the gap, but there were only tunnels boring deep into the riftwall, an invitation to the unwary, but nothing useful to Zepp.

It looked frightening, but Zepp had come equipped. He pulled a coil of lightweight, Meshkarian line out of his pack and rigged a lifeline, one and of the rope he tied around his waist while the rest he looped around a projection on the parapet. The crater wasn't too deep, a dozen hands, and there was even something of a lip at the bottom for him to stand on. It was the long, sheer drop to the rocks below that made crossing more than just a chore.

He picked his way across the gap carefully, his hearts squeezing hard and sweat running from his forehead in endless streams. He slipped in the loose rock at the bottom of the crater, and his feet went out from under him in a shower of sand.

For an endless instant he found himself swinging out over the empty air on the end of his safety line. Than he slammed into the cliff face almost hard enough to jar his grip on the line. But he didn't let go and after a few minutes of heavy breathing, he worked his way back up onto the stairway on the far side of the gap. He sat down on the steps a good distance from the edge and tried to regain his nerve.

This was not as easy as he had thought it would be.

He looked down at the rift floor once more and wondered why the walls of the valley looked so much higher from up here than they did from down below, then he continued on his way.

The cavernous hall of the main fortress made Zepp feel as small and insignificant as a newborn frog in the middle of the mud flats. Its ceiling arched eighty-eight hands overhead, the far wall was eighty-eight yards away and the rear of the chamber disappeared into the shadows – the Hall of the Seedkeepers could fit in here with room to spare.

The air was filled with the sound of water pouring from the ceiling and running out crevices in the cavern floor. The front of the chamber was a gaping wound, blasted out by missiles and bombs, framing a bright blue sky that burned Zepp's eyes as he turned from peering into the dark depths of the cavern.

And dominating the scene were four black shapes, rising forty hands from the floor, spaced equally from one end of the hell to the other – the mighty guns of the Red Monkeys.

Their barrels were split, their breeches were plugged, their traverses were demolished. Great flakes of brown rust peeled from their sides. The ends of the barrels were streaked with the droppings of generations of winged halflings. Trucks and railroad tracks lay at their side and trailed off into the rear of the hall, silent attendants to the eternal sleep of the mighty battery,

Zepp had a hard time connecting this gargantuan artillery with the Red Monkeys of Suridash. Was this awesome power lying dormant in their workshops? Or were the familiar residents of his home just weak specters of this inglorious past?

He was struck then by a sudden realization.

This place was a monument to the transience of power in Chamal's swiftly flowing stream of history. Nothing could endure the winds of change that blew through Zepp's race.

There was an irresistible trend towards chaos and decay in everything and everyone on Chamal. It undermined every attempt to rise above the planet's genetic curse. Every structure on the planet was founded on that quicksand and could not be expected to last the lifetime of the builders.

Even the masters of these great war machines had fallen from their pinnacle.

And upon that fact rested the sick genius of Tedrak's plan.

As Zepp crossed the wide hall, ha realized that this was a fitting home for the pilgrim called Griddle. For the first time since he had learned the details of his mission he believed that it might have a chance.

If Griddle really had the power Whirlpitt claimed he did, then the plan could work.

And if it did, Zepp realized, then even as he betrayed his race, he would be fulfilling its destiny. Griddle, with Zepp's help, would only be unleashing the inner spirit of Chamal – and all the chaos that that terrible spirit could create.

CHAPTER ELEVEN

The night Griddle and his littermates were born in a small Meshkarian fishing village, lightning struck a nearby barn, the neighbor's house, the village temple, and three fishing boats. There was an earthquake, a landslide, and two bank failures the next day, and that week, three day's catch spoiled from fungus in the ice house. It wasn't until years later that anyone made the connection.

Once it was clear that Griddle would grow beyond a halfling and that he had the wits to benefit from it, his parents started him in school.

In the first week the school bell cracked – in the second it fell from the bell tower and narrowly missed crushing the teacher to death

Griddle was a curious student at first, but after a while he grew inattentive and occasionally unruly. When the teacher finally went to discipline him with an old-fashioned ironwood stick, the stick broke, flew up in his face, and gave him a cut that required five stitches to close.

That was only the beginning.

Within a month, two fishing boats had sunk – the first in shallow water without loss of its crew, the second a more serious tragedy with no survivors. Then, all over town, the plumbing began to go bad. First at the schoolhouse, then in the small homes where the villagers lived, and finally in the drainage pipes beneath the streets. A rash of small accidents followed – falling ladders, colliding trucks, minor fires, leaking boats, broken planks on the docks, exploding engines, spilled paint, spoiled vegetables, and rotting fish.

When the electricity began to flicker and fail, the villagers finally grew suspicious. They had heard stories of this before and they knew what was going on.

It was a jinx.

It took them a few weeks to figure who. A lot of suspects were suggested – mostly out of jealousy, anger, or petty rivalries. But after talking to the schoolteacher and recalling the disasters following Griddle's birth, they identified the culprit.

Griddle didn't look dangerous. He was little more than four hands tall, a tailless creature with floppy ears and blue fur that grew in irregular patches around his face. His nose was a moist, black button, and four long, white whiskers grew out of either side of his face.

He didn't know what he had done or how he had done it – but he was guilty nevertheless. His was a rare talent, one that didn't present itself to ready view,

Old sailors recognized it right away. Griddle was a Jonah, a bad luck charm, an enforcer of chaos. When he was around, anything that could go wrong, did – immediately. It was a psychic defense mechanism over which he had no control.

Whenever he felt threatened, things went wrong.

He was as much a victim of this strange power as his neighbors, but in a way he was even less fortunate. At least they could rid themselves of the nuisance.

There was a short, sharp debate over his fate – the majority of the villagers wanted to kill him before more misfortune struck, but they were restrained by the older, wiser heads among them who knew that killing him was easier said than done. Griddle's power was a highly effective defense and in the past others like him had been very difficult to dispatch.

They allowed him to leave town, promising a cruel and unsympathetic reception if he should ever return. Young, inexperienced, and afraid, Griddle began his hapless pilgrimage.

He never stayed long in any one place – it seldom took long for his new neighbors to recognize him for what he was. Plumbing would go foul, electrical power would behave erratically, accidents would increase, and soon he would he on his way again.

For a while he wandered alone in the hilltops, foraging for food, protected from danger by his wild talent, which seemed to guide him to fallen fruit or freshly slaughtered wildlife when he neglected his own nourishment,

In little more than a year, he had worked his way around half the circumference of the sea from the village of his birth. He realized that if he continued to follow the coastline, he would return there within another year, to suffer the awful fate that had been promised him, so he turned northwards instead.

He descended into the rainforest where many before had gone and never returned. But despite the dangers lurking there, he survived. He reached the edge of the tropical belt within another year and struck off across the desert.

There was something strongly self-destructive in the little pilgrim – an outcast wherever he went, there was little joy in his life. He thought he might find relief from his suffering in the burning desert, but he was wrong. After a few days of delirious wanderings, he stumbled into an oasis filled with the pack animals of a desert caravan.

They tried to kill him, but when a pistol blew up in the face of the first attacker and the second cut himself on his own sword, they decided he was a charmed creature and allowed him to follow them to

Suridash – at a safe distance.

His stay in the city of Jobe was longer than any he had ever been allowed since leaving home – but it was also the least comfortable. The Red Monkeys bought him from the desert traders and spent six months studying his unconscious defenses.

At the end of that time, even they had grown tired of the environment he created and he was sent on his way once more.

It was the same story wherever he went, as he worked his way haphazardly towards the rift, growing used to the need for constant emigration. He moved through the Blue Monkey civilization rapidly. The crowded floor of the rift gave him little sanctuary – word of his passing traveled much faster than he could. But when he learned of the fortress complex carved into the riftwall, he knew he had come to the end of his pilgrimage.

He passed through Ring Pang Do briefly, tempting fate most dearly as the enraged inhabitants of the city attempted what the villagers of his birthplace had been afraid to. They were as unsuccessful as the desert traders had been and once more he was on his way – but this time only on the brief journey to the south where he found the Red Monkey fortress.

And it was there that Zepp found him.

* * *

Zepp found Griddle's small room at the far end of the hall. A fireplace in the corner was cold, filled with ashes and charcoal and a half-consumed chair. A narrow window set deep into the wall provided just enough light for Zepp to avoid bumping into the wobbly table in the middle of the room. The only other furnishings were a three-legged stool, a straw-filled mattress and a chair with uneven legs to match the table.

The pilgrim himself wasn't there at the moment, but there was plenty of evidence of his recent departure, so Zepp sat down to await his return.

He didn't have to wait long. Within a few minutes, his ears perked up at the sound of scuffling in the outer cavern. Then Griddle strode through the door unsuspectingly.

It took him a moment to notice Zepp's presence, but when he did he backed up quickly against the wall and a deep, painful moan was wrenched out of him.

The moan was enough to frighten the wits out of Zepp. He stood up quickly and backed himself against the opposite wall. They stood facing one another like that for an endless moment, frozen in mutual terror, gripped by deep-seated fear responses.

Zepp was the first to recover his wits. "Who are you?" he asked quickly, using the common tongue of Suridash.

He was afraid Griddle would run from the room, but he did not. After Zepp repeated the question, Griddle seemed to understand.

"My name is Griddle," he said, relaxing his guard. "You're from Suridash, aren't you? I recognize the tongue."

"That's right," Zepp replied. He introduced himself and started to tell Griddle his story – not his true story, but one invented for this occasion. Whirlpitt had given him specific instructions not to challenge Griddle head on. He was to be circumspect, cautious, presenting himself as a refugee from the impending doom who had stumbled on Griddle by accident. He was careful not to raise any suspicions in the pilgrim, not to nut him on his guard in any way.

Griddle responded by embracing this unexpected companionship

– much to Zepp's surprise. He prattled on about his life in the galleries of the ancient fortress, his sufferings in Suridash at the hands of the Red Monkeys, and his opinions of the alien invaders.

"You're the first of the refugees to make it up this far," Griddle said, his words accented slightly by Meshkarian pronunciation. "I'll bet you didn't know that the winglings were warning you away, did you? This calls for a celebration. Do you want a drink?"

Zepp's eyes widened and he nodded. He had expected a much less trusting creature. Put Griddle's defenses were so effective, he didn't need to worry about threats from strangers.

"Drink a toast to the avenging angels. They've turned the whole world into outcasts just like me and you. We should start a new clan – the clan of the outsiders. You can be the first member. You can live here with my friends the winglings. You'll have to be careful, though – I'm afraid things tend to get kind of messy around me."

He lifted a wooden jar to his mouth and swallowed hard, passing the drink to Zepp.

Griddle peppered Zepp with questions – what was he doing so far from home, what was happening in the cities, was there really a deathship out there to meet the angels?

"I was following the Way of Jobe on a pilgrimage," Zepp told him. "The cities are in shambles, the roads crowded with refugees. And there is such a ship out there – it's called *Deragathon*, *'Killer of Angels.'"*

Griddle's face twitched with nervous energy, he was always rubbing his nose or his ear with one hand, and he barely seemed to listen to the answers to his questions. Zepp felt a pang of sympathy for this unfortunate pilgrim. The two of them had a lot in common.

"Tell me," Griddle asked, "how did you find your way through the tunnels on your way up here?"

"I didn't," Zepp answered. "I came up the stairs in the cliff face."

Griddle's mouth opened wide. "But ... but how did you get past the hole at level 20?"

"That wasn't hard," he said, explaining the rope trick, "But what worries me is how I'm going to get back down,"

Griddle's face fell with disappointment. "Back down? Aren't you going to stay here? What about the Clan of the Outsiders?"

Zepp gasped. He realized too late that he had said the wrong thing. He had to act quickly now, or he would lose his opportunity.

He reached into his pack and withdrew a small, cloth bag, dumping its contents onto the table. There was a small vial filled with clear liquid and a cylinder wrapped with paper.

"I really hate to do this," he said apologetically.

"What is that stuff?" Griddle asked, a ragged edge of fear creeping into his voice. "Who are you? What do you want?"

The little pilgrim grew animated and upset. Zepp had to be careful now – Whirlpitt had been very stern in his directions. There was a way around Griddle's defenses: slow, deliberate actions, carefully planned and carefully executed. Zepp couldn't panic now or all would be lost.

"Were going on a little trip," he said as he drank the liquid in the vial – a counteragent for the contents of the paper cylinder.

"I know who you are! The Red Monkeys sent you after me."

"No, not exactly. But they did send a package for you," Zepp said, his voice turned hoarse from the bitter liquid.

"You'd better be careful," Griddle warned, "You don't know what I can do to you. I have special powers, you know,"

"I know, but I don't think they'll stop me today."

Zepp pulled the string out of one end of the cylinder and dropped it onto the floor. It was a gas canister, fabricated by the Red Monkeys and designed to be absolutely Griddle-proof,

Zepp hoped that it would work. Whirlpitt hadn't told him what to do if it failed.

Griddle's face twisted with fear as the canister spit out a single puff of thick smoke. The smoke rushed up to the ceiling and the cylinder fell silent.

Griddle laughed. "See, I told you. It won't work. Nothing ever works right when I'm around."

But the Red Monkeys were smarter than that. Once the string had been pulled, the casing around the bomb began to dissolve. The canister split open like a ripe melon and smoke filled the chamber.

Griddle dropped to the ground like a stone.

* * *

Zepp stood at the edge of the crater that interrupted the stairway and stared down the precipice at the ground eighty-eight hands below. Griddle lay on the steps behind him in a deep and unshakable stupor. According to Whirlpitt, he would remain that way for at least twelve hours, but less than eighteen. The Red Monkeys had insisted that the drug would also inhibit Griddle's defenses, although it complicated the problem of transporting the pilgrim.

Griddle was no heavyweight, but even so Zepp was glad he was going down the stairway and not up. The pack helped distribute the dead load of the unconscious body across his shoulders, but only halfway down the cliff his ankles and feet were beginning to ache from the jarring impact of the added weight.

And now he had reached the point that he had feared most – the wide crater in the wall that he had barely been able to traverse on the way up.

How was he going to get Griddle down to the valley floor without killing them both?

A few minutes of studying the problem and Zepp thought he had the solution – it was just a matter of careful rigging. But would it be that simple? Zepp was by no means convinced of the effectiveness of the sleeping gas. Griddle's power might not be countered by the gas at all. Every time he had scraped his hands or banged his knee on rough stone, he thought it was the jinx at work.

Getting Griddle this far down the riftwall from his airy perch had been an ordeal of nerve, not muscle. All he needed now was some fatal misstep to send him down the cliff face to his doom.

He took his time, transferring the pack to sleeping pilgrim, lacing the rope through its straps, coiling it around the parapet as he had done before. When he had checked everything three times, he lowered himself down to the narrow lip and scrambled up the opposite side,

His preparations made him feel a bit more secure than he had – by tying Griddle into the rope, he insured that Griddle would share his fate if anything went wrong. Whether it was that or the Red Monkey drug, Zepp didn't know, but he reached the stairway on the far side of the crater without incident. Now if anything went wrong it would be Griddle's neck, not his own.

He pulled on the line, dragging Griddle to the edge of the stairs. A coil wrapped around the parapet kept him secure until Zepp gave the line some slack and the pilgrim slipped over the edge. By alternately taking in and letting out the line, he soon worked Griddle to the other side. Then he put the pack back on his own shoulders and tossed the rope over the side – he wouldn't need it again.

As he paused to catch his breath and ready himself for the remainder of the journey, Zepp looked out once more on the Great Rift Valley as it was cloaking itself in shadow while the pale sun settled in the west. Lights were flickering to life in the spreading darkness and the valley floor began to look almost transparent. What remained of the Red Monkey hydroelectric system provided ample power for this part of the valley. Towns and villages stood as beacons of blue and yellow linked together by the bright ribbons of the canal network. Ring Pang Do was a bright bonfire in the north, sprawling across both banks of the Daughter of All Rivers. Other cities glowed in the distance up and down the river. The rift was full of life, no part of it unsettled or unworked. That was the thing that astonished Zepp the most, coming from a small desert city where the broad expanse of land was lifeless and barren.

On the edge of the city, Zepp saw a bright firefly flash into being, grow to a bright blaze and rise from the valley floor on a pillar of flame. It accelerated quickly, climbing to the sky on a towering column of smoke. A hissing, crackling roar filled the air, lingering for several minutes after the rocket disappeared toward the south.

Zepp's next destination was the rocket's source – the shuttle port outside the Blue Monkey capital. If all went well, the next time a breathtaking launch like that took place, he and Griddle would be aboard.

* * *

The train rolled past endless squalid slums, tin and plastic shacks, steaming waterways, smoldering cook-fires and gray creatures with mangy fur. The morning sun filtered through sparse treetops, burning off the fog along the riverbank. Throughout the car, soldiers were stirring, jostled by sudden stops and jerky starts as the train made its way through the city. Zepp had slept poorly, wishing more than once that he had been gassed instead of Griddle.

At the front of the car a trio of unicorns played cards. All night long Zepp had listened to them celebrating their good luck and cursing their bad. The fact that they had anything to celebrate at all encouraged him – he decided Griddle's powers must have been suppressed by the Red Monkey gas.

The car was filled with a burst of golden light as it crossed the Daughter of All Rivers on a rattling railway bridge, the sun reflecting off the churning waters a few hands below. That brought Zepp wide awake and in a few minutes he was beginning to worry how much time he had before the sleeping gas wore off and Griddle became dangerous.

He inspected the pilgrim carefully as he lay unmoving on the floor. He still seemed comatose and a few sharp prods to the ribs produced no response, he was safe for now,

If they could just get to the shuttle port without incident, all would be well.

The rail yard was a monstrous mess, a swirling sea of bodies pressing against the fences and walls as thousands of frightened Rifters tried to board trains bound for the uplands. Cars packed and overflowing with flesh and fur rolled by slowly in the opposite direction as they entered the yard. It was nearly half an hour before they reached the station. They stopped alongside a worm-eaten platform jammed with desperate-looking creatures clutching the last of their possessions in ragged bundles or carrying weeping children on their backs.

Zepp had grown used to the uncountable masses that choked the streets of Ring Pang Do, but he had never become accustomed to the massive suffering that they endured. To see them fleeing in mindless fear was almost more than he could bear.

Soldiers fired their guns in the air as the train rolled to a stop, holding the throng back from the cars until the passengers had disembarked from the other side. Zepp dragged Griddle behind him, a shoulder under one arm, as he hurried out of the car. He paused once on the platform, looking around to get his bearings and plan his next move.

The soldiers who had shared the car formed up into loose ranks and began a slow march towards the nearest gate – but lagging behind were the three card-players who spotted Zepp and Griddle and came by to offer help.

Zepp had a hard time understanding their words, but they recognized the bright plastic badge that identified him as a member of the crew of the *Deragathon* and that was enough for them. They talked quickly among themselves, pointing at Griddle who lay in a heap on the ground and laughed uproariously. With a few graphic charades Zepp was able to convey the impression that he and Griddle had bean up late the night before drinking and now they had to get to the rocket base before the next launch.

The soldiers solved the transportation problem with startling ingenuity. One of them approached a cargo handler, drew a thick, black root from his pocket and asked him for a light. He lit the root, blowing green smoke into the air, carrying on lengthy conversation with the handler – a slave with a steel ring around his wrist. In the meantime, behind the handler's back, the other two soldiers were liberating a wheeled cart.

By the time the handler caught on, they were gone. The handler ran after them while Zepp and the third soldier carried Griddle off between them. They rendezvoused with the other two on the edge of the yard, dropped Griddle onto the cart and made their way into the city, catching up in a few minutes to the infantry company.

They trudged along the crowded streets of the city, taking turns at the cart with Griddle. Ring Pang Do was a mixture of ancient Red Monkey architecture rising above unfinished, neglected tenements interspersed with thick forest. But even the woods were thick with bamboo shacks and plastic nests where tree-dwellers made their homes and businesses.

There was the same mix of breeds here that Zepp could find at home, but the variety was not as great; most of these were forest creatures from the temperate zones north of the desert.

Most of them moved about quickly, still engrossed in the daily business of a large city despite the danger that grew closer with every hour. Here and there were other companies of soldiers, slave-masters leading strings of merchandise in chains, or the bobbing palanquin of a Blue Monkey aristocrat. There weren't many monkeys in the general population of the rift but they wielded a power that had been forged long ago by their crimson-coated forebears. How long that power would last after the next few days was anybody's guess.

The rocket port was on the northern edge of the city, a broad, flat plain, far from the bustling rush of buildings at the main gate. A trio of fat spaceships shimmered in the distance, flanked by cranes and gantries and separated from one another by a league of empty space.

Zepp had parted company with the soldiers a few leagues back, but he knew the way from where they had left him and there was less traffic here on the outskirts of town. There ware also many more signs of the panic that was sweeping the rift and, by all reports, every other so-called civilized spot on Chamal – looters running freely through the streets, burning and smoking buildings only recently abandoned by their owners, refugees streaming out of the city on foot, soldiers standing guard over a few intact warehouses and workshops.

Zepp was not worried by this, although he knew he should be. Fatigue poisons kept him anesthetized much like the Red Monkey gas kept Griddle asleep.

He wheeled the cart that carried his unwilling companion through the gate to the rocket port and showed his travel orders to the guard, receiving in return a queer look, but no questions. The orders were specific, no questions were to be asked and the two of them were to be passed through without delay.

The guard made a show of inspecting the orders carefully, then he stamped and initialed them and gave them back.

They went on to the cargo and boarding area where wagons filled with cargo and passengers were pulled by snorting draft teams out to the rockets. At one end of the field giant fuel tanks rested in wooden and bamboo frames. The control tower and communications shacks nestled in the treetops forty-four hands above the field, constructed of bamboo and straw and accessible only by climbing the trees themselves.

A Blue Monkey official put them on a wagon filled with a mix of Rifter-types all wearing *Deragathon* badges and a short time later they began the slow trip out to a tall, gray rocket streaked with red and brown stains, leaking steam from vents amidships.

His companions in the wagon gave Zepp a hand with Griddle as they climbed a wooden ladder to the side door. On the way up, Griddle moaned several times, giving Zepp a serious scare.

What would happen if the gas wore off before the rocket lifted off?

They climbed into the cramped cabin and a crewman led Zepp to his seat while a companion helped carry Griddle up to his. There was barely enough room to breath inside the craft. Zepp and Griddle were strapped into leather couches mounted on heavy springs on opposite sides of the central passageway.

Zepp looked over at the pilgrim while the other passengers were being secured. Suddenly Griddle's eyes popped open.

Zepp tried to sit up, but heavy straps restrained him – a good thing too, since there was no room for him to move like that without smashing his head on the braces above him.

"Where am I?" Griddle asked with a yawn.

It was too late. Down below, he could hear the complaints of the crewmen trying to shut the airlock door. His heart sank as he craned his neck to see what the matter was. Things were starting to go wrong. They'd never get off the ground.

Then Griddle's eyes closed, the bolts on the airlock door slammed shut and Zepp's ears popped as the cabin pressure went up.

Zepp's hearts squeezed and his ears roared as he lay there, his eyes locked on Griddle's face, watching for some sign of consciousness. But the only thing he heard or saw was a loud snore, a twitching smile, and the creaking of the cryogenic fuel tanks warming in the morning sun.

A few minutes later, a buzzer sounded in the cockpit overhead, the cabin rang with sound of pumps, turbines, and motors coming to life, and with a booming explosion that sounded like the end of the world itself, the rocket threw itself into the sky.

CHAPTER TWELVE

In **the long** and ragged history of Chamal the science of flight just never seemed to get off the ground.

There were two main reasons for this.

First, evolution had skipped right over reptiles and birds, so there were no graceful flocks of larks and starlings to inspire the chamalian heart to dreams of flight.

And second, the flying creatures that did arise on the planet became intelligent enemies of the groundlings who might have been interested in taking to the air. They were jealous of their mastery of the sky and did not take lightly to interference from below.

Whenever some bright engineer managed to divine the principals of aerodynamics and construct a glider or balloon – not a difficult task for smarter chamalians – he found himself the target of attack from the winglings of Arkaria or old Shipar.

The fledgling aviators were quickly discouraged when these winged creatures began disassembling their crude flying machines in midair.

Rockets, on the other hand, were much more appropriate to the chamalian character. No Arkarian could stop a fiery missile as it blazed through the sky. The violent relations between most chamalian breeds made rockets and missiles important objects of interest. And chamalians were such good chemists.

The greatest attraction of the rocket, however, was the feeling it gave of escape up and out of the confining habitats of Chamal.

Zepp had recognized this feeling the first time he went up in one of the expensive machines. He discovered it again as the shuttle lifted itself out of the rift valley and across the smoky peaks of Kwikorak.

Through the tiny window beside his head he could see his world dropping away below him as the rocket turned slowly about its long axis. He recognized the volcanic ridge of Shipar to the south, poking up through high clouds. As they gained altitude, he could see the deep green rainforests that wrapped the world, mottled by the heaping white cumulus clouds of tropical rainstorms that kept the rainforest steaming and alive.

The battering of the rocket's engines stopped after several minutes, leaving Zepp with a queasy feeling as they fell into orbit.

And a moment after that, Griddle awoke

"Where am I? What's going on? Who did this to me?" he screamed loudly as he struggled against the straps that held him in his seat.

Zepp turned to him and told him to stop yelling. "Remember me?" he asked. "I guess your power isn't foolproof, is it?"

Griddle calmed down once he recognized Zepp.

"We're in a rocket on our way up to the *Deragathon*. If you don't keep quiet, we'll drop you off before we get there. And you'd better keep your defenses under control, because if something goes wrong aboard this rocket, it won't do any of us any good."

"I can't control it. Don't you understand? If I could, my life would be a lot easier," Griddle said with a whine. "Put don't worry, it takes time to do its work – unless I'm threatened, that is. So if you leave me alone, it'll let you alone."

"That's good. Just relax. This is the easy part, you know. When we get aboard the ship, things will start to get tough."

"Do you know what you're getting us into?" Griddle asked. "When things go wrong around me it isn't pretty."

"I know what will happen if we fail," Zepp said. "And that won't be pretty either."

Griddle moaned. "I should have known something like this would happen to me sooner or later. This is all I've ever gotten from life anyway."

"Ah, shut up," Zepp snapped. "You're not the only with problems."

As Griddle turned his head away, Zepp looked out the window one more time. Now he could look back up range towards the rift valley as they passed over the sickly gray-green salt flats at the bottom of the Arkarian basin.

By straining his eyes he could make out the narrow arm of the sea that curled southward from the ocean. Falling away behind them at a furious pace was the city of Suridash and everything Zepp held familiar.

Although he had seen his homeland from this vintage point before, for the first time he felt like he was leaving it behind forever. He just didn't know if he should he sorrowful or glad.

More than half an hour after liftoff, the shuttle made its rendezvous with *Deragathon*, providing Zepp with a spectacular view of the awesome machinery of death catching the bright sunlight and spraying it across the star-spangled darkness of space.

Below them were the boundless briars of the Underworld, but Zepp's attention was drawn to the majestic spaceship that turned slowly in the distance,

The ship was a technical marvel, a monument to the ferocious energies of a dozen races sparked by an unusual new experience – cooperation.

There was no precedent for the work that had cone into this

vessel. Nothing like it had ever been done in so little time, with so little conflict, and with so many participants in the history of Chamal.

The construction of the ship was not without incident, of course – but there had been only a few cases of brutal, spontaneous murder, a minimum of wildcat strikes, a case or two of sabotage, and only the expected bickering among the major parties supporting the venture.

The real problems were being saved for after the defeat of the angels.

Eight times eight-eight workers had helped put the *Deragathon* together – less than eighty-eight had perished in the process. There had been only one serious accident – and explosion that destroyed a four-deck module and set back work by a week – and now, with the angels only two days away from arrival, better than half of the ship's systems ware operational.

The ship was eight times eight-eight hands long from the bulb of a bridge at the bow to the massive cones of the rocket engines at the stern. The keel consisted of a thrust beam of heavy steel, cross-shaped, anchored in the engine template at one end and the rear of the bridge at the other. The rest of the ship was attached to the keel, a series of odd-shaped modules held together by stress-beams and guy wires.

A central shaft ran down the keel for two-thirds of its length, a cylinder eighty hands in diameter divided into sections by eight airtight bulkheads. Below that were the fuel tanks, above it the bridge.

On either side of the amidships line were two sets of four giant spokes. Each spoke ended in a cylindrical containment eighty hands in diameter and eight decks deep. There was a containment for each of the major allies – outfitted and maintained by the owners with exclusive rights of territory and sovereignty, self-contained and self-supporting.

This was the solution the admiralty board had found for the fears and suspicions that even the spirit of cooperation could not allay.

The ship spun slowly, once a minute, providing enough artificial gravity to hold things down and prevent motion sickness, but not much more than that.

Between the containments and bridge was the operations center – several decks of communications, navigation and electronic warfare equipment. Between the contaminants and the fuel tanks was a larger section containing the life support section, the shuttle and the flight decks and engineering center where the large thrusters for maneuvering in orbit were controlled.

The ship was commanded by both an admiral from Meshkar and an admiralty board made up of representatives from each of the allies. Rikabar had demanded command of the vessel at first, but it was outvoted by the others.

While Rikabar was isolated at the far end of its stormy ocean, Meshkar occupied a more central position, providing it with contacts among nearly all of the allies. Rikabar was compensated with control over the operations division and the responsibility for navigation, communication, and electronic warfare.

Suridash was given the unenvied task of administrative coordination, while overall weapons control was assigned to the Blue Monkeys. The cave-apes of the upper rift were in charge of life support, and the Arkarians cheerfully took on the duties of flight operations.

None of the different groups was forthcoming with information about the size of their detachments or the exact technical details of their weapons systems, but there were at least twice eight times eighty-eight chamalians of nearly every description aboard.

Zepp's rocket closed in the final distance with its maneuvering engines hissing loudly. He considered what lay ahead of him in the next two days.

The fate of his world trembled in the balance and one mistake could send it plunging over into the abyss. He still wasn't sure if he was acting as a savior or a traitor. And worst of all, he might never know.

The only thing he knew for sure was that there was no turning back.

* * *

Admiral Purdee of Meshkar, commanding officer of the *Deragathon*, was sitting on the vessel's bridge before a wide bank of various-sized video screens monitoring the operations of his command when the messenger-of-the-watch arrived.

The news did not make him happy.

"Admiral, sir," the messenger said. "Ensign Pim awaits your permission to enter the bridge."

Purdee heaved a great, somewhat affected sigh aimed at impressing the messenger with his displeasure. "All right, send him in."

Admiral Purdee was commander of all the hordes of Blue Monkey gunners, Vegetarian engineers, cave-ape chemists, and Jobian clerks, but all the power in the world could not rid him of his greatest burden – his first-born, full-grown son, Ensign Pim.

While other Meshkarians looked forward to passing their heritage on to their children – often even with some pleasure – Purdee was saddled with a son like Pim. The roots of his disappointment were immediately obvious when the ensign joined his father before the screens on the bridge.

Purdee was an imposing-looking leader – at seven hands he towered over his subordinates. His coat of shaggy golden fur was immaculately groomed and fell from his head and arms in long curls. His polished hooves were shod in a pair of steel and rubber deck shoes, and his uniform with its broad shoulder boards kept razor-sharp creases and rigid starched collars. And projecting from the middle of his high forehead was a single, twisting horn one hand long that was the object of many a wild tale among the crew and junior officers.

Pim, on the other hand, carried the genes of what, in a less-developed form, his father called a hedgehog. He was short and round, his shoulders drooped, his stomach bulged, and his head was the shape of a cannonball. His short, brown fur stood straight out from his skin all over his body, making his uniform look almost inflated. He couldn't go more than eight minutes without his shirt coming out of his trousers. And to top it all off, he gave off a smell that was hard to ignore when he came near – even those with nostril flaps confessed that after a short time their eyes began to water.

But whatever Purdee's personal inclinations towards his son might be, it was his duty to educate him in his trade, to pass on his knowledge and insight to his descendants. After all, that was what had made Meshkar the power that it was – indeed it was what held the cities of Meshkar together – putting duty above self and passing on the inheritance.

"Good watch, Father – I mean, admiral, sir," Pim said. "I've came as instructed."

Purdee frowned as he inspected his son's uniform and bearing with a professional eye, but what could he do – nature had given him so little to work with.

"Yes, ensign. Good watch to you," he replied with stiff formality. He hesitated for a moment, casting his eyes about the immediate area, than said, "Here, son. Station yourself over here by the rail while we talk."

Pim moved a few hands away while the admiral reached out to a ventilator fan and redirected its draft. A wave of disgruntled murmuring swept through the crewmembers downwind of them, but a scowl from Purdee silenced them quickly.

Once satisfied and comfortable, Purdee began. "There is much I have to teach you and little time for it. In the next few days I will be very busy and there will be no chance for us to talk. You realize the importance of this mission, don't you?"

"Yes, sir. The creatures from beyond our solar system are very different from us – alien enough that most of what we do on this world will seem like a horrible perversion of nature to them – just us they seem like a horrible perversion of nature to us. After all, if we cannot get along with the Rikabarians and the Arkarians and the rainforest-dwellers and the desert people, how could we possibly co-exist with creatures like these. They will surely seek to destroy us sooner or later. It is only prudent that we strike first."

"Yes that sums it up well. However, there are those among our company who do not agree with us entirely in that interpretation. Rikabar and the Rifter cave-apes are the only ones who share our view of the crisis. There are two other factions."

"Two? I thought there was only the threat of disloyalty from Suridash or Arkaria."

"No, my son. Those two are dubious compatriots in this

adventure, it is true. And they are not alone – if our spies among the slave groups are correct. But they only represent only one extreme.

"The other end of the spectrum rests with the carnivorous lords of Birhat and the snowmen of Kwikorak. They – along with Shipar and the Blue Monkeys – are rabidly xenophobic. They hate and fear all outsiders – and that includes us and each other and sometimes even themselves. They will not hesitate to destroy every trace of the angels, eliminating their valuable technology along with the real threat. The problem they present is two-fold."

"Again I only anticipate half the problem, sir. I see that we must hold these groups back and restrain their more destructive impulses. But what is the other problem?"

"That comes when we have captured the angels and locked them in our hold. It is surprising that such powerful enemies as we chamalians are to one another have menaced to assemble this force at all. It is not a stable venture. Do not expect our unity to last past the capture of the angels. It is my most difficult task until we meet the invaders to keep the crew disciplined and orderly and away from each other's throats – and believe me, it is not a duty I would wish upon my worst enemy.

"Consider this, my son. We have had to construct this vessel so that it is comfortable for each of the parties involved. Each of them has his own life support system to maintain pressure and temperature to their liking. They have each carted aboard their weapons and equipment and whatever other devices they desired – without interference from anyone. Who knows what has been smuggled onto our ship? Each of them has demanded his own power supplies with different technical specifications to run their different equipment because no-one would agree to a single standard. My job has been complicated by the admiralty board over there by the communications nest – " He waved at the knot of eight creatures of wildly varied forms on the far side of the command framework. " – and as you can surmise, they cannot see eye-to-eye on even the smallest detail.

"And worse yet, everyone is out to get everyone else. The Rikabarians hate the Birhat. The Blue Monkeys are not at all fond of the cave-apes and are hated by their slaves. Kwikorak and Shipar are age-old enemies who have been lobbing missiles at each other for four times eighty-eight years. We may have a slave mutiny on our hands before long. Arkaria and Suridash are up to their usual tricks with some sort of intrigue – for all we know, they may be ready to make a deal with the angels, as revolting as that sounds.

"You cannot imagine, my son, how much I look forward to the day when the angels are locked securely inside our hold and we can get on with the elimination of all of the foreign bastards from wherever they are."

Purdee realized he had raised his voice and attracted the attention of a crewman nearby. He caught himself and pressed his lips together tightly, saying no more.

"Is it possible, father – I mean, admiral, sir, that the other races on this ship are anticipating the same thing?" Rim asked quietly.

His father looked off into the distance, staring at nothing in particular. "More than that, ensign. It is certain."

* * *

Getting Griddle aboard *Deragathon* was no problem. Once the rocket had docked and the restraining straps were undone, Zepp pulled himself across the central passage and put his head close to Griddle's.

"I'm only going to warn you once," he said. "If you make any trouble, if you don't follow me and do exactly as I say, there are a dozen, big, hairy monsters aboard that ship who will toss you into the nearest airlock and pump you dry. Maybe your jinx will. Stop them and maybe it won't, but if I were you I wouldn't want to put it to the test. Understand?"

Griddle nodded meekly, his eyes nearly bulging out of his head at all the strange sights. Zepp thought he looked dazed, still sleepy from the knockout gas. He softened his tone.

"I'm not going to hurt you, and neither is anyone else if you follow orders. Believe me, I'm as scared as you are, and I hate this just as much as you do. But it's something that has to be done."

"Where are we?" Griddle asked. He still couldn't make sense out of what had happened to him. Zepp sighed in exasperation.

"I told you that once already," he said.

"You did? I guess I forgot."

"We are on a Blue Monkey space shuttle, about to board the *Deragathon*."

"You mean the deathship that's going to meet the angels?"

Zepp nodded. Griddle squirmed in his seat.

"I don't want to go!" he cried. "I know about ships and creatures like me. If they find out what I am, they'll kill me. I know, the sailors in the village where I was born told me all about it. They told me that if they ever caught me aboard one of their fishing boats they'd carve me up for bait. Send me back! Don't take me aboard!"

Zepp slapped his hand across the pilgrims mouth. "Stop that! Remember what I said about making trouble. Nobody knows who or what you are, and nobody is going to find out unless you tell them."

Griddle's eyes welled up with tears, and Zepp removed his hand from his mouth,

"But they'll know," he said in a whisper. "Just as soon as things start to break down. They always do. They always find me and send me on my way. But up here they'll just drop me out the window and let me fall back into the rainforest."

"There won't be time," Zepp said. "We're only two days away from contact with the angels. By the time anyone figures out what's wrong, we'll be home again – or what passes for home."

Griddle whimpered. "Are you sure?"

"Positive. Trust me. Just hurry up before they start asking questions about you.

"But why? Why do you want me here?"

Zepp frowned and shook his head. "Its a long story, too long to explain right now. Come with me end I'll tell you everything you need to know later. All right?"

Griddle nodded and sniffed loudly. He let Zepp unstrap him and they were on their way.

Zepp made his way across the landing bay carefully, Griddle in tow behind him like a bag of dirty laundry, bobbing in the draft, weightless as a balloon. The crowded compartment vibrated with the rumble of the spin bearing that separated it from the rest of the vessel.

The lower half of the ship – the shuttle deck, the flight deck and the engines – remained stationary while the upper half turned slowly shout the keel. Separating the two halves was the giant spin bearing and an air seal that oozed green oil.

Zepp and Griddle passed through the slowly turning support beams and made their way up the central passageway.

"Where are we going now?" Griddle asked – the first of innumerable questions with which he badgered Zepp. There was so much to see and so much to explain that Zepp grew tired of them quickly. And Griddle seemed uninterested in the answers and paid little attention to them.

"We're heading for the admin department – in the Suridash can. That's where our berthing area is. We're off-watch for now, but I have to be at work in four hours and I haven't slept in a day and a half."

"I'm not tired," Griddle said.

"That doesn't matter. Sleepy or not, you'll have to stay there until we meet with Whirlpitt."

"Who's Whirlpitt?"

Zepp shook his head. "You don't want to know."

They threaded their way through the passageway that ran through the middle of the ship. Countless figures floated past them, moving fore and aft on their own business, some manhandling heavy equipment, others rushing about with message folders.

"I feel dizzy," Griddle complained.

"You'll get used to it. It'll be all right once we get down inside the containment."

The inside of the chamalian spaceship was a riot of metal and plastic fittings and machinery, much of it incomplete or uninstalled.

Copper pipes came to an abrupt end along the bulkheads without valves or joints. Wires and cables hung loose in junction boxes or danced like snakes at the end of conduits.

Bright colored stripes were painted along the bulkheads to help newcomers find their way around, but they had never been connected, led nowhere, and were useless for anything but decoration. Here and there distracted shipfitters had wasted hours carving ornate scrollwork into the ship's structural braces or burning murals into the bulkheads with welding torches – one depicted the *Deragathon* blasting apart the alien spaceship.

The crew was an assortment of chamalian forms broader even than the streets of Suridash held. Zepp could identify most of them, but there were several types that had arrived aboard in the few weeks he had spent on the surface of Chamal.

Zepp filled Griddle in on the essentials of life aboard an orbiting spaceship as they moved. "The main passageway here is open territory. Anyone can use it – like the shuttles, the bridge, operations, and the flight deck. That means almost anything can show up along here – Blue Monkeys, Birhat panthers, even the admiral himself. You have to be careful about what you say or do through here. Keep to yourself and stay out of everyone's way."

"Who are the hip guys with the helmets?" Griddle asked as they passed an aggressive-looking feline-type who watched over the hatch in the thick airtight bulkhead.

"Those are the masters-at-arms. They're here to keep fights from breaking out when some of the more hostile groups mix together – you know, like Kwikorak and Shipar. They won't bother you as long as you have one of these red passes," Zepp waved the plastic tag he wore around his neck on a chain. Griddle looked down at his own, "You can't use this passageway without one. The MAA's will grab you so fast it'll make your head spin.

They reached a widening in the passageway where bright lights pushed away all the shadows. The claustrophobic feeling of the lower levels of the ship was banished.

Around the circumference of the outer hull were four wide

circular openings, each painted with a different color, each well-marked with signs and symbols identifying whose territory lay beyond the threshold.

"What's in there?" Griddle asked timidly.

"Those are the containments – the entryways to the containments. You have to go down a long tunnel to get to the heart of them. The ship is spinning around its axis – you can't feel it up here, but out at the edge, it's got quite a lot of push. You'll see what I mean.

"There's eight of these things – one for Kwikorak, Shipar, Meshkar and Rikabar and one for Suridash, Arkaria, Birhat and the Rifters. Ours is the next level up from here."

They passed through another airtight bulkhead and a similar wide space awaited them. Zepp led his companion towards the orange orifice.

"They're all laid out the same way. Command and control at the top, living quarters in the middle, operations and weapons at the bottom – the outermost level. Each one's six or eight decks high. Most of the crew never leaves their containments, except for admin and the engineers – we're in admin. Stay away from everyone's containment but ours – you're not color-blind, are you? Good, remember, we're orange. And don't go wandering around the containment without me.

"Be careful as we go down the tube, " he warned Griddle. "It'll be a little bumpy and you'll land on the deck at the other end – feet first or whatever else you point that direction."

Zepp led the way as they entered the shaft. They stopped for a few minutes in a compartment a few feet down the passageway – a checkpoint to insure against trespass by foreign crewmembers – and presented their orders and ID tags, then they continued down the tube.

The illusion of gravity created by the spin of the *Deragathon* was just that, an illusion. Instead of falling smoothly down the shaft like rocks down a rain gutter, they had to propel themselves along, bumping and bounding against the trailing edge of the rotating passageway in increasingly harder impacts.

Zepp had learned the trick of negotiating the tube, shoving off on what his eyes told him was a collision course with the opposite side of the tube. Griddle just took it in the rear.

Zepp managed to halt their motion at the end of the tube in order to avoid a total catastrophe, grabbing the safety ring at the lip of the tube and blocking Griddle before he plunged by.

Then he let Griddle drop the few hands to the deck, following him with a practiced leap. He could tell Griddle was surprised when he didn't fall straight down, hut instead hit the deck three hands away.

"Are you all right?" he asked as he helped the pilgrim to his feet. Griddle whimpered and his knees shook, but he was unharmed, and he followed obediently as Zepp led the way to the berthing area.

* * *

"Here we are," Zepp announced as they entered a compartment six hands high, thirty deep and forty wide with canvass hammocks stretched tightly on metal frames all occupied by slumbering, snoring figures.

"Are all the rooms this small?" Griddle asked.

Zepp, who had grown used to the cramped quarters and didn't think the berthing area was that small, brushed off the question.

"Come with me," he said.

He took Griddle to a tiny compartment off the rear of the berthing area. "This is something I've wanted to do since I met you," he said. "Take off your clothes and climb inside."

"What?" Griddle yapped.

"Don't ask questions, just do as you're told." He pulled the straps from Griddle's shoulders and the other complied.

"What is this?"

"It's something you need desperately" Zepp said. "A shower."

An expression of horror struck Griddle's face and he hesitated at the threshold to the compartment. "Go on in," Zepp said. "It won't hurt you a bit."

"It won't work. You'll see. It'll break down as soon as I step inside. Don't waste your time."

"If it does, it does, now got in there."

Zepp set the controls on the elaborate space-shower and shut the door behind Griddle. At first, nothing happened.

"See, I told you so," Griddle called from inside.

Then Zepp pounded on the door a couple times to get the shower started – a trick he had learned when he first came aboard.

Griddle's screams were drowned out by the sound of rushing water.

CHAPTER THIRTEEN

Zepp slept poorly despite his fatigue. He tossed and turned all through the watch, awakening several times. And each time he awoke, he turned to see the silent figure of Griddle, sitting on the bunk across from his, awake, but motionless.

Before long, before Zepp wanted it, the lights flashed on and the master-at-arms came through the berthing area, snarling and snapping, shaking the crew out of their bunks.

Zepp found Griddle a disposable paper coverall like his own, tore off the excess material from the overlong pants legs, and helped him dress.

Then they went down to the mess deck, a level below the berthing area, where dozens of furry and fuzzy creatures wolfed down hot porridge and bitter-root tea.

Griddle ate quickly and without delicacy. When he was through, gray porridge stuck to his whiskers, his ear and his chin.

"Wipe your face" Zepp told him. "As soon as you're finished we have to go talk to Whirlpitt."

"Is he your chief?" Griddle asked. "I'll bet he's stern and serious – chiefs always are. They're insiders, all of them. They don't see things the way outsiders like us do. They don't see things at all sometimes. Are you going to tell me why you brought me up here?"

"Later," Zepp said.

As they were getting up to leave, a loud scream cut through the babble of the mess deck. Up at the steam line where the porridge was being dished out, a gray-furred crewman with short antlers was clutching his hand to his breast while the teapot sprayed hot liquid freely into the air. The mess cooks were converging on the machine while the fellow with antlers moaned in pain. One of them slipped on the wet deck and did a slow-motion, low-G dive against the wall.

As they dropped their steel bowls into the bin at the scullery, Griddle gave a sheepish grin and looked up at Zepp.

"Its starting," he said.

* * *

Whirlpitt's office was almost as small as the shower Zepp had tossed Griddle into the night before – there was barely enough room for the two of them to stand side by side in front of Whirlpitt's desk.

The small, black eyes of Tedrak's assistant narrowed as he studied Griddle carefully. Zepp searched for some expression in his face, but there was nothing but a cold, hard void without compassion.

"So this is our dangerous saboteur," he said after a moment's silent reflection. "What has he done so far, Zepp?"

"Not much. The teapot sprung a leak on the mess deck this morning and he took credit for it, but I don't know one way or the other."

Whirlpitt hissed. "That's a start. Tell me, Griddle, do you recall your visit to Suridash – your stay with the Red Monkeys?"

Griddle winced and shuddered, but said nothing.

"They also remember quite a bit about you. It makes very interesting reading. Listen carefully, Zepp, this information might be very valuable in the next few days.

"Griddle, the Red Monkeys made quite a thorough study of your ... knack. I doubt if they told you much about their findings, but you should be aware of what it is you do and why.

"At the root of your strange talent is a highly sophisticated principle of physics. Most of the time, the scientists tell me, energy cannot be created or destroyed – only transformed. But did you know that when the interval of time is too small to he measured – so small as to be almost instantaneous – tremendous amounts of energy can be released – actually created out of nothingness. There is something inside you, Griddle, that can release this energy – something similar to the ability of the telepaths to read the thoughts of the angels. It is not something you can control, but it works to protect you.

"It is most effective on small mechanical and electrical devices. Incipient metal fatigue, crystal defects, loose wires and worn parts are most vulnerable to your power. At the crucial instant, vital machinery fails, accidents occur, systems malfunction, all without visible cause. And a new vessel filled with untried and untested equipment is overripe for an assault by your insidious influence"

"The Red Monkeys documented your effect on your environment very carefully. It is cumulative over a period of time – that is, the longer you are around, the worse things get. And it is highly dependent on proximity – you must get close to the machinery in order to affect it. After that, the natural tendency of order to collapse into chaos takes over.

"Therefore, Zepp, your duty for the time being will be to escort our friend here around the *Deragathon*. Take him to every vital area in the ship – leave no place untouched. By the time we meet the angels, this vessel should not even be able to signal its surrender, the disorder will be so complete.

"Now go!"

Zepp and Griddle hurried from the cramped office and made their way through crowded corridors to the print shop. Griddle was quiet at first, but when he and Zepp were alone, he stopped and faced Zepp with a sad but defiant expression.

"Will you tell me what we're doing now?" He asked.

"We're going to deliver the daily operations order to the ship's departments. They're in those mesh bins over there."

"That's not what I mean. You want to sabotage this ship, don't you? That's why you brought me up here, isn't it?"

Zepp looked around to see if anyone was within earshot. "Has it taken you this long to figure it out?"

"I thought so."

"Do you have any objections? Because it won't do you much good if you do."

"But isn't that betraying our whole world?"

"So? What has the world ever done for you?"

"Nothing," Griddle replied. "But it's my world, too. Why are you doing it?"

"You're not the only one with problems," Zepp said, "I'm only doing what I have to. Are you with me or do we go back to Whirlpitt and tell him you won't cooperate?"

Griddle frowned in thoughtful silence for a moment, then his nervous twitching returned.

"I guess I'm with you," he said. "For now, anyway."

* * *

Mitrak the Prayermaster made the call to prayer in the middle of the first morning watch by blowing on a prayer horn made from his grandfather's antler. He was a foreboding figure even to his fellow highlanders. Seven hands tall, with a shaggy coat of white fur, he had sharp fangs protruding from his mouth, fiery red eyes, and powerful limbs.

His authority came from both his size and his spiritual purity. As an acolyte, he had spent three years in a pressurized retreat on the lip of a volcanic crater meditating on the plasma flux in a Kwikorak energy beam. He began the morning prayer with a brief mantra from the riddle he had set for himself before leaving Kwikorak – he was trying to figure out a way to boost output on the energy beam without blowing out the plasma flow.

Mitrak was one of the second echelon of leaders in the Kwikorak contingent, and his watch this morning consisted of a trio of lazy, overfed guards at the pressure lock leading to the main body of the *Deragathon*. The environmental parameters in the Kwikorak containment were somewhat different from the majority of the vessel. They liked their air thin and cold, the way it was back home. Heavy refrigeration coils, caked with white frost, kept the entry checkpoint comfortable in the untempered sunlight of space.

The guards followed the prayer without zeal, which Mitrak noted for further mention to their section leader and spiritual overlord. He would see to it that their attitudes were improved after a little special discipline.

In the middle of the ritual, the buzzer at the pressure lock sounded – someone wanted to pass through. Mitrak ignored it and continued the prayer.

"May the Spirit of the Void smite our foes. May the Avenging Angels of the alien Spirit be struck with mortal fear. May our warriors be touched by the breath of God. May our victory be swift and complete. May our energy beams be strong and true. And may the enemy inflict severe and debilitating casualties on our unholy rivals from Shipar."

The buzzer sounded again as Mitrak cut the air with his ritual dagger. He sheathed the small blade and ended the prayer, slapping the switch for the surveillance cameras inside the lock.

There were two messengers from Admin waiting there with a bundle between them. He went to the door and slid it open with a mighty shove.

"What is your business here?" he demanded.

The metal box strapped to his belt squeaked out a translation in the lowlander tongue used by the Admin servants. The translator was an invention of a High Meditator back home in Kwikorak.

The messengers – a green ape and a blue-furred, rabbity creature – shivered violently enough to lift themselves off the deck in the negligible illusion of gravity here near the keel. One of them babbled a reply to Mitrak's question.

"Messengers from Admin with the daily oporder," the translator barked at his belt. The highlanders were the only ones aboard the ship with these devices – it never occurred to them to share their gadgetry.

Mitrak sneered and pulled the bag away from the blue messenger, almost taking him with it. He pulled out a copy and looked it over quickly. It was just as the messenger had indicated. He inspected the bag – nothing suspicious there. He was cautious, however. Rumors had been thick through the ship. Plotters and schemers were everywhere.

When he was satisfied with the innocence of the package, he ordered the pair away.

They refused.

The translator squawked with a protest. "Sign the receipt, frog-breath."

The green ape looked confused and his mate quivered with apparent fear. The translator squealed with foreign tongues. Mitrak drew back a pawful of retractable claws as if ready to strike, but the ape did not flinch.

If he had known what the translator had added to his request he might have been more fearful. Instead, he held out the receipt and a stylus, motioning to Mitrak to sign.

The translator began to chant the opening lines of the morning prayer. Mitrak grew puzzled as the gadget made a new sound. He spoke into it at length, describing the ape's unholy ancestry in detail. The translator repeated his words perfectly, in the highland tongue, not translating a thing.

He pulled the instrument from his belt and shook it, pushing buttons and barking out oaths. Finally he threw it against the bulkhead where it smashed into pieces.

He grabbed the receipt from the messenger's hand, scribbled his initials on it, and thrust it back. Then he waved at the pair from Admin and pointed at the door. They got the message and fled.

He looked down at the pieces of the translator lying on the deck. The High Meditator would not he pleased.

* * *

Tartok of Birhat stretched his lithe, cat-like body, extending himself by more than half his normal standing height and rippling tight bunches of cable-like muscles under loose skin. He yawned, revealing a mouth full of sharp, ragged teeth.

His brown fur, thick with round, yellow spots, looked faded and unnatural in the harsh, fluorescent lighting, but the effect of his display on the cage of plump, ovine grazers was undiminished.

They cowered and bleated and crowded into one corner of the cage.

"They've little to fear from you, Tartok," jibed Eltok, Tartok's older cousin. "They know they are earmarked for the victory celebration, but I'm afraid there will be little left of them for the Outer Clan once the rest of us have had our feast. Don't they make your mouth water?"

Tartok muttered an answer. His blood always boiled at the sight of Eltok. As a member of the Middle Clan, Eltok was his senior in more than age, as well as an object of much jealousy on Tartok's part. Tartok was a member of the Outer Clan – neither of his parents had been predator cats and he had spent his youth as an outcast, scavenging on the outskirts of the camps of the Tokmir clan until he reached adulthood and was allowed to join. Eltok's father was a member of the Inner Clan, one of the few truebreeds whose parents were often close relatives – his mother was not. He was always acutely aware of his own status and he made Tartok bear the burden of his insecurity and envy.

What angered Tartok most was that there was nothing ha could do to resolve the situation. The two were clansmen and would have to suffer with one another until one of than died.

Tartok focused his eyes on the grazers in the cage, trying to ignore his cousin, but the other would not let him off so easy.

There was one creature that did not shake with fear, a female who stood like a rock in the midst of her fellows. She caught Tartok's eye with a defiant gaze. She had unusual eyes, deep and knowing, flashing with the light of wisdom..

"There's one for you, cousin," Eltok taunted. "She looks as plump and pleasing as they come. Juicy and tender, with a good liver."

Tartok ignored the remarks. His eyes had caught other details of the female – the lines of her round, young body, the curving flanks, the full breasts covered with soft fur, the eyes that burned so boldly. In her own way she was quite beautiful.

Tartok wasn't the only who had noticed that. Eltok also saw both the beauty and the light in Tartok's eyes.

"Ho-ho. I see she tempts other appetites in my cousin. You shouldn't harbor forbidden desires, Tartok. They'll only get you in trouble."

Tartok turned away from the cage and glared at his cousin. His face turned red under the fur and he bared his teeth. Eltok just laughed.

Tartok left the compartment with a single bound, leaping through the hatch in the overhead and climbing the tube toward the center of the ship. He was supposed to be on duty now anyway and perhaps a few hours on watch would rid him of his humiliation.

The clans of Birhat were unusual even for Chamal. They were technologically advanced, but they lacked many of the outer trappings of their more civilized cousins. They lacked permanent settlements – with the single exception of the castle of Smirtar, home of the grand patriarch of all the clans. Their technology was mostly derivative, pirated from the rift and from Rikabar before the Vegetarians took power.

Their contingent provided *Deragathon* with manpower for less technical duties – ship's maintenance and boarding parties. They also supplied a battery of sophisticated weapons – projectile streamers that were deadly against fragile spacecraft.

Tartok's status as an Outer Clansman made him a junior officer in the Birhat chain-of-command, responsible for maintaining order among the slaves and underlings, commander of a projectile streamer when the battle was joined.

When he reached the top of the entry tube, he found the guards holding a pair of messengers from Admin. It wouldn't be to Birhat's advantage for the lower ranks to eat a messenger from an ally. Only a few of the Birhat cats were allowed out of the containment to mingle with the rest of the crew. Those orders came from Smirtar himself and were a condition imposed on Birhat by the alliance before they were allowed aboard.

Although the gunners were eying the two messengers hungrily, Tartok was not concerned. Everyone in the Birhat contingent was well-fed and there was little chance of a slip in discipline. The penalties were too great.

The messengers had a mesh bag filled with book-sized documents – the daily oporder. He knew the routine. He checked over one of the books carefully, then reached out a claw to hook the receipt from the green ape's hand.

He was about to sign when a loud commotion boiled up out of the tube from below.

First to emerge was a fat, red-furred grazer, its tongue flapping from an open mouth, its short legs pumping furiously but to little effect as it overshot the edge of the doorway and caromed off one wall.

Following it was a trio of Tartok's clansmen, their bodies flexing and contracting in great leaps as if they were bounding across the steppes of home.

The two messengers from Admin ducked back towards the hub of the ship as the parade rushed past. Tartok grinned at them apologetically, and murmured, "Breakfast."

Somehow it must have escaped from the galley. That was bad form – someone would have to pay. Perhaps a slave had released him to create disorder. You could never trust those jackals.

The grazer made a squealing sound as it realized there was no escape – the pair from Admin blocked its way into the rest of the ship and the third cat had stopped in the passage back into the containment.

It bounced off the walls a few times, then grabbed the leg of desk that stood at the end of the compartment. It screamed in protest as the others grabbed it by the legs and pulled it from hiding. Tartok noticed tears in its eyes as they carried it back below. He signed the receipt and the messengers were on their way.

* * *

Pirr-Click-Wheet hovered between the deck and ceiling in the spacious flight deck, a pair of smaller attendants keeping station above and behind him. The Arkarian despised the confining compartments of the spacecruiser. The flight deck was the only place he felt comfortable, the only place with room for him to stretch his wings. He held his position on the gentle ventilations of the overhead blowers as surely as if were riding a desert thermal.

He looked over the band of co-conspirators mustered before him – a band of Blue Monkey slaves – and his target – their simian slave master.

While they looked innocent enough, there was a serious scheme afoot. Both Pirr-Click-Wheet and the slaves were more than they appeared to be.

The slaves were part of the flight deck crew assigned to haul rocket-propelled fighters into position for launch. But this morningwatch, they were also a band of assassins preparing to eliminate another Blue Monkey master, clearing the way for a mutiny that was planned for the following day. The plot had been prepared by the Arkarians and was being led by Pirr-Click-Wheet, a member of the Arkarian Cult of the Lost Argument.

He did not speak the languages of the slaves, but he made the proper recognition signals and the plan was set in motion. The moving crew attached the harnesses and detached the restraining straps on a nearby fighter and began moving it in the direction of the huge airlock doors at the edge of the flight deck. In the meantime, a pair of large, but seemingly slow-witted handlers flanked the Blue Monkey master at his perch on a workbench beside the door, arguing over which rocket-plane was to be moved next.

Although Jobe and his descendants never knew it, the wandering prophet of Suridash had left an unusual legacy to the winged beasts of Arkaria. The Cult of the Lost Argument had been founded generations ago by the Arkarian who discovered one night that his race was not the only one blessed with the spark of wisdom. The shock to the Arkarian sense of self-importance was still sweeping through the society of the fliers. The cult had become a revolutionary movement, motivated by the self-doubt and self-criticism that the Lost Argument had spawned. Its members were radical individualists, committed to personal freedom and opposed to authority of any kind. Few outsiders knew of the cult – the fliers were secretive and clannish to an extreme even for Chamal.

Among those few were the mutinous slaves of the rift who had plotted for years against their Blue Monkey masters. While the Rifter underclass had differences of opinion with the Arkarians, they were agreed on one principle – the Blue Monkeys should not gain control of the *Deragathon* when the battle was over. To that end, they had joined forces in an alliance of sabotage and sedition, intent on denying the space vessel to the Blue Monkeys and to the other extremists in the alliance – the highlanders of Shipar and Kwikorak and the Birhat cats. The cult considered those fanatics to be the worst threat to Chamal – rabid xenophobes, all of them, who would kill anything or anyone who crossed their path.

The Arkarian saw what was coming long before the slave master caught on.

The fighter – one of twelve on this deck, half the ship's complement – was fully fueled and armed. It took quite a large effort to overcome its inertia and get that mass moving.

It took an equally large effort to stop it.

Any miscalculation in direction of the effort and the results could he disastrous – but this was no miscalculation. The plane moved slowly, a few fingers per second, but there was a lot of momentum behind it. The Blue Monkey, distracted by the two slaves, did not notice the path it was on until it was too late.

Instead of a safe and easy course to the spotting circle, it was bearing down on the workbench beside the airlock.

Pirr-Click-Wheet noted silently the moment when a reverse tug should have been applied. Instead of straining in their harnesses, the flight crew was drifting along behind the plane, their eyes casting around suspiciously.

When the Blue Monkey realized what was up, it was too late. He squirmed to escape the inevitable impact, but the slaves on either flank held him down. At the last minute, they dashed aside, leaving the slavemaster to be squashed like a bug on a rock.

The nose of the fighter struck the wall and buried itself in the thin metal, the body following slowly and surely, as if mounted on a gigantic press.

The impact with the wall absorbed enough energy to stop the fighter. It sat there, its wings resting on the workbench, the air whistling loudly as it escaped around the edges of the hole where the nose was buried. A globule of dark blood drifted up from the wreckage where the Blue Monkey's broken body lay and was swept away on the draft.

The entire flight deck broke out in confused activity as sirens and horns went off in alarm. Flight crews from neighboring planes flew across the hangar, grabbing cross-beams and stanchions to stop themselves at the scene of the accident, but there was nothing they could do now but patch the leaks and repair the plane.

In the midst of the commotion only Pirr-Click-Wheet noticed a second Blue Monkey body drift out from under the wreckage, a fatal bruise across his forehead. These slaves were bold.

The Arkarian scanned the area with keen eyes – eyes that were accustomed to picking out rodents on the desert from two leagues up. Were there any witnesses to the incident?

He saw two strangers near the control shack. Who were they?

A green ape and a root-eater with mangy fur – he recognized one of them as a messenger for those Suridashers in Admin. He struggled inwardly for a moment. Should he let them go after watching such blatant sabotage? If he did, their master, Whirlpitt would surely know of the Arkarian scheming.

He cursed again the memory of the wingless one, Jobe, and all the pain he had caused for generations of doubt-plagued Arkarians, but he could not ignore the debt his family owed the pilgrim from Suridash. The Cult of the Lost Argument was also the Cult of Lost Causes. He let the pair from Admin pass on their way unmolested and turned to the urgent repairs before him.

* * *

Later that morning, Zepp told Griddle his story while they waited for the print shop to catch up with their deliveries.

"I don't like this ship," Griddle said. "Did you see what happened in the last place? We could have been killed."

"What about your curse?" Zepp sneered. "Wouldn't it have protected us?"

Griddle sulked at the rejection in Zepp's voice. "I don't think so – not against a real accident like that."

"That was no accident."

"Anyway, it's not like I can turn it off and on."

Zepp shook his head woefully. "Is that why this plan isn't working?"

"What do you mean?"

"Just what I said. So far all you've done is ruin the teapot and some snowman's translator. And you've watched a couple of accidents. I can't see how bad plumbing is going to stop the ship or do anything else. If you ask me, this is a scatterbrain idea and it had been from the beginning."

"Then why blame me?"

"I'm not blaming you, it's just that – "

"It's the story of my life. It's not my fault and I always get blamed. Everybody hates me because of what happens when I'm around, and now you hate me because you don't think it's enough. If you knew how much I've had to go through because of something I never asked for and never wanted – "

"You're not the only one with problems," Zepp said. "You don't know what I've gone through."

"Oh yeah? Like what?" Griddle asked.

Zepp told him.

He told him about Sheverek, the death squad, the assassination, and the night of passionate terror and terrible passion with his three sisters.

He told the pilgrim with the odd accent and the nervous twitch about the shame and the guilt and the fear that he would be discovered.

Griddle was sympathetic. For the first time he didn't ask a lot of empty-headed questions.

"You really are an outsider, just like me," he said. "We really should belong to the outsider's clan."

"The outsider's clan? Is that something you made up or is there really such a thing?"

"I started it, but it's real. Outsiders like us are different. Most of the breeds on our planet are insiders, so were kind of unique. We can see into their world, but they can't see out at ours. They're obsessed with what they have, with what they want and with what they think they want. You have to make them feel important or they'll hate you. Outsiders are free – insiders aren't. We know things that they don't."

Zepp chewed over that for a few minutes. There were hidden

depths in this pilgrim. And he realized that the two of them had even more in common than he first had thought.

"I think almost everyone on this ship is an insider. And I know something they don't," Zepp said with a sudden smile.

"What's that?" Griddle asked back.

"I know what the angels are like. I know what they can do. They're the real outsiders, those angels. More than even you or me."

"What do you mean?"

"It's a long story," Zepp said. Then he went on to tell it.

* * *

Months earlier, just before Zepp had left for the rift and his training as a spaceman, a pair of burly, wall-armed guards had appeared at the Rat Patrol garage to escort him to the high tower where Tezar the psychic lived. Tezar had learned about Zepp and his mission through his clairvoyant vision and had decided to meet him before his departure.

"I was really scared at first," Zepp told Griddle. "He started off by saying, 'I know who you are and what you've done.'"

Tezar's gaze, however, had been compassionate. "You have nothing to fear from me. But you must admit that for a youngster, you've gotten yourself into an awful lot of trouble. Believe me, I sympathize with your suffering – that's the reason I had you brought here today. I believe I can ease it just a bit."

He offered Zepp a seat and the small green ape allowed a leather easy chair to swallow him up.

"First of all, about your indiscretion with your sisters – let me tell you something about Jobe's commandments. It may take you some time to realize it, but the taboo against incest is only partly about breeding. The problem with our race is that we are too ingrown, too bound up with ourselves and whatever is familiar to us. Only a few of us, like Jobe and like you, have the chance to strike out into the unknown and come to grips with the world. Jobe knew that and that's why his tribe is forbidden to breed too closely with one another. To force them out of the immediate family.

"You have broken that prohibition and until you atone for it, you will he plagued with guilt, but now you have a chance to atone. Your mission will take you far from what is familiar and test you sorely, but if you survive, the guilt will pass."

Then the grizzled soothsayer told the wide-eyed Zepp, "Fear not, you are not betraying your world. These angels are more important to us than you can imagine."

Tezar had studied the angels for months – in his own mysterious way – and he told Zepp all he knew. It took him a long time to describe the strange race from the stars and Zepp could hardly believe what he heard.

The angels had suffered great wars and upheavals, like the fall of the Red Monkeys in the rift, but on a planetary scale. Their machinery, both material and social, had driven them mad. But in finding their way back to sanity, this race had overcome much in its nature that had been irrational – proving a point that Zepp had a hard time understanding at first.

But it was a point about that Tezar felt strongly, as was evidenced when Whirlpitt interrupted the meeting.

"Are you filling our young friend's head with more of your nonsense, old one?" Whirlpitt asked. "Or are you trying to subvert Tedrak's plan?"

"Neither one, you son of a salamander. I'm trying to provide him with some necessary knowledge so he can make a reasonable decision when the time cones."

"Decisions? Ha! All this one needs to do is follow orders without question and all will be well. What has he been telling you, Zepp?"

Zepp fidgeted and stammered, "Just about the angels, sir. What they're like and – "

"I was just about to point out what these strange creatures can do for our world and our race. There's nothing wrong with that, is there? After all, isn't that the reason Tedrak has embarked on this perilous enterprise?"

Whirlpitt said nothing, but sneered at the wizened old creature.

"The problem with you, Whirlpitt, is that you see everything in the narrow perspective of brute force and material power. Knowledge means nothing to you unless you can exploit it for your own purposes. That is the difference between you and the creatures in that faraway starship. If we are not to be overpowered by them, we must acquire a new respect for knowledge and for those who wield it. Force alone will not be of any help to us."

"Very well, then. Enlighten us both. What is so special about the angels?" Whirlpitt said as he took a seat before the cold fireplace.

"Let me ask you a question first. You are an expert in the ways of our world. You have some knowledge, I'll admit. Give us a piece of it and I'll show you what is special about these creatures and about ourselves."

Whirlpitt nodded in ascent.

"Explain to me, then, what makes our species fight? Why are there endless wars, interminable conflicts, a continuous struggle for power. Why is reason so foreign and brutality so natural to us? What is the root cause of the spread of terror that today threatens to destroy our world?"

Whirlpitt hissed. "That's an easy enough question. The answer is simple. War and conflict are our inborn nature. We carry our wild roots too close to the surface. It has always been like this on our world – if not even worse than it is now. After all, we are so much more civilized than our ancestors. If anything, they must have been more warlike, more barbaric and wild. It is a curse we all must bear, one that cannot be overcome and that will eventually destroy us and our world – despite the angels and all their fantastic knowledge."

Tezar paced back and forth below a slowly spinning fan in the ceiling, shaking his head. "I'm sorry, Whirlpitt. What you have said is wrong. Your knowledge about the world is wide, but it is not deep. There are other reasons for our curse – and ways to overcome it."

Whirlpitt snorted in; disbelief. "Prove your case, old one – if you can."

Zepp watched silently and with a little bit of confusion. He had never considered such weighty questions before, but he was curious about what Tezar had to say. As it was, he agreed with Whirlpitt – at least he explained all that Zepp had seen in his short life.

How could Tezar possibly disagree?

"First, you see things from wrong end. You assume that the way things are now is the way they have always been. They have not.

"Our wars and our barbarism grow worse as we grow farther and farther from the soil that gave us birth. It is not our wild roots that make us mad but our rapid rise from them. Can you imagine anything more barbaric than what the Royal Onion Party is doing in Rikabar? Weren't the Red Monkeys at the peak of the power when the great revolt took them? Aren't the tribes of the Underworld peaceful in a way no modern tribe can match – not even Suridash?

"No, Whirlpitt. The problem is knowledge. Self-knowledge. It is the curse of the gods that we know who and what we are. They gave us the moral sense to separate us from the wild beasts with which their seed has mingled. That is our curse – to be separated from the world and a part of it, both at the same time. It tears us in two, drives us mad, makes us powerless, and drives us to seek power. Each of us is alone in the world, but we cannot escape from it. The overwhelming isolation drives us ever stronger to search for power.

"That is why we build empires, exploit others, accumulate wealth, form tribes, clans and cities. That is why we are constantly at war with one another. The endless drive for power that can never be satisfied, the emptiness of greed and desire, the will to kill and destroy, these all grow out of the unbearable tension within each of us. Look within yourself and know the truth, Whirlpitt. Deny me if you can." Tezar sipped from his cup of bitterroot tea and squinted at Whirlpitt.

"Your vision of the world is only partly true. You use it to hide from the truth, but your self-knowledge betrays you. It strips away the false front of power and leaves you weak and impotent. Knowledge defeats power – knowledge is endless, power is not. The more you seek power, the more you become its object, the more powerless you become. The more you seek knowledge, the more power becomes your subject.

"This I know better than anyone. You think your power keeps me a prisoner, but it does not. My knowledge of the world sets me free, freer than you will aver be.

"That is what the angels bring us, Zepp – knowledge. The knowledge to set us free. These angels have suffered like we have.

They have learned a powerful lesson from their suffering – one that we had better study if we are to survive. The violence within us is our responsibility and not an inherited evil. They have overcome it and they can show us a way to overcome it ourselves. This is the hope of Tedrak's plan. There is a slim chance of its success, but it is the only hope our world may have. If the angels survive first contact with us, they will have both the knowledge and the power to change this planet completely.

Whirlpitt looked up with surprise, the first expression he had shown in Tezar's long harangue. Previous to that, he had listened and accepted the charges without flinching and without objection.

"What is this?" he asked sharply. "Have you been holding something back from us, old one?"

"Only knowledge, Whirlpitt. You place so little value on that, aren't you?"

"What knowledge is this?"

"The angels have," Tezar explained, "machines that can sort out the seed of the gods, place it before them like the entrails of a frog, measure it kernel by kernel, know it intimately as a husband knows his wife, and see each and every bit of it, down to the tiniest part. And knowing that seed, knowing which part gives us red eyes or blue, green fur or gray, long legs or short, the gift of speech or the power of flight, the angels can intervene and control the seed of the gods itself. They can breed true the traits of every chamalian. They can sort out the chaos that plagues our world. They can fulfill the grand design of Jobe to recover the original seed that the god spilled in the Garden. These angels can make us right."

Whirlpitt had little to say to that. He ordered Tezar to keep him informed on the subject and he and Zepp left Tezar, winding their way down the long staircase to the foot of the tower. Before separating, though, Whirlpitt had given Zepp a final warning.

"If you breathe one word of this encounter to another soul, youngling, " he said in a harsh whisper, "I will have your small green head on my breakfast table."

Zepp was sufficiently cowed, but at that moment, although he still didn't quite understand what Tezar had said, he knew that he had been right.

* * *

Zepp was less enthusiastic than Tezar had been as he repeated the psychic's words to Griddle, but the Meshkarian was no less awed. His eyes were wide and his mouth open as he listened to the tale.

"Can the angels really do all that" he asked, when Zepp was finished.

"If Tezar is right, they can. I'll believe it when I see it, though."

"Is that why you're not afraid to commit treason against the whole planet?" Griddle asked innocently.

"I do what I have to do," Zepp answered with obvious irritation. "And right now I have to deliver a load of orders to the Meshkar containment. Come on, let's go."

As they returned to the print shop, Griddle asked Zepp one more question. He was trembling a little as he asked it and the words came out slowly.

"Do you think that maybe – if they're so powerful – that the angels might be able to help me? I mean, fix it so everyone doesn't hate me anymore? So I'm not a jinx?"

Zepp paused and thought about it for a moment, then he shook his head. "I don't know, kid. Maybe, if they're all that powerful. It seems like it should be easier than sorting out the seed of the gods. But I don't really know.'

Griddle sighed, then followed Zepp down the passageway.

CHAPTER FOURTEEN

Meshkar's **containment** **was** **more** comfortable than Kwikorak's and less threatening than Birhat's. It was warm and humid, but not unpleasant. Potted plants and creeping vines filled the empty spaces of the entryway and small speakers in the corners of the room broadcast the sound of chirping insects and rasping frogs.

Zepp and Griddle were met by Meshkarian ensign with stiff brown fur, a rumpled uniform and simple-looking, round face. It was Ensign Pim, the admiral's son.

"What's this?" he asked in the Suridash common tongue, Zepp was surprised to hear his own language being spoken by a foreigner, hut he knew that Meshkarian officers were well-educated and versatile in dealing with other races. They did not rely on machines or servants as intermediaries.

They handed over their package and he signed the receipt, but before he dismissed them, he looked them over with an eye that betrayed his simple appearance.

"You two are from Suridash. My father tells me your city is up to some kind of intrigue. Have you heard anything about it?"

Zepp's knees grew weak and his hearts started to squeeze. He stammered, "Uh, no, sir. Not us. Why ask us what our masters are up to? We're always the last to know what's going on."

"Sometimes servants overhear things they weren't meant to," Pim said. "And you must get all over the ship during your duties. I thought you might know something."

Zepp shook his head vigorously, repeating his denials as he turned to go, but Pim stopped them one more time. "What about you?" he asked Griddle.

Zepp had thought they were going to get out of this safely until that moment, but now he wasn't sure. He froze in his tracks and awaited his doom. His fate was in Griddle's hands.

"Me?" Griddle said with a shrug. "I don't know nothing."

"Very well, go on your way. But if you should hear something, contact me."

When they were back out in the central passageway, Zepp stopped to catch his breath. "I don't believe it," he said. "That little hedgehog must be telepathic or something. I thought we were cooked."

Griddle just shrugged. "Why? I wasn't going to tell him anything."

Zepp looked surprised. "Does that mean you're on our side?"

"It means I know better than to let anyone know what I am."

* * *

Elger Carlonzia rubbed his eyes where the edge of the goggles cut into his skin. These damned outlanders kept the lights so wastefully bright. It was only a marginal improvement over the posting in the desert at Suridash. Becoming a space warrior on the front line of the apocalypse was not his idea. But since Suridash had played such an important role in organizing the *Deragathon's* construction, the party officials had decided that their agent with the tradetown there should be assigned to space duty to maintain relations with them. He cursed his luck – he had always counted on the Suridash assignment to keep him out of harm's way.

Now he had to race from the bridge to the operations section to the Rikabar containment or back to the bridge four or five times a day. The lights were always on somewhere, so he had to wear those torture devices over his eyes to deep the glare out.

Ha was on his way back to the containment for a welcome off-watch relaxation, making his way slowly down the central passageway while others flew past him. If it weren't for the goggles and the lights, he'd be soaring in the weightlessness too.

Just as he was about to enter the passageway down to the Vegetarian containment, a pair of messengers emerged. It took a moment for the wheels to click into place in his memory, but when they did, he let out a yell. "You! You were the one who stole my pistol back in Suridash!"

Carlonzia never forgot a thief.

Zepp was stunned when the Rikabarian grabbed him by the arm – he didn't recognize Carlonzia – he'd never seen him in the light. That day in the Tradetown, six months ago, all he had seen was a shadow behind a bright light. But he recognized the voice and the accusation was correct.

But why was he here now?

Zepp saw the malice in Carlonzia's face and struggled against his grip. He broke loose and shot down the passageway like a rocket.

"Come on, Griddle," he yelled. "Run for it."

Griddle was still awkward in the weightlessness of the central passage. It was a few seconds before he got started, just long enough for Carlonzia to react.

"Wait! Come back here, you little thief," he shouted as he took off after them. Zepp looked back and saw the larger creature gaining on his companion. He stopped abruptly to let Griddle by, hoping to delay the Rikabarian himself.

Just then, a pack of pups knee-high to Zepp boiled out of the side passage Griddle had just passed – an engineering crew led by a Rifter cave-ape. They filled the central passageway and blocked the Vegetarian from further pursuit. Zepp and Griddle kept going without looking beck.

When they got to the Admin section and Zepp could talk without gasping, he explained to Griddle who Carlonzia was. "I guess your curse comes in handy sometimes."

Griddle just smiled weakly.

* * *

Lunch was a warm gruel with graincakes on the side. While they sat eating, the lights overhead flickered on and off several times – and each time everyone looked up for a minute and then went on eating. Before the meal was finished, one of the cooks came running through the mess dock with a vacuum squeegee to mop up a growing pool of water in the galley where a blocked deck drain was overflowing. And when they returned to the berthing area, the door was sprung on its frame and would not shut tight.

"It's starting," Griddle said with unconcealed pride.

"Are you sure?" Zepp asked. "This is a new ship. These things happen all the time – ever since I first came up here."

Just then, the toilets exploded and water began gushing out onto the decks.

"Yes," Griddle said. "Im sure."

A few minutes later they were in Whirlpitt's office, receiving their orders for the afternoon.

"Take this file to the bridge and deliver it to M'Kei, the Chorai delegate to the admiralty board. It's his turn to look over the admiral's shoulder this watch and this is a perfect opportunity to get you two onto the bridge."

They were gone in a flash.

The entrance to the bridge lay at the head of the keel with a broad open chamber separating it from the rest of the ship – a security zone covered by a pair of fearful-looking guns in blisters on the forward bulkhead. To reach the entrance, Zepp and Griddle had to climb a short, latticework accessway under the watch of a squad of heavily armed guards. Like the rest of the ship, incomplete fittings and unfinished wiring were hanging loose everywhere.

Zepp and Griddle climbed along the steel bars until stopped by the corporal of the guard. Although he had been attached to the *Deragathon* for several weeks, he had never been to the bridge before. It took a special entrance order signed by Whirlpitt to pass the two of them into the nerve center of the mighty spacecraft.

They floated through a short tunnel and then emerged at the rear of the bridge.

Zepp was awe-struck.

The spherical control center was almost eighty-eight hands in diameter with heavy scaffolding spread through its volume like weeds in a fishpool, supporting all the equipment and control stations. Overhead was a dome of thick, clear plastic and beyond it Zepp could see a riot of bright stars stretching across the sky with glaring golden sunlight reflecting off the framework.

Dozens of creatures scrambled about the area – cave-apes, Rikabarian woodfolk, Meshkarian officers, winged Arkarians, Blue Monkeys, great-toothed cats from Birhat, some were watchstanders glued to their posts, awaiting the alien menace, others were technicians, working feverishly to install their arcane apparatus at the last minute.

Zepp's attention was drawn to posts spaced regularly around the circumference of the bridge where the Meshkar marines stood guard.

The marines were bred for strength and ferocity – chains and collars held the white-furred beasts in place as they strained like wild animals. Indeed, they were wild animals, held barely under the control of their masters.

A squad flanked each side of the entranceway where Zepp and Griddle stood. They were close enough for Zepp to see their razor-sharp teeth, the spurs on their ankles and wrists, and the angry-looking swords they carried at their belts.

At the focus of all the frenetic activity was a sparsely furnished framework at the center of the sphere, elevated above the surrounding stations, where a dozen uniformed officers held themselves in relaxed readiness. Even from here Zepp could recognize Admiral Purdee by the slender horn projecting from his forehead.

He and Griddle made their way past brightly lit consoles, video monitors with views of the vessel inside and out, incomprehensible control panels manned by odd beasts the like of which Zepp had never seen before.

Zepp was overwhelmed by the vast and unusual prospects of the bridge and the clear signs of authority of the Admiral and his staff. Before he could approach the exalted command party, he had to present his signed orders to yet another guard who had him await the permission of the duty officer before he could deliver his burden.

The duty officer was another tall, graceful Meshkarian who looked at Zepp and Griddle suspiciously.

"Does it take two of you to deliver a single file?" he asked airily.

"No, sir," Zepp replied. "I'm breaking him in as messenger. He pointed at Griddle with a jerk of his thumb.

M'Kai, the delegate from Suridash, intervened quickly and gave Zepp an icy stare. "It is not necessary to answer such questions, youngling. Your manner is quite impertinent."

Zepp blushed beneath his fur and withered beneath the Chorai's glare.

"Here, give me your message and be gone. Do not waste our time at this crucial hour."

Without speaking, Zepp handed the file over to M'Kai and once the initialed receipt was in his hand, he was gone, Griddle bobbing and weaving in his wake, trying to catch up.

Once the bridge was far behind him, Zepp spoke. "Whose side is he on, anyway. I thought I was going to die. Did you sea those marines? What do you think – were we there long enough to have any effect?" He almost sounded like Griddle.

"I don't know," Griddle answered. "I don't think so. Sometimes it takes longer, you know."

"Well it better not take too long," Zepp said. "We're running out of time real fast."

* * *

That evening, before supper, Zepp received a visit from his cousins, who lived in another berthing area in the containment. Ever since the incident with the keys months earlier, Zepp's clansmen had treated him with cold suspicion. Nothing had ever been said aloud to him, but he could see the distrust in their eyes.

Tonight was different – the hostility was open arid alive.

They pressed him back into the berthing area and forced him to sit on his bunk while they confronted him.

Fripp began. "We have just received word from home, cousin. Your three sisters have given birth. Each litter was six pups. Three of the pups in each litter have bright green fur just like yours."

Zepp's soul sank. He was torn between joy and fear.

Longo continued. "You can see the questions this raises, cousin. Times have changed, but the law is the law. What have you to say for yourself? Where were you the night the keys were stolen?"

Zepp put up a feeble defense. "You can't prove anything. My sisters are my mother's children. They carry the same seed as Uncle Tapp. There is no reason they should not bear young that resemble him. You know that as well as I."

"But why so many, cousin?" Fripp asked with a sneer. "Something smells of vile taboo here. If these pups are not yours, why are you so agitated?"

"I'm agitated because my clansmen treat me like a criminal. If three of us were to ask you these questions, Fripp, would you be so calm? How do we know what you were doing that night?"

"I know where I was. That is why have come to you. I have no guilt – you are the one who must answer the questions."

"I'll answer questions put to me by a family council, not by a few mistrusting cousins who are jealous of my position on this ship. If you have suspicions, voice them at the appropriate time and place. And anyway, you should be asking my sisters who is responsible for their pups, not me."

Zepp's cousins sneered, but saw that nothing would be resolved here.

"You wait, cousin," Groz said. "When we return to Suridash, there will be a judgment. Then you will answer our questions and then we will see who faces the blessed knife."

Zepp watched as they stomped through the berthing area and up onto the mess deck. When he was sure they were gone, he buried his head in the hard little pillow at the end of his bunk and screamed.

* * *

There was no hot supper that evening. The cook dished out cold graincakes left over from lunch. An orange-furred technician had his head buried in the microwave oven, cursing Meshkarian gadgets, and the cook wore a bandage over a burn on his paw.

While Zepp and Griddle passed through the steamless steam line, the tea-pot sprung another leak and cold tea splashed onto the deck.

As they sat down to eat, the rear of the mess deck erupted in a wave of rushing, screaming crewmen as clouds of white steam poured out of the scullery.

But the real disaster struck when they returned to the berthing area. Its name was Androkar.

Androkar was the master-at-arms for the berthing area – responsible for order, discipline and, above all, cleanliness. And thanks to Griddle's effect on the plumbing in their berthing area, he was in a foul mood.

He was a devil-cat whose gene-strain had emigrated from the upper rift valley generations ago. He carried all those traits that had made his breed masters of their domain long before technology removed their critical edge in size and weaponry. He massed more than Zepp and Griddle combined. His tough hide was seamed with scars, his long tail ended in a spiked burr, and two curved horns only a few fingers long stuck out of his low, heavy brow.

He came into the compartment with an angry leer on his face, poking at crewmembers at random, pushing them against a wall. He passed by Zepp, and poked at Griddle. Zepp protested.

"What's going on?" he demanded.

Androkar snarled and released a guttural yap. A bald-pated interpreter Zepp knew from his training days in Ring Pang Do intervened.

"It's a cleaning detail," he explained. "Your friend has been picked to stay here and help clean up the mess from the plumbing. Don't argue with him if you know what's good for you."

"He can't do that!" Zepp yelped. "Griddle, come with me. We'll go see Whirlpitt and stop this."

Griddle started to follow Zepp, but the devil-cat swatted him with his book-sized paw, claws mercifully retracted.

Zepp stared Androkar in the face, watched the skin around his bloodshot eyes twitch, a vein in his temple throb, and the long, pointed tongue lick the long, pointed teeth.

Androkar was obviously on the ragged edge of madness and should never have been brought up into space. Zepp realized that he would just as soon swallow Griddle for breakfast and use Zepp's bones to clean his teeth as listen to any arguments. What he needed most, Zepp decided, was a heavy dose of incense or Red Monkey sleeping gas to calm him down.

Zepp exercised the better part of valor and backed down.

"You wait here," he told Griddle. "Do whatever he says, and I'll get Whirlpitt to take care of it."

Griddle just frowned at him and scratched the floor with his toes.

But there was no relief at Whirlpitt's office. Zepp couldn't get in to see him. "We're too busy, right now," the clerk outside his office said. "The admiral is going to call away drills in about two minutes and we have to get ready. Come back afterwards, or better yet, tomorrow."

Zepp slumped to the floor. What could he do? There was no place to go. He waited for the drills to start, afraid that the scheming was about to come apart, dooming him and his world.

* * *

By the end of the watch, Zepp was exhausted. He had been run ragged by the drills – his billet for Final Attack stations was as emergency messenger and when the normal internal communications channels broke down, or in this case simulated a breakdown, he was sent from one end of the vessel to the other – over and over again.

He barely had time to worry about Griddle, but when he returned to the berthing area, his worries returned – with compound interest.

The compartment was full of sewage. It covered the deck, bubbling up out of the head at odd moments for no apparent reason. In the middle of the soggy, smelly mess was Griddle, armed with a vacuum squeegee, trying to clean it up. But every time he pumped the squeegee, instead of going through the hose and into the canister, the sewage squirted out the opposite end.

Towering over him was Androkar, well past psychopathic rage and far into blood frenzy. His eyes glazed, his lips were curled back and foam flecked the corners of his mouth. He was incoherent and completely unable to figure out what was going wrong. All he seemed to know was that Griddle was responsible.

Zepp just stood back and watched as Griddle kept up the futile performance. Finally, his back turned to the grunting master-at-arms,

Griddle gave in.

"I've had it," he proclaimed, throwing the squeegee onto the deck with a splash.

That was enough to set Androkar off. He was simply not constituted to handle defiance of that sort – or any other sort.

Zepp let out a screech when he saw the razor-sharp claws extend from the devil-cat's paw. Androkar reached out his long arm to take a lethal swipe at Griddle that should have sliced him like a piece of sausage. But the wet deck worked against the enraged cat, his center of gravity drifted perilously away from his base of stability, and he went down on his tail in the sewage.

He jumped for another go at the jinx, who was too stunned to run away from certain death, but the big laces on Androkar's sandals got in the way this time, and he went down on his face in the sewage.

Finally he sat up – his frenzy still unquenched – and without attempting to stand, he grabbed the vacuum squeegee and swung at Griddle with it. Griddle ducked and the squeegee split open along its length with predictable results.

The sewage that was left in the squeegee sailed upwards, hit the overhead and rained back down onto Androkar.

Zepp could see the skin under the devil-cat's fur turn scarlet. For a moment, he looked like a machine whose gears were all bound up, and Zepp expected to see smoke come pouring out of his ears. Then Androkar grew silent, ceased his snarling and spitting, rose carefully to his feet, and stomped out of the compartment.

Zepp's shipmates followed the devil-cat at a distance to see how far he went and returned a moment later to signal all clear.

Zepp realized that his hearts were squeezing tightly in his chest as he helped Griddle clean himself up.

"That was close," he said. "You almost ended it right there."

Griddle was unfazed. "Him? He doesn't scare me. Did you see what happened? Bring him back and I'll do it again. Let me at him."

"Don't get too brave. He did that all to himself. If he hadn't been so furious, he might have connected with those claws of his. Then we'd be picking pieces of you up off the deck."

"He never would have come close," Griddle protested. "That's my curse. I've seen his kind before. They can't hurt me. I'm protected. Just ask Whirlpitt and his Red Monkey friends, they'll tell you. When I am attacked, the curse takes over. Just warn him that next time, it won't be so gentle on him."

"I don't know. If there is a next time, I don't want to be around. And if you were smarter, neither would you."

Unfortunately, both Zepp and Griddle were around when Androkar re-appeared.

It was just before lights cut. The berthing area was full of Zepp's shipmates, trying to get to sleep after a grueling day of drill and practice, trying to pretend they were not frightened by the confrontation with fate that was fast approaching. Zepp was reading over his last letter from his sisters while keeping one eye on Griddle.

There was a commotion in the front of the compartment, but at first, Zepp couldn't see what it was.

Then he caught sight of the devil-cat's unmistakable countenance above the heads of the others.

"Griddle!" he hissed in a harsh whisper. "It's Androkar!"

From the front of the berthing area came the squeal of frightened creatures, and above it all a single, high-pitched voice cried out, "Oh my gods! He's got a death ray!"

CHAPTER FIFTEEN

The compartment burst into frantic activity. Those behind the devil cat rushed through the door and up to the mess deck. A few of Zepp's bunkmates took refuge in the head and the showers. Others ducked under their hammocks or tried to stuff themselves into the tiny lockers between the bunks. The lights went out.

Zepp heard Griddle's whimpering voice cry out, "Zepp, what do we do now?"

"Keep quiet or you'll draw his fire. Maybe we can get out while it's dark."

Androkar's first shot was high and wide. The death ray spit its deadly stream of microwaves along with a spot of light for aiming. The weapon was so big it took both of the cat's hands to carry and fire it, and where the beam hit the plastic locker across the compartment a small circle turned black, bubbled, and smoked. Zepp gasped and a few others hiding beneath their hammocks whined.

He could hear the high-pitched scream of the power pack recharging itself for the next shot. It stopped, and in seconds the death-ray lanced out again. It must have hit near someone, because Zepp heard a scream and the patter of running feat across the deck.

The scream of the power pack returned. Zepp realized that he had a chance to move while the death-ray was recharging, but it didn't help if Griddle didn't know that.

He waited for the next shot to come. This one hit the deck only a few hands away from him. Zepp seized his opportunity to move to where he had last seen Griddle, next to a row of lockers on the forward bulkhead. But when he got there, Griddle was gone.

Androkar heard Zepp move and fired the next shot in his direction. Zepp thanked the fact that he had never grown very tall as the deadly beamed seared the plastic a few digits above his head.

Where was Griddle?

"Hey, you big pussycat! You can't hit what you're aiming at, can you!" The voice came from the darkness on the far side of the compartment. There he was.

Androkar fired at the voice, but the aiming light revealed nothing. It swept the bulkhead, waiting for the charge to build up again, but no target appeared.

Suddenly Griddle popped up again, standing in the middle of the lighted doorway. The aiming light centered on his chest. Zepp cried out, but Griddle dropped to the deck just before Androkar fired. The shot hit the wall outside the door.

"Griddle, are you crazy? He's going to kill you!" Zepp yelled.

"He can't hit me. Can you, you overgrown sap?" he taunted.

Androkar must have been completely mad by this point. His next act showed he had lost all sense – he fired the death-ray before the power pack was finished recharging.

The room filled with a sudden flash of light. Androkar let out a blood-chilling shriek and the death-ray dropped to the deck. The gun had shorted out and overheated.

Zepp could see the dull, red glow of the hand grip lying on the deck. Androkar moaned. Then the lights came back on.

A dozen crewmen entered the compartment quickly, not Zepp's bunkmates, but an armed party ready to deal with the insane devil-cat. They came in at a crouch, but their caution was unnecessary. Androkar was curled up on the deck, nursing his singed and blackened hands.

After the advance guard came a pair of medics, one of whom went to Androkar while the other searched the compartment for more casualties. There were none.

Zepp was overjoyed when he finally saw the slender figure of Whirlpitt stride into the berthing area. Now that he was here, the trouble was over. He stepped forward, ready to report to their superior, motioning Griddle to join him.

Whirlpitt cast his cold gaze over the carnage, the blistered walls, the melted plastic lockers, the injured figure on the deck. He issued his orders quickly and without deliberation.

"Take this one to the sick bay," he said, pointing at Androkar. Then he turned to the beaming face of Zepp and his sullen partner, Griddle. "And take these two to the brig."

* * *

The brig of the admin section was not far from Zepp's berthing area. It was sparsely equipped – no hammocks, no furniture, no lights, just a sanitary sink in one corner and a heavy steel door with one window. There weren't even blankets to take away the chill of the metal deck and walls.

And to make matters worse – or perhaps to make Zepp more uncomfortable – he and Griddle were bound together by a long, noisy piece of shiny chain, with a shackle at each end, one wrapped around Zepp's right wrist, the other around Griddle's left wrist.

All through the night, every time one of them stirred or twisted in his sleep, the chain clanked loudly against the deck and pulled the other's arm. Neither of them got much rest.

Zepp had just dozed off or the fifteenth time when the door

swung open and hit him in the rear. He leapt to his feet and Griddle stumbled aside. The light pouring into the cell blinded him at first, but after a few seconds he recognized their visitor – it was Whirlpitt.

"Shhh!" the minister hissed. "It is still off-watch. The guards are asleep and it would not be good to wake them."

"What's going on?" Zepp asked in a loud whisper.

"No time to explain," Whirlpitt said. "You must go. Leave here. Trust me, Zepp, this is part of Tedrak's plan. You and your companion must escape and hide yourselves. You must complete your mission. For now, go to the flight deck and wait for my messenger. He will give you further instructions when he finds you. Be careful not to be caught – although with Griddle along, that is unlikely. Now quickly, be off with you.

Griddle protested as Zepp pulled him to his feet. Whirlpitt waited by the door while Zepp stuck his head out and looked around the corridor. He was too tired to question his orders and too discouraged to turn down freedom. But a growing suspicion gnawed at the back of his mind.

"Why are you doing this?" he asked.

"No time for questions now," he said. "You'll need these." He handed them each a red tag, access passes for the main passageway. "Now get going."

They started off through the half-lit passageway, the chain clinking as they walked. Zepp stopped and grasped the chain with his hand, then told Griddle to do the same. By keeping it taut between them, they stifled much of its betraying jingle. A few minutes later, they were through the entryway and on their way to the flight deck.

* * *

The admiral's cabin was a plush chamber connected by a short passage to the bridge. Purdee slumbered peacefully in a freefall sleeping bag strung before colorful tapestries with soft red lighting. An altar filled one end of the cabin, decorated with relics and pictures of his ancestors – sea captains and fleet commanders for eight generations. Despite the weighty responsibilities of his office, he managed to sleep well – a trick he had learned years ago as a young ensign.

But this watch, his sleep was disturbed by a persistent buzzing from the wall phone near his sleeping bag. It took him a while to respond because normally calls could not come in on that phone while he slept – nobody was allowed to disturb the admiral without going through his aide, who would enter the cabin personally to wake the admiral. His eyes blinked widely as he smoothed his silky mane, then he picked up the receiver, ready to blast the caller with quiet rage, but he did not.

"Admiral Purdee, this is Whirlpitt, the administration officer from Suridash. I'm afraid we have en emergency here that required that I call you like this. I'm sorry if I disturbed you."

Purdue only grumbled. "Emergency? What's the matter? You must call the bridge and talk to – "

"This is the only way. Admiral, I'm afraid we have a jinx aboard the ship. A jonah. Are you familiar with this breed of pest?"

Of course he was. Sailors had told tales going back to prehistory of the havoc caused by the bad luck charmers. Purdee was not at all pleased. "A jinx? How? When? What has happened?" he stammered.

"This evenwatch, sir, in our section. We had him in the brig, but I'm afraid I have some had news: He's escaped. I've already passed the word to the admiralty board and notified my superiors."

"You what?" the admiral said. "Are you mad? Do you know what this means?"

"Is something wrong, sir?" Whirlpitt asked smoothly. Purdee cursed the slippery Suridasher. He was no fool – this was part of some plot.

"Where are you?" he demanded.

"I'm trying to track down the jinx and his companion, sir. They are chained together, so I doubt if they can get very far. Never mind trying to find me, sir, you'd better go after the jinx. Don't you think so?"

"Why you – you – "

"I'm afraid I must hurry, admiral. The search parties are already forming up and I don't think it would he a good idea to delay the pursuit. I'm sorry if this has disturbed you. Good watch, sir." There was a click and the connection was severed.

For a moment, Purdee hung in his bag while his blood boiled. "Blast Whirlpitt! Blast Suridash! Blast that bastard Tedrak!" he muttered over and over. Then he called for the duty officer and ordered *Deragathon* to general quarters.

* * *

The *Deragathon* fell endlessly in its orbit, smashing into sunlight from out of the broad shadow of Chamal just as the sun rose over the city of Suridash. On board the mighty warship, the watch was changing, adding to the already confused situation created by the escape of Zepp and Griddle.

And on the bridge, Admiral Purdee tried to cope with it all.

The commanders of the several factions from the planet below crowded the quarterdeck where Purdee held his station, all trying to speak at once. The babble increased as their interpreters and translating machines all tried to interpret and translate at once. Added to this were the periodic announcements of the bridge crew and the emergency reports of the adjutant who was monitoring the search for the jinx. It was to this last officer that Purdee was paying most attention.

"The party from Meshkar has reported that the fugitives have entered the life-support section, sir," he said with a loud military voice that cut through the noise. "Three parties are in direct pursuit, while another is trying to head them off at the far end of the life-support plant."

"Very well," Purdee replied as the admiralty board argued among themselves over who would speak first. From the bits and snatches he overheard, they all appeared to be blaming each other for aiding the treachery committed by Suridash – which happened to be the only power not represented on the bridge.

There were threats and counter-threats, charges and counter-charges, and a few tempers seemed to be so near the breaking point that Purdee expected open violence to erupt at any moment.

The admiral was only mildly distracted by the arrival of Ensign Pim, whose distinctive perfume made itself known swiftly to the bellicose debaters who filled the framework – all of them struggling to stay in place in the near weightlessness of the bridge. He was even pleased when the disputes were stifled as the admiralty board adjusted to the change in atmosphere.

"Good watch, sir," Pim said. "I have been informed that we have a serious disturbance below decks."

"Yes, we do, unfortunately," Purdee said. "But it will soon be under control. At least I sincerely hope so."

A moment later, the crowd on the quarterdeck was joined by three cave-apes – identical except for size – who converged on the adjutant. They conversed in a series of sputtering and snarling growls, then the adjutant turned to the admiral.

"Sir," the officer said, "the life-support officer, his assistant, and his superior have made an official complaint about the foreign search parties invading their section. They insist that you recall the parties and leave the security of the life-support plant to them. They say that if you do not, they will shut the plant down and let the rest of us struggle on without them."

"Is that what they say?" the Admiral asked disparagingly. His blood pressure was beginning to rise now, despite his best efforts at self-control. "You tell them that if they carry out such a threat, I will have all three of them ejected from the ship through the nearest airlock."

The adjutant relayed Purdee's comments through the interpreter and the three cave-apes frowned, argued among themselves for a minute, then made their reply.

"The cave-apes' engineering officer has changed his mind, sir," the adjutant reported. "He now requests that you ask the foreign search parties to exit the life-support section as soon as possible to avoid interfering with its delicate operation.

"That's better," Purdee said. "Relay his request to the others and tell them that I recommend that they comply. And warn them that if they refuse, I will let the cave-apes deal with them personally." Then to his son, he remarked, "You just have to reason with these creatures, that's all."

Pim nodded, hut said nothing.

Another crisis followed on the heels of the first. The Rikabarian consul approached the admiral with a fierce expression across his bushy squirrel face. Purdee, familiar with the tongue of the leaf-eaters, needed no interpreter.

"I wish to lodge an immediate protest. Search parties of our detestable enemies from Birhat have seized upon this confusion to enter our living module by force. Unless they are stopped, as a matter of policy, we must retaliate with force."

Purdee sighed. He had been waiting for this. He issued an order for the Birhat representative to appear and confronted the officer, a fat and toothy tomcat, with the charges.

"A vile a slanderous lie," was the reply. "They're only making this accusation to justify an attack on us. Our safety is your responsibility, admiral."

Purdee scratched at the base of his horn as the clamor of the creatures jamming the quarterdeck reached a new crescendo. It was finally getting to be too much for him.

"Silence!" he commanded with a tone of undeniable authority. "Your petty bickering has gone too far. You are jeopardizing the mission of this ship. I will have an end to this foolishness, or you will all regret the day you were born. Unless my orders are obeyed immediately and without exception, I will cut off the oxygen supply to the containment module of the offenders. And do not doubt that I have the power to do such a thing."

The admiralty board fell silent as Purdee returned to his seat at the center of the command framework. There was a rush of soft voices echoed by the murmuring of interpreters as they discussed this new development. Beside Purdee, Pim spoke in a confidential tone. "Sir, I do not wish to criticize or sound impertinent, but I believe it is possible that you have miscalculated. "

The Admiral harrumphed. "What do you mean?"

"Notice the admiralty board, sir. See the new look of suspicion that has come over them? I believe they have realized that if you can cut off their air now, you can do so in the future. The threat may keep them in line for the moment, but in the long run, you may have diminished your authority."

Purdee was surprised – but only because he wasn't used to receiving such an analysis from his son. The boy was wrong, of course, though perceptive

"Not if I actually do it," he said.

* * *

In the life-support section, Zepp and Griddle busily gave their pursuers the slip among the narrow scaffolds and bulky machinery. They hid behind huge blowers as the search parties passed them by. They watched as the cave-ape technicians chased the packs of Birhat cats and Meshkarian deckhands out of their domain. They ducked behind the evaporators and scrubbers and circulating pumps as the same technicians searched the plant for the hapless pair.

Then, as the technicians seemed to pop up everywhere, threatening to surround them, alarms began to sound – sirens , buzzers, bells. The cave-apes rushed to tend to their machinery and Zepp and Griddle rushed to take advantage of their sudden opportunity for escape.

A moment later, they were out of the life-support section and into the main passageway again, alone and unharnessed.

CHAPTER SIXTEEN

The search parties were getting dangerous.

Packs of angry, fearful chamalians roamed the corridors of the vessel, armed to the teeth with weapons of every kind – slug-throwers, death-rays, spring-loaded dart pistols, Red Monkey revolvers, swords, knives, and boomerangs. It wasn't safe for the officers and crewmen of the ship to move about, let alone Zepp and Griddle.

During the negotiations over the *Deragathon*, the members of the alliance had agreed to limit the number of small arms aboard the warship – for everyone's protection. But the agreement was only as good as the word of the chamalians who had made it – which was worthless as ever. No rational – or irrational – chamalian would voluntarily limit themselves like that. Every group had smuggled what it thought to be the minimum number of weapons necessary for its own security – and their lockers were bulging with arms.

Lights and ventilators were going haywire throughout the ship. The air pressure was dropping in the Arkarian section and rising in the Kwikorak tank. Foul odors were issuing from the fresh air blowers in the main passageway. The water in the Blue Monkeys containment was coming cut of the spouts a dirty, brown drip.

Admiral Purdee railed at the cave-ape engineers, but they just shrugged him off. "It's not our fault," they said. "We didn't let the saboteurs and search parties into the life-support section. It's up to you to keep those things from happening, not us."

Purdee's forehead turned purple around the base of his horn and he tipped his chin down to aim the stiletto-like point at the senior cave-ape's chest, but his adjutant and his son restrained him.

"Remember the angels," Pim said softly. "Even now, they are making the course adjustments to assume orbit, in a few minutes we will have an intercept point and we will have to shift our own orbit."

Purdee relaxed and returned to his seat, strapped himself in and awaited the next crisis. It could not be long in coming.

* * *

"Zepp, slow down for a minute, Griddle pleaded with a whine. Zepp didn't slack off as they rushed down a short side-passage to avoid some unseen commotion ahead. "Please," he asked. "Just for a minute."

"Alright," Zepp said as they drifted to a halt, hugging the red-painted deck that indicated "Down" in case the vessel fired its main engines. "What's the matter?"

"I jut want to catch my breath, that's all." He was wheezing from the exertion of maneuvering in free-fall. Zepp was not surprised. Griddle had never looked very healthy to him – he supposed that living in the wet caves of a Red Monkey fortress didn't help any.

Zepp poked his head around the corner and looked up and down the next corridor. It ran parallel to the main passageway, but only for forty-four hands or so before it came to an end at a wide, locked door. There was no one around.

When he looked back at Griddle, he saw large tears welling up at the corners of his eyes and rolling down his face, soaking into the short fur. He was trying hard to avoid making any noise.

"What's wrong?" Zepp asked.

"I'm scared. I've never been so scared in my whole life. I'm so scared it hurts. I don't know what to do." He sobbed once, then held it back.

Zepp felt his throat grow tight. He felt sorry for the poor creature.

Suddenly from up the passageway Zepp had just inspected came the sound of a crash, like a door being forced open, then a loud war cry. A half dozen hand-guns popped and cracked and heavy, slow bullets buried themselves in the metal bulkhead a few digits away from Zepp.

He moved without thinking, dragging Griddle along behind him. There wasn't even time to think. They flew through the narrow side-passage, back towards the central shaft of the ship, without even touching the wails.

Once in the main passageway, he went south, even though he know that somehow he would have to rely on Griddle's curse for protection.

They made it as far as an airtight bulkhead before their pursuers came spilling out of the passage they had just vacated. Zepp was about to open the heavy pressure-door when the long handle swung up past the thick, rubber seals, nearly knocking him on the chin, and a second armed party came rushing through the door.

Zepp and Griddle jumped back, cowering behind the door as eight rodent-faced Rikabarians filed through, each carrying a knife and a dart-pistol. None of them saw the pair as they rushed into the passageway.

Zepp peeked around the door and saw to his delight that the first party, which had not overlooked its quarry, consisted of Birhat panthers.

Then the lights went out.

Before the shooting even began, Zepp and Griddle were through the doorway. They could still hear the shooting when they reached the next airtight bulkhead to the south.

* * *

The flight deck was bustling with last minute activity as the Blue Monkey slaves manhandled the small fighters into their launching docks. Zepp and Griddle watched as a team of twenty halflings supervised by a harsh-voiced monkey detached the cables securing one fighter to the deck, run thin lines through their harnesses and tackle, and pull the craft into position.

When they were through, five of the halflings dropped out of the team, fell back until they were behind their supervisor, then grabbed the monkey without warning. As Zepp watched in silent amazement, they carried the helpless officer to the nearest airlock, stuffed him inside, and cycled the lock.

"Did you see that?" Zepp asked.

"See what?" Griddle said.

They crouched behind a cluster of heavy equipment that was strapped to one wall, trying do remain unnoticed and inconspicuous. They had little fear of discovery for the moment, though, since everyone on the flight deck was too busy to pay attention to anything but the heavy craft that were their responsibility.

They had been there only a few minutes when a pupling with short, blue fur, long, spindly arms, and an oversized head came scampering across the wide chamber. When he finally reached Zepp and Griddle, he stopped and rubbed his face and head frantically, looking around the flight deck with wide, round eyes. He stood only two hands tall.

"Tiki, Tiki, Tiki," he said, beating himself on the chest. His voice was high and shrill and at first Zepp was silent with yonder at the small creature with the gift of speech. Then he held out a plastic tag tied to his wrist with a piece of string.

"Follow him," it said. It was signed: "Whirlpitt."

"Zepp, " he said, pointing to himself. "Griddle," he said, repeating the gesture with the pilgrim.

"Come, come, come," Tiki ordered, tugging on Zepp's arm. They followed the pupling cautiously, keeping one eye on their rear flank.

"Not much for conversation, is he?" Griddle remarked.

They let Tiki lead the way around the flight deck, then through a door and up a passageway that took them upwards once more. They didn't have far to travel, however, as Tiki soon stopped in the middle of the corridor and began chirping, "Open, open, open."

Zepp looked around for a door but there was none. Then he realized that the pup was pointing at a scuttle plate set into the bulkhead and held in place by a dozen large-headed bolts. A tiny recess beside the scuttle held a wrench secured to the wall with a length of metal cable. It fit the bolts and a moment later, the plate was open. Beyond the small opening was an impenetrable darkness, and Zepp was afraid of what Tiki would order them to do next.

"What's that?" Griddle asked.

"It's a void," Zepp said. "An empty water tank. It's awfully dark."

"Come, come, come," Tiki said as he jumped through the opening. Zepp did not follow right away, but hesitated. He inspected the plate and the rim of the opening. He wanted to see if he could open the scuttleplate in order to escape, should it be necessary.

The last thing he wanted to do was lock himself into a cold and empty coffin at the urging of a witless pupling. The scuttle plate was equipped with a quick release bar that unsealed the entire frame into which the scuttle was set. It could be opened easily from inside the void without light or tools. Zepp poked his head through the hole and peered into the gloom, trying to judge the size of the compartment. A dim reflection could be seen a dozen hands away and he could hear Tiki scratching at the far wall, repeating his instructions. "Come, come, come," his tinny voice echoing in the emptiness.

Zepp took the time to release the scuttle's frame, replace the bolts, and close the door behind Griddle to avoid leaving a trail for the search parties to follow – if they survived one another.

Griddle moaned slightly as the light vanished, but Zepp pulled him along to the other side of the void. In the dark, near Tiki, he found another quick-release bar on another scuttleplate, which he quickly slid open. Dim red light spilled into the void and Zepp, Griddle, and Tiki climbed through the second opening. They found themselves in the middle of a short corridor lit by red offwatch lights that glowed dully overhead.

The corridor was only fifteen hands long and closed at both ends. A single doorway stood in the middle of the wall opposite the scuttleplate. There was nowhere else to go but through it, so they did. On the other side was a machine shop. Zepp recognized the shapes of tools, lathes, drill-presses even in the limited light. Some of the equipment was still wrapped in protective foil and a fine layer of dust covered the decks and benches.

But the most amazing thing of all was that there was no other exit to the shop. The only doorway was the one in which the trio of fugitives now stood. Zepp looked back at each end of the corridor where featureless metal walls blocked the way. He looked at the small scuttle that led back to the rest of the ship.

He turned a switch and light filled the compartment. Then he noticed a note on a work-bench in the middle of the shop. He pulled it down and read through it quickly.

"Whirlpitt's been here before us. He says this place hasn't been touched since the ship was built. They sealed off the passageway and never came back to put in the doors. Typical!"

"Does that mean that we're safe?" Griddle asked.

"We are for now," Zepp said. "Whirlpitt says to stay here until he gets in touch with us."

"Good," Griddle said. "I'm going to sleep." He took his end of the chain that bound them together and hooked it around the jig of lathe. Drifting in near weightlessness, he was asleep and snoring loudly in less than a minute.

* * *

Horns hooted throughout the ship, warning that the main engines were about to fire. For the next three minutes, everyone aboard *Deragathon* scrambled to tie down loose gear, secure heavy equipment, and find a solid place to stand. In the central passageway, the mad dash for the security of the "red" decks was even more frantic, since the acceleration of the vessel would leave those unfortunates in the wrong position high, dry and without support.

In the machine shop, Griddle snoozed unsuspectingly. But on the bridge, the admiral, his staff, and the admiralty board took their posts for thrust stations.

The powerful engines fired and *Deragathon's* orbit began to change.

Purdee and the ship's engineers held their breath. Although there had been drill after drill testing the integrity of the big ship under acceleration, it was always risky to put new strains on the vessel. Shifting loads, the continuing changes brought about by the vessel's spin, the different tensions and strains put on the cables that held the structure together, combined to make firing the main engines an incalculable gamble.

The ship held together. Griddle bounced onto the deck in the machine shop and awoke with a start. Damage control parties rushed to critical spots to brace against new vectors. Tools and other gear became deadly missiles. Crewmen in the spinning containment modules were forced to hold tight against conflicting accelerations as decks seemed to tilt at crazy angles. But the ship held together.

The acceleration lasted several minutes. It was followed by another of a half a minute, and then a third only a few seconds in length. Then the "All Clear" was sounded. By then, the warship was in a new orbit – one that would intersect with that of the alien vessel in only a few hours.

Things were returning to a closer semblance of order now. The bloody collision of Birhat and Rikabarian search parties near the flight deck had thrown a chill into the admiralty board. The armed parties had been recalled at last to their proper stations. Nobody would admit that the arms they carried were in violation of an early agreement. Admiral Purdee took the time to speak to the ship's company over the internal address system, seeking to rally the crew for the assault that would soon be upon them.

"Wiselings of every race!" he began, his words echoed by the murmuring and babbling of interpreters that filled the compartments and passageways of the ship. 'The hour of our glory is rapidly approaching. In a short time, the fate of our entire world will depend on your swift and fearless actions. The menace of the angels will be no match for our valiant crew – but it is up to you to perform your duties with the utmost alacrity. Be brave, my cousins, be courageous, be bold, and victory will he ours."

A chorus of cheers rumbled through the metal walls of the ship as the crew responded.

"But I warn you all," Purdee continued. "If you surrender to your own selfishness, if you seek revenge against your cousins, if you slacken in discipline, if you hesitate in obedience to commands, if you fail, then our planet and all its peoples will pay the forfeit. And you shall have more reason to fear my wrath and the wrath of your clansmen than any invader from the stars."

There was a murmur of approval from the admiralty board, but the rest of the ship was silent.

"Now onward to our destiny," Purdee announced as he flipped off his microphone with flair. It was still several seconds before the sound of the interpreters' voices ceased.

The adjutant approached the admiral and said, "I request permission to launch the fighters."

"Permission granted," Purdee replied. The quartermaster sent the command to the flight deck and loudspeakers there rang with his amplified voice.

"All hands man your flight stations!"

The Arkarian officer in charge of the flight control center secured the door of his compartment against attack and watched through a wide window as the mutiny began.

The flight crews for the space fighters were made up of Blue Monkey slaves – no noble monkey would ever risk death in such flimsy contraptions when there were slaves to be sent, in this case, they were two families of tree-dwellers from the rift valley: foxbats, who ruled the night woods and whose high-pitched screams struck fear into the hearts of all who lived on the forest floor, and flying squirrels, whose gliding acrobatics in the tall trees of the rift were the envy of even their simian masters. For centuries uncounted, both clans had suffered under the yoke of Red and Blue Monkeys. Now the tables were reversed.

With the aid of Arkarians like Pirr-Click-Wheet and other members of the Cult of the Lost Argument the revolt swept the flight deck. Their ranks depleted by secret ambushes, the Blue Monkey officers couldn't muster a decent defense. They fought desperately, but their only line of retreat – into the flight control center – was cut off by the Arkarians within. It was all over in a few minutes, so quickly that all involved were surprised they had won so easily.

The foxbats and the squirrels manned their fighters, the flight crews topped off their fuel tanks and charged up their accumulators, and the tiny spaceships were launched.

On the bridge, the Arkarian member of the admiralty board gripped a rail with his toes, spread his wings wide, and announced to the admiral: "The fighters have been launched, sir."

"Very good," Purdee replied.

"But I regret to say that I must inform you that the flight crews have mutinied, slain their superior officers, and deserted in their fighters. We must conclude that we have lost their strike capability for the remainder of the engagement."

Purdee sputtered and fumed. "Order the weapons officer to arm his batteries. I want those fighters destroyed!"

"Aye, aye, sir," the adjutant replied.

But the Arkarian shook his head. "I doubt if that will do much good, admiral. The only equipment we have that is capable of tracking so many small targets is the flight control radar itself and I'm afraid that was disabled in the mutiny."

That was a bald-faced lie, of course, but within a few minutes, down on the flight deck, Pirr-Click-Wheet would make it the truth before the lie was found out.

Purdee slumped in his seat – a difficult thing to do in the weightlessness of the bridge. Ensign Pim tried to comfort him, but it did no good. "So much for your brave speech, father," Pim said.

"Go away," Purdee responded. "You make my nose hurt."

CHAPTER SEVENTEEN

Tartok considered himself lucky. He was not the first one to enter the Birhat containment. Instead, he followed his cousin Eltok by a few hands, that meant the difference between life and death.

They had been searching the ship with a party of armed jackal slaves, trying to run down the Suridash jinx and his co-conspirator. But they found nothing but a band of Vegetarian vandals who exchanged fire with them and then retreated into their own containment. Although Eltok led a few of the braver souls in the search party as far as the entry checkpoint, they were driven back by a hail of bullets.

Eltok and his fire team covered the party's rear as they withdrew across the central passageway and into their own turf. Once inside they secured the pressure door against intruders and dived down the tube to report to their leaders. Eltok went first.

They didn't suspect a thing until they reached the upper level of the module and Eltok was cut in half by a murderous crossfire as he dropped to the deck. Tartok managed to stop himself a few digits from the hatchway, wrenching a muscle in his arm and a bullet fragment scratching one knee in the process.

There were only four slaves in the party under Tartok's command. He looked them over carefully. He didn't know who was shooting down below, but he had a good idea – the Birhat clan elders had warned of the dangers of a slave mutiny. Tartok wasn't sure if he could trust the creatures at his side.

They hadn't shot at him yet – that was a good sign. He wondered if he should disarm them or order them to help drive off the rebels he knew must be below. They didn't look too steady – crammed together here at the bottom of the long passage with the smell of gunpowder, death, and fear thick in their faces.

Then an idea struck him. "You," he said grabbing the slave nearest him. "Go in there and find out what's happened. If those are slaves down there., they won't harm you. Stay where I can see you and tell me what you see."

The poor beast hesitated and Tartok bared his teeth. These jackals were such cowards. The slave dropped through the opening and landed in a crouch on the deck. "Don't shoot!" he yelled. "The masters are all dead."

A feminine voice with a harsh edge answered him. "Stay where you are!" There was the sound of someone moving in the compartment, and Tartok could see the jackal's eyes following them out of his own sight.

"Come," female slave said. "Join with us. The hour of our liberation is at hand. Help us seize the vessel from our masters."

"But what about the angels?" Tartok's slave asked. "Who will protect us from their vengeance?"

"Have no fear. Their vengeance is for those who have oppressed us for so long. Slaves will be spared when the angels arrive."

Then the jackal made a fatal error – he looked up at Tartok with a questioning glance. The female slave was no fool, and an instant later bullets ripped through the jackal's body.

Tartok reacted quickly. He grabbed the three remaining slaves and shoved them down into the chamber of death, following quickly on their heels. "Shoot!" he cried. "Shoot or you're all dead!"

They dropped into the compartment in a blaze of fire. Guns

cracked from passageways to the left and right. Tartok's gunmen fell bleeding to the deck, but miraculously he remained unscathed.

The remaining rebels fled for the lower levels of the containment, insuring Tartok's survival for the moment. But the thing that surprised the Birhat cat was the identity of the rebel leader. He had just a glimpse of her as she dropped through the hatchway in the center of the compartment. It was the beautiful lamb chop he had seen in the cage – the one reserved as first course in the victory banquet.

* * *

Carlonzia peered into the darkened checkpoint where only a short time ago Vegetarians and Birhat crewmen had exchanged fire. He could see the damage done by the firefight – shattered lighting, broken furniture, the bodies of dead and wounded Vegetarians. His blood boiled at the treachery of the predator cats. The party never should have accepted the compromise that had allowed them aboard the ship.

It was safe now. Nothing stirred, and the safety doors on the far side of the compartment were shut and secure. He put on his goggles and switched on the battle lanterns, ordering the repair party behind him into the chamber to clean up.

The first of Carlonzia's problems was solved, now he went on to the next one. While the repair party secured the way out of the Rikabarian containment, he led a team of well-armed soldiers cautiously into the central passageway. On the opposite side of the heavy keel of *Deragathon* was the entrance to the Birhat containment. He looked up and down to the airtight bulkheads above and below the entrances and saw nothing dangerous, no lurking panthers or their wolfish lackeys. His view of the entrance to Birhat territory was blocked by the keel, and he sent one of his soldiers out into the passageway to reconnoiter.

When the sentry reported that the way was clear. Carlonzia ordered the rest of his squad out of the tube and across the axis of the ship.

He waited in the central passageway while the squad disappeared down the tube. There was no sound or signal from the squad for several minutes, then a burst of gunfire echoed out of the passage. A short time later a messenger appeared and gave Carlonzia some encouraging news. "The Birhat slaves are in revolt," he said. "The panthers are fighting for their lives. You can see bodies everywhere."

Carlonzia returned to the Rikabar checkpoint and relayed the information to his commanders and called for reinforcement. A short time later, a whole platoon of Rikabarian warriors was infiltrating the Birhat containment and the second of Carlonzia's problems was being dealt with. Now he could turn his attention to his primary duty – the defeat of the angels and the security of his homeland.

Within a few minutes he was on his way to the operations section – the nerve center of the *Deragathon*. Much of the equipment there, navigation, communications, and data processing equipment that gathered and relayed information about the alien vessel to the bridge, was owned and operated by Rikabar. It was Carlonzia's post for the attack on the alien ship. Ahead of him was a small guard of Vegetarian security police, behind him a half dozen loyal party members whose politics were unquestionable. When they entered the operations section, a fearful silence fell over the watchstanders and their officers. The security police took us their positions, and

Carlonzia drew a list from the pouch at his belt.

One by one, he read the names on the list and one by one the party loyalists took the place of those named. It was a Vegetarian tradition. Before battle, the ranks were purged of the politically unreliable – or the politically least reliable. Everyone knew it was coming, and everyone knew there was nothing they could do about it. It had kept them on their toes for weeks now, all of them anxious to perform without failure and avoid the purge. A few of those removed from duty whimpered or whined, but there was no resistance. The outlanders from Meshkar and Suridash just looked on with puzzlement. Carlonzia looked at them with scorn. They were not sure what was going on, but they didn't look good about it.

When Carlonzia was through, the security police escorted the unfortunate watchstanders out of the section and operations resumed. Them was a sigh of relief from the Vegetarians who remained and a subdued murmuring among their foreign allies. Carlonzia took his position at the plotting table where the orbits of the *Deragathon* and the angels' ship were being tracked. There was nothing left for him now but to wait.

* * *

The *Deragathon* fell silently through space, high above the ragged gash of the rift valley, on its way towards the snow-capped heights of Kwikorak. On the bridge Admiral Purdee listened to reports of disorder from below decks. They did not improve his mood. The Birhat rebellion worried him – he didn't want to lose the projectile streamers in the cat's containment.

Then word was passed that the a squad of Rikabarian troopers had entered the Birhat module. All hell broke loose on the command framework as the Birhat representative on the board attacked the Rikabarian member. The adjutant had to separate the two of them, getting his face scratched in the process by the Birhat panther's razor-sharp claws. The wound was not serious but the howls of protest wore. Each side accused the other in provoking the incident. Each side claimed that the other had invaded his territory first.

Purdee could care less. He made his position clear. He was waiting to sacrifice both parties if they could not deal with each other in a disciplined manner. He was willing to start with the members of the admiralty board if necessary. That quieted the argument, but there was no satisfaction for Birhat and the Rikabarian kept to one side of the framework far from his adversary.

While Purdee and his staff monitored the progress of the mutiny, word arrived of a disturbance in the Vegetarian module. Purdee summoned the Rikabarian representative and demanded an explanation. "We are purging our unreliables before the battle, sir. It is a common party procedure. I wouldn't think of engaging in combat without absolute loyalty in the ranks. You can see what happens when those precautions are not taken, can't you?" he said, eying the Birhat cat on the far side of the framework.

Purdee scowled, but the was nothing he could do – either about the purge or the insolence of the Vegetarian. It was purely an internal matter and he had a hard enough time tending to problems that were rightfully his.

* * *

As violence and chaos spread through the ship, Zepp and Griddle remained safe in the sanctuary of the misplaced machine shop. Griddle snored loudly, moaning occasionally at nightmares that could be no more horrible than the grim reality around them. The only other sound was the rumble of the spin bearings, not far aft of the shop. The single battle lantern that Zepp had left on did little to dispel the gloom. The heavy equipment bolted to the deck cast ominous shadows that that lurched and danced when the engines lit off and the decks tilted and the lantern swayed on its hook.

Zepp did not sleep – he could not. His brain was alive with the echoing images or the pursuit and escape of the last hours. Although safe and secure for the moment, his future was certainly in jeopardy. Other images flooded his mind. Death stared him straight in the face. He wondered how it would come. Would the world explode at once in a flash of light as some terrible weapon destroyed the *Deragathon*? Or would it simply fade away as the chamber they occupied grew cold, dark, and airless while the vessel orbited lifelessly above Chamal?

This was the end of the world – at least as far as he was concerned. Whether the angels finished off the planet below hardly mattered anymore. It was a strange feeling – a freedom unlike anything Zepp had over experienced. There was nothing compelling him to action anymore. The shapeless fears, the threat of death or mutilation at the hands of his cousins, the blackmail by Tedrak end Whirlpitt, all these seemed distant and irrelevant. They could only kill him once. Now he understood how Griddle must have felt as Androkar blasted away at them with the death ray.

He felt almost invulnerable, reckless and unafraid.

The more he thought about it, the stronger it became.

He didn't have to worry about following Whirlpitt's orders anymore. He didn't have to be afraid of discovery by his cousins. He didn't have to fear death. Death was almost preferable to a life that belonged to others, a life that continued at their whim or that served their wills. He was not born to that kind of life, he knew that much for sure – his Uncle Tapp had told him so many times when he was young. It was only his youth and inexperience that had made him an object for the plans of others.

But that was over now.

An inner strength Zepp had never known before had finally emerged after all the trials and sufferings he had experienced in the past six months. He had finally come into wisdom.

The change had been coming for a long time. It was fueled partly by the crisis caused by the arrival of the angels, partly by the new challenges that Zepp had faced adapting to his new life as a space crewman, and partly by the natural changes in is own biology. He had entered another of the phases in chamalian growth when the mind grasps and devours new experiences whole, forming a new appreciation of the world and his place in it.

New possibilities and options now presented themselves to him – to anyone with the wits and imagination to recognize them. It was like seeing clearly for the first time in his life.

He was almost crushed when he realized the terrible irony of it. How could he feel all these great and wonderful new feelings in the final hour of his life? But the nagging, skeptical voice of this new reservoir of hope kept him asking questions. Was this really the last hour of his life? Was death so certain? There had to be something he could do.

In the past, in times of crisis, Zepp's only problem had been mustering the courage to push ahead on a path that had already been laid out for him. This situation was different – the path was not so clear or obvious. Not yet, anyway. Now he had to decide for himself just what to do.

He wrestled with his dilemma for a short time, then he leaped to his feet, propelling himself skyward until the chain brought him to a sudden halt inches from the ceiling, yanking Griddle from his slumber. The pilgrim responded with a deep, moaning shout.

"Come on," Zepp said as he recovered his balance in the middle of the compartment. We've got to get moving. We can't stay here any longer.'

"Why?" Griddle asked. "Did Whirlpitt call? Where are we going?"

"Forget Whirlpitt. I'm in charge now. We're going to go to the bridge – maybe there we can stop this madness before it's too late."

"No, thanks," Griddle said. He tried to cross his arms over his chest but the chain got in the way. He postured defiantly, but comically, too. "You go – I'll stay here."

"Uh-uh, " Zepp replied, shaking his head. "You're coming with me. I need you. Alone I won't last eight minutes out there. With you attached to me, I've got a chance."

"But why? Why don't we stay here where it's safe? We can wait until it's all over and then come out. Isn't that better?"

"If we stay here, we die. At least we have a chance if we go back out. If we can only get to the bridge, your curse will stop the admiral from damaging the angels' ship. And that'll keep the angels from destroying us."

Griddle's face revealed the fear inside him as he broke into tears. "But I don't want to go out there, Zepp. We can get killed. You can get killed. What would I do if they got you and not me. At least here, it'll all be over at once. If they catch us alive, they may torture us for days. I don't want to risk my life for the rest of the world – I hate the rest of the world. It's nothing I care about. All it's ever done since I was born is hurt me."

Zepp's throat grew tight at the sight of his companion's anguish. "It'll be all right, Griddle. Trust me. I told you how I got us past the gap in the stairway back in the riftwall fort, remember? As long as we're chained together, we're both safe. Have faith in your curse. Even if it hasn't sabotaged the ship the way Tedrak planned, it's kept us alive so far, hasn't it?"

Griddle sniffled, wiped his eyes with his arm and said, "I guess it has. But I'm still scared."

"I am too," Zepp said. "But sometimes you've got to do what you know is right no matter how you feel. Otherwise you'll be scared forever and have to live your life in a cave in the riftwall. Is that what you want?"

"Nobody ever bothered me up there," the pilgrim said, "Until you showed up."

Zepp frowned in exasperation. "Look," he said. "You've got to help me with this. If you don't do it for Chamal, do it for the angels. It means just as much to them as it does to us."

"The angels?"

"That's right. They're part of the clan of the outsiders, just like you and me, aren't they?"

Griddle nodded meekly. "I guess if anybody is, they are."

"Well, then, how can you turn your back on fellow clansmen. They need us, they need us to stop the *Deragathon* before it does something they can't ignore. Before it forces them to do something to Chamal that we can't ignore. We're the only hope for them, Griddle. Whose side are you on: The selfish, paranoid maniacs who've punished you all your life for something that's not your fault – or the side of the angels?"

It was not question Griddle could answer. He looked down at the floor, jingled the chain, and chewed on his lower lip.

"Are you coming with me or not?" Zepp asked after a moment, giving him a question he could respond to.

"It guess I'm coming with you," he said at last. "Let's go."

Zepp smiled and rubbed his face, then took the chain is one hand and grabbed the battle lantern with the other.

At that instant, in the corridor outside the machine shop, a stream of light and sparks erupted from the wall with a loud hiss. Zepp and Griddle jumped with surprise and ducked behind a drill press, one on either side with the chain wrapped around the base. Then Zepp approached the doorway cautiously and looked for the source of the sparks.

"They're cutting through the wall!" he shouted. "Whirlpitt must have told them where we were hiding."

"What do we do now?"

Zepp looked around the compartment quickly, then returned to the drill press, stripped the foil wrapping off and threw it over his back and Griddle's.

"Run for it!" he yelled. They leapt into the spray of sparks from the cutting torch. Zepp noticed that the line had grown only a few digits so far and he was satisfied that it would be half an hour before anyone got into the passageway. He sent Griddle through the scuttle plate first, holding the foil blanket to protect them. A metal fragment landed on his arm and another sent a plume of smoke coming up from the singed fur. Then he climbed into the void and they were on the run again.

* * *

Tartok huddled in a dark corridor in the outermost level at the Birhat containment. He was alone now, the rest of his jackal slaves had been separated from him as they fought their way through the mutineers, pursuing the killers of Eltok. A short distance away, a mattress burned, filling the corridor with a layer of smoke. He was waiting for the mutineers to make their next move. He had overcome their rear guard on the deck above and tossed the burning mattress down here in order to clear the rest of them out of the way. He was still unharmed, despite the ferocious fire of the rebels. Quick reflexes and alert vision had kept him safe. The fighting had yet to make much an emotional impact on him. He had been too busy just trying to stay alive. He wasn't about to mourn the death of Eltok – too many worthier clansmen had shared his fate, as Tartok had seen while making his way through the containment. He didn't even have time to think ahead, to anticipate the slaves' objective. He just kept close and followed their howls as they descended deeper into the nodule.

Twice he had caught a glimpse of the sharp-eyed female who led the mutineers. Each time he had raised his weapon to fire and each time he had hesitated just a moment too long. Then, as the deck began to rumble with a familiar vibration, Tartok realized what she and her fellow slaves had been after. The walls began to hum from the great transformers and coil that formed the heart of the Birhat projectile streamer. He was on his feet before the sound of scrap metal pouring through the pipes exploded around him – a slinking, rattling cacophony as the streamers fired.

The control booth was only a short distance away. Tartok was there with a leap of his lithe, powerful body. The slinking roar of metal on metal sounded again. He wondered what they could be firing at as he smashed through the door. The compartment was small, sandwiched in between the two magnetic accelerators that pumped the metal scrap into space. A clear plastic dome in the deck looked out on a slowly turning sky filled with bright stars and the curving horizon of Chamal.

There were three rebels in the chamber – two at the control consoles and the female leader in the gunner's seat above the dome.

Tartok reached out with one paw and ripped a slave from the controls, tearing open his shoulder at the same time. The other turned to face him just in time to catch a pair of bullets in the chest. The female looked up from the gun sights and glared at him with those alluring, hate-filled eyes.

Then she shot him.

Tartok fell back against the control panels, a fire burning in his side. He was surprised that dying could be so painful – and incomplete. Then he was filled with rage at the creature who had shot him. He knew he wasn't finished yet, his strength was still with him.

The female turned back to the sights and yanked on the triggers, filling the compartment with an almost unbearable roar. Eighty-eight pounds of metal poured out into space like the spray from a fire hose.

Tartok sprung.

The rebel leader never saw him coming. He collided with her and saw red from the pain in his side. He looked down, through the dome, and saw the stream of metal splattering against the hull of the *Deragathon* itself. It meant no more to him than the splash of wine from a falling cup, even though he could see the sparks fly and the plume of atmosphere jetting out from punctured bulkheads. Then the pretty lamb who had led her fellows so far leered at him, her face digits from his. He gripped her in his arms. They were together at last.

She tried to break away, her pistol clenched in one hand, but it was no use. Tartok was much too strong for her. He pinned her arms to her side and bared his teeth. He was consumed with rage, hunger, and lust. He didn't know which to satisfy first. He never made the choice.

The female fired her gun, again and again, until it was empty. The bullets never came near Tartok, smashing instead against the plastic dome at his feet. Air whistled through the holes. The crack came slowly, then widened under the pressure of the containment's atmosphere. It exploded with a pop and the air began rushing out.

The female struggled against Tartok's grip. He kept a hold on her, but on nothing else. An instant later the two of them were sucked out into space, clutched in each other's embrace.

* * *

The bridge of the *Deragathon* grew dark for a brief moment as the vessel crossed into Chamal's shadow. One minute the chamber was lit by the golden abundance of sunlight, the next it turned harsh and glaring as the artificial light switched on.

Admiral Purdee sat in his command chair and brooded. Far below him, the upper rift valley, Kwikorak and the eastern rainforest were slipping past the terminator. Night was falling down there – a night that for many would be their last. Purdee had received a number of messages from the surface to that effect. He feared for all those below him who would pass the hours until dawn in a strange, uncertain hell.

Already in the lands that had passed into the night, in Rikabar and Birhat, the looting, the burning, and the wanton killing went on, suffering beyond belief – even for Chamal – was inflicted on the weak and the powerless as all moral control dissolved under the threat of the immanent apocalypse. If the world did not end before dawn – and for many it would – then millions of depraved souls would wish it had. The knowledge lay heavily on Purdee's mind.

He was not reassured when the adjutant came to him with a report of more discord within the shaky alliance that manned the ship.

"More bad news," he announced. "Shipar has decided to retaliate against Suridash for trying to sabotage the mission and has cut off their electrical power."

"So? I don't care what happens to those traitors anymore They have no weapons anyway."

"Yes sir, I agree. However, without power to the admin section, we are without internal communications. While emergency systems will suffice for weapons control, we are unable to follow the progress of the Rifter mutiny or the Birhat stave revolt."

Purdee closed his eyes and shook his head wearily. The adjutant kept a wary eve on the point of Purdee's horn as it traced a small circle in the air. "It's just as well. I would rather not know about those things anyway. See what you can do about restoring power, but take your time. There are more urgent problems demanding our attention."

"Aye, aye, sir," the adjutant replied with a sigh of relief. He was just a step away from his commander when the clatter of metal striking metal sounded to the right.

All eyes on the bridge turned to the source of the sound. There was a loud crack, followed by a chilling whistle – the certain sound of a breach in the pressure hull. A wave of panic seemed about to boil up from the bridge crew.

Then a loud boom shook the bridge and orange flames belched

from the southern rim of the chamber. Purdee looked to the source of the flame and saw that it came from his cabin. "Oh, no!" he cried with a cracking voice.

He was just beginning to feel the air slip past him as it rushed out into space through what was left of his cabin when the heavy, airtight blast door slid shut, sealing the leak and ending the panic.

Gone were the portraits of his ancestors, his family shrine, the relics, the swords, medals, and badges that he had accumulated in a lifetime of naval service.

He turned his face away from the admiralty board and his staff, burying it in his hands and hiding the tears. "What next?" he sobbed. "What next?"

And the angels were still an hour away.

CHAPTER EIGHTEEN

Zepp dragged Griddle along behind him as they made their way through the cloying darkness of the empty void and back to the flight deck. Tiki ran off as soon as they were through the scuttle as Zepp had expected him to. He was no doubt going to inform Whirlpitt of their escape from the machine shop.

The flight deck was a grisly scene. The carnage of the mutiny floated between the deck and the overhead, bodies drifting on the gentle currents of air accumulated around the louvered intakes of the ventilation system. Zepp felt his stomach churn, and Griddle gagged as they hurried through the hangar and on to the main passage without opposition.

Griddle was willing but barely able to move himself as Zepp propelled them along the passageway at high speed, gripping the railings along its length with his free hand and with his feet while Griddle bobbed and bounced at the end of the chain.

Zepp's senses were alive and alert in a way he had never known before. Colors were brighter and clearer than he had ever seen, every little sound registered sharply on his ears, he opened his inner nostrils and drank in the rich variety of smells that filled the air – machine oil, ozone, sweat and blood, burning insulation and gunpowder. Every line and edge of the ship's structure seemed sharp enough to cut himself on.

He was filled with a sense of potency, of strength and boldness, in spite of his fear. He was able to hold his doubts and anxieties at bay with the irresistible force of sweet reason. He knew there was every chance of failure and a horrible death but he knew that there was also a chance of success.

They pressed on.

It didn't take long to run into the rear of a small firefight – one of many such battles going on throughout the lower half of the ship. The Rifter mutineers had fought their way as far as the third airtight bulkhead above the flight deck. On the near side, their backs to Griddle and Zepp, a pack of striped and armored insectivores were trading shots with a knot of cave-apes from the life-support plant. The cave-apes were not about to let the insurgents foul up the only thing that kept the crew – and themselves – alive in the hostile environment of space.

Zepp barely slowed down as he approached the fighting. He yelled out a warning instead. "The jinx! The jinx! Run for your lives, the jinx is coming!"

Both parties turned their attention to the two fugitives. Their eyes opened wide, their mouths were framed with horror. By the time Zepp and Griddle were among them, they had broken ranks and begun to flee. The pair was past the airtight bulkhead in an instant, leaving a confused mob behind them.

There were more Rifter slaves in the passageway beyond them. Zepp could see them through the windows in the airtight doors. Speed and surprise worked to disrupt them just as easily as the first group. They rushed past side passages jammed with armed squads and avenging assassins, narrowly avoiding them and their deadly attentions. But there were more horrors than he had expected.

Chamalians flailed themselves with electrical cables, slashed at their own arms and legs with sharp metal, beat their heads against the walls and tore at each other with tooth and nail. They wailed mournfully, surrounded by clouds of their own blood. They scrawled epitaphs on the bulkheads. They sang haunting deathsongs, chanted battle poems, and cried at the end of the world.

The whole crew seemed to have gone mad. Rifters battled each other unchecked, slaves fighting slaves, while Blue monkeys floated lifelessly in the crowded passageway. Birhat cats and Imperial Vegetarians attacked at close quarters with such ferocity that it was difficult to tell who was the carnivore and who was not.

All the hostility and antagonism and hate of a thousand years of fetid chamalian history had been transplanted onto the *Deragathon*. All the cooperation and organization that had brought them up into space to meet the threat of the angels had disintegrated. Tedrak's vision of Armageddon was being acted out on this small stage, high in orbit above the surface of Chamal.

All the fear and antipathy, the distrust and suspicion, the revulsion and self-disgust had boiled to the surface at once. The end of the world was rushing down on them all, the ultimate release from the last compunctions against destructive slaughter. Fueled by blind panic, all of Zepp's distant cousins were joining in an orgy of mutual destruction that shocked him to the bottom of his soul.

He thanked his stars that he had been blessed by fate and had been born into the tribe of Jobe. Otherwise, he would have joined in, immersing himself in the bloodlust that had seized the crew of the warship, vanquishing the terrible foe that every chamalian fought all his life. The enemy here was not the angels who grew closer every minute, it was the alien within every one of them. It was not the foreigners, the other chamalians, each of them a constant reminder of the fragmented diversity of the cursed race, it was the spark of self-consciousness, the light that could not be extinguished, the seed of the gods, that was at the source of all the problems of Chamal. Zepp could see that old Tezar knew the chamalian soul well in all its tragic despair. He could see for himself now what the seed of the gods had done to his kinsmen. It drove those who possessed it mad, forced upon them the awareness of their unsevered links with nature even as it set them apart from it forever.

It forced awareness upon a race barely ready for it. It showed the truth about themselves – that they had been cast out of the garden, but could never leave it. It presented them with a riddle they could not solve, made them isolated while they were still tied to a corrupt world.

But Zepp knew something that they did not. He had learned, as Jobe had learned before him, that there was only one solution to the problem of life on Chamal.

The source of the cures was the source of the curse.

The spark of light had to be carried forward, the seed of the gods had to be nurtured, the spark of reason had to be sustained. More than that, it had to be spread, given fuel, stoked and tended, until it was bight blaze that pushed away the darkness clouding the chamalian soul.

It could not be done by a single soul. Even the tribe of Jobe had difficulty serving the seed of the gods and the memory of its patriarch. But with the help of the angels, the light could be brought to a whole world. If only their first meting was not spoiled by the madness that threatened to destroy *Deragathon* and with all of Chamal.

Zepp pushed on, closer and closer to the bridge, despite the hazards ahead of him.

* * *

Midway up the length of the vessel, Zepp thought the end had come. He and Griddle slid aside the airtight door and passed into the next section of the ship only to discover a mass of Blue Monkeys waiting to trap their mutinous slaves as soon as they appeared.

Zepp stopped quickly and reversed course, but not before the monkeys spotted them. They set of in pursuit just as he slammed the door shut against a clattering barrage of poisoned darts.

He got as far as the next bulkhead before they came through the door – unfortunately they didn't have the same handicap to rapid movement that Zepp did. He scrambled to open the airtight door and escape into the section below, but he knew there wasn't enough time. He was about to say his prayers when the acceleration alarm hooted loudly.

Seconds later, the decks rumbled with the thunder from *Deragathon's* mighty engines. The long free-fall chamber suddenly became a high-ceilinged vault – with Zepp standing on the floor and the monkeys high above, clawing the air ineffectually for support. The acceleration was not great, but the fall was a long one, by the time the monkeys crashed into the bulkhead around him, they were moving at nearly fifteen hands a second. None of them were in any shape to stop Zepp and Griddle as they ducked down a side passage to get around the rest of the squad up ahead.

Zepp was almost excited when he discovered that the side passage led to the operations section.

The fighting and the lunacy had passed this department by. The navigation, communications, and electronics stations were still manned and in order. Arkarians, Meshkarians, and Rikabarians bustled up and down the corridors, paying no attention to Zepp and his companion. These breeds were made of sterner stuff, and their leaders employed tougher discipline than the races below decks.

But as they moved along, treading lightly, upwards towards the bridge, all that changed. First, emergency alarms began to sound as they passed rooms filled with dark figures and flashing lights.

Then the lighting strips in the walls began to flicker on and off. Repair technicians came rushing up the corridor, stumbling into one another, doing damage with heavy tool boxes to the unfortunates at the head of the line. Zepp looked at Griddle quizzically and Griddle returned a broad grin. Then, from the back of the commotion, three familiar faces appeared – Zepp's cousins.

"The judgment is upon you, cousin!" Fripp called.

"You will not survive this battle!" threatened Lingo.

"My blade is sharp and ready!" warned Groz.

Zepp scampered away, looking for a place to hide, Griddle was yanked along behind him, taken by surprise. They ducked into a large, dimly lit compartment where watchstanders bent over radar scanners filled with orange and white blobs. Overbearing superiors huddled next to the plotting boards tracking the approach of the angels.

One by one the radar scanners began to black out and wisps of smoke curled up from the innards. Someone in the back grabbed a fire extinguisher and sprayed his equipment. At the head of room a ring-tailed creature with large eyes turned to Zepp and Griddle, chilling the small, green ape down to the end of his tail.

"It's you again!" the officer said. It was Elger Carlonzia – Zepp recognized the voice and now the face that he had glimpsed briefly the day before.

Carlonzia barked orders to guards as Zepp and Griddle made a leap for the exit. One brave soul rose to bar their way, but the chain between them grew taut as they diverged slightly, caught the guard in the neck and threw him to the floor. The rest of the guards got in each other's way and stumbled around is the semidarkness, providing the pair with just enough time to escape safely. A few minutes later, they emerged from the upper end of the operations section only a few hands from the entrance to the bridge.

Their goal was within reach.

Zepp pushed off towards the sentry post with Griddle in tow. The pilgrim had shown remarkable courage so far, but it looked as though he was nearing its end. His eyes were jammed shut and his ears were quivering with fear. Zepp felt a burst of sympathy. But he knew there was no other way to end this nightmare.

Just as they came within sight of the sentries, the wide doors to the main passageway slid open with a crash. A handful of Rifter slaves burst through, pursued by a trio of Blue Monkeys backed up by a squad of spotted Birhat cats.

The sentries joined the running gunfight, shooting at both sides, taking a few hits themselves and filling the space in front of them with blue smoke and fire.

Zepp was quick to take advantage of the opening. A moment later, he and Griddle were past the guards and inside the short tunnel that led to the ship's nerve center.

He paused to catch his breath and rally his partner. When Griddle finally opened his eyes and gave him a smile, Zepp gritted his teeth and pushed through into the eye of the storm.

He was the least surprised at what followed.

* * *

Admiral Purdee sat alone and unattended, silently conversing with his ancestors. "Oh ancient ones, whose spirits wander the foggy night, what have I done to warrant your disfavor? Why have I been punished with the burden of command aboard this asylum? Have I not defended the honor of you r city and your heritage? Have I not followed the correct path, nurtured the family fortune, taught my son – source of embarrassment though he is – the ways of our people? What then was my crime? How have I sinned?"

His plaintive questions went unanswered.

The angels' starship was only minutes away now. The riots below decks were spreading to more and vital areas – operations, engineering, weapons control. He asked his long-dead forefathers to grant him a swift completion to his ordeal. His prayers were answered, but not in way that he expected.

Behind him, at the entrance to the bridge, a scuffle had broken out. He looked up to see a sentry carom off the bulkhead as a small green ape came shooting into the chamber, dragging what looked like a bag of dirty laundry behind him. On closer examination, Purdee realized the ape's cargo was a smallish creature of undetermined form. He wondered who would dare to disturb the ship's command center at this sensitive moment. Whoever it was, he would be severely punished for this transgression.

The ape came bounding up the middle of the bridge, past the control stations and the stunned watchstanders, along the latticed tower that led to the command framework, right up to the assembled admiralty board itself.

He stopped barely fifteen hands from the admiral, anchoring

himself to the deck grating with his toes while his companion floated freely in the air behind him.

"Everyone stay back!" the ape commanded. "This miserable bag of bones beside me is the Suridash jinx. Anyone who tries to harm us risks his life and the admiral's. Stay back or pay the price!"

The bridge crew fell silent, except for the snarling and snapping of the Meshkar marines straining at their leashes. Everyone waited for the admiral to say or do something. Obviously he could not allow a pair of petty saboteurs to threaten him like this.

He reached for the control that would release the marines. A flip of a switch, a gesture from him, and the ferocious beasts would fall upon the intruders and rend the flesh from their bones.

The tension in the chamber grew as all eyes focused on the strange confrontation at its center. On one side of the framework was the admiral, a purple glow to his skin as his blood pressure climbed higher and higher. On the other, the two saboteurs held firm, a look of grim determination in the ape's eyes.

"This has gone far enough, admiral," the ape said. "I'm not going to let you attack the angels. Too much depends on them to let you and the rest of these lunatics screw it up."

Beside the admiral, in a barely audible whisper, Ensign Pim gave words of warning of his own. "If you release the marines, father, you will never recover the command of the bridge in time to meet the angels."

Purdee cursed the truth his son spoke, but he knew the youngling was right. If the marines were let loose, the watchstanders would desert their posts, officers would flee, and it would he many minutes before order could he restored. He was stymied. What could he do to end the standoff?

Before he came up with an answer, the problem was solved for him.

The Rifter space-fighters, commandeered by the mutineers from the Blue Monkeys, came flashing by the *Deragathon* without warning. Their cannons blasted away at the mother ship. Bullets splattered against the outer windows of the bridge, high above Purdee's head, but failed to penetrate the inner glass that held back the vacuum of space. Below them, external sensors, electronics, radar antennae, and running lights were stripped from the hull of the ship by the intense gunfire.

Then the entire bridge shook with the suppressed thump and violent shudder of a major explosion somewhere below decks. Alarms began to ring, horns hooted. The *Deragathon* wobbled sickly on its axis, sending everyone on the bridge reeling in a wide arc.

"They've hit the Rifter containment!" someone shouted.

"We're spinning out of control'" another cried.

"We're all doomed!" yelled a third voice, others echoing agreement.

Through the splintered cracks in the windows overhead, Purdee could see warped steel, wrecked equipment, and Blue Monkeys drifting by. More alarms went off, the loudest and most insistent of them close by Purdee, the board, and the two saboteurs.

The green ape looked about nervously in the noise and confusion, realizing that he had been upstaged. Purdee's son and his adjutant came up behind him and took both him and his companion by surprise, grasping them quietly and without a struggle. The ape was surprised, but he did not look defeated. His companion's eyes rolled back and he went limp.

Purdee regained command of the situation swiftly. "Have the

engineers dump fuel and regain the ship's balance! Seal off the Rifter containment! I want a damage report immediately."

He turned to Zepp and Griddle, his deadly horn aimed at their hearts. "Take these two away," he ordered. "They can he tortured to death slowly when we have more time."

The marines fell back to a more relaxed stance and a squad of sentries converged on the saboteurs. But before they could take the hapless pair away, the sound of gunfire echoed from the entrance to the bridge. A gunman – a squirrelly type with blue fur – rushed through the doorway, only to he shot by an alert guard.

The admiral released a pair of his marines and pointed to the doorway. They were through the exit in an instant, ready to stabilize the situation and repel the mutineers. The guards surrounding the two saboteurs closer at hand held their place.

"It will do no more harm to keep them here for now," Purdee said. "but if they move, shoot to kill."

Reports began to flow in from all sides, now. The watchstanders who had panicked were relieved by more reliable crewmembers – and if Purdee had his way, they would suffer the same fate as the two interlopers before him.

The engineers worked frantically to get the ship back on an even keel. The Rifter containment had been split from end to end and was a total loss.

The angels' ship had long been in sight as the orbits of the two spacecraft slowly converged. In a few minutes it would be in range of *Deragathon*'s weapons.

The adjutant reviewed the systems that remained functioning after the fighter attack. "Navigation, communications with the surface, at least one of the Kwikorak energy beams and Shipar's anti-ship missiles are still operational, sir. Everything else is out of commission or out of communication with the bridge."

Purdee frowned and wrinkled his brow at the base of his horn. It was a distressing situation. He had lost almost all of his combat effectiveness and he had yet to engage the enemy.

"Very well," he said. "At least we have a horn left."

He returned to his seat and fastened himself in with the strap. Then in a loud and commanding voice he announced to the bridge crew: "Steady now, my comrades. The angels are almost within our reach. This is the moment of glory. Let us pray to our gods and to our ancestors, summon up our courage, and concentrate our will. The final assault is upon us. Let us be victorious – or let us not live to see defeat!"

* * *

Datascreens all over *Cousteau* were tuned to the command channel, the direct feed from the bridge with the battle computer's annotated view of space ahead of the vessel and the dry, nasal voice of Captain Newton P. Fletcher in a droning commentary.

"I am reminded at this time," Fletcher said, "of the cinedrama fantasies of the early nuclear age – the flying saucers invading the earth and the valiant, if somewhat overemotional, defense of the planet by the military. It is my hope to avoid such a confrontation here, as you all know."

His round, hairless face filled the screen – much to the annoyance of those glued to the datascreens who were hungry for the sight of the alien creatures who until now had existed only as voices on the radio and, less often, images in a video. Over his bald pate, he wore a blue baseball cap with the *Cousteau*'s patch and a chrome-plated eagle on the front. The hat was a half-size too large and kept slipping down his forehead, stopped only by a pair of large wire-framed glasses.

"Just like the men-of-war in which Captain Cook or Darwin once sailed, we have the capacity to destroy the angels below without hesitation. But as scientists, we see such an act as personally and morally objectionable. I would hate to be forced into it. But luckily we have Lieutenant Barrett with us to handle just this problem."

The picture changed to show the boyish face of the Space Corps officer, James Barrett, the *Cousteau*'s weapons officer and the only military man aboard the ship. He grinned at the crew through the screen, then switched back to the battle computer's readout – eliciting cheers from the more critical viewers in the starship's labs and lounges.

"While I ... uh ... supervise from my post, Jim here will operate the battle computer and fend off any action the angels may make that are of an offensive nature. What's our status now, Jim?" Captain Fletcher asked as he stuffed his briar with pipeweed.

"The alien ship is about five points to port, moving off to the south – belay that, she's just making a course adjustment now. I'll bet she's matching our orbit. They've got some kind of electronic countermeasures up – jamming our radar – but the mass detectors have her pinpointed. We should start seeing some action from her in the next few minutes."

"Well keep monitoring her, Jim. Let us know if the situation changes. In the meantime, let me take this opportunity to thank those of you who have worked so hard on the inbound leg to study our new friends at one remove. You have put in long and tireless hours and we all owe you – "

"Heads up, Captain?" Barrett called suddenly. "Here comes something – about twenty small contacts moving at high velocity. Looks like rocket-powered fighter craft coming in from behind the big ship."

The display from the battle computer flashed a sharp warning as the fighters appeared, guns blazing, on either side of the alien ship.

"It looks like some kind of weapons fire from them now, but they're still a long ways off to engage us. Wow! They're shooting at each other! What do you make of that?"

Fletcher puffed on his pipe, making a sucking sound that echoed throughout the ship. "Beats me, Jim. There's so little we know about these creatures and so much we don't know. If anyone has any ideas about this significance of this, give us a call up here, by all means."

Then the display let up with a flash of red light and a window announced: "Major hit on target Alfa."

"Holy cow!" Barrett yelled. "You may find this hard to believe, skipper, but something just blew up on the mother chip. Below the kiloton range, but a major hit. She's still alive, but that blowout must have shaken them up quite a bit."

Then a new voice spoke up from the datascreen. "Val Nordland, here in the cultural survey section," he said. "We've managed to identify over a thousand language groups on the planet's radios, captain, and we think we've isolated at least a dozen separate technological cultures down there. This is just a guess, but I wouldn't be surprised if some of them are in disagreement over how to handle our arrival. We could be involved in an internal conflict here. Something more to watch our step over."

"Thanks, Mr. Nordland," Fletcher said. "I'll keep that in mind."

"They're closing to within a hundred kilometers, sir," Barrett announced. "The big ship's moving real slow relative to us, but those fighters are still coming in at a hell of a clip."

"You don't think they could be a threat to us, do you?"

"Could be, sir. Oops – some of them are putting the brakes on now, but not all of them. The rest should be here in just a minute. I'm going over to full defensive mode, captain. Screens are up. And just a note here, the jamming stopped when the mother ship was hit."

As the fighters came within close range of the *Cousteau* the tracking systems beeped softly and Fletcher ducked instinctively. Apparently not all of the fighters were targeting the big ship.

The fighters were visible through the spacecraft's windows for a brief moment as they sped past. From behind the bridge came a distant crackling sound.

"What was that?" Fletcher asked sharply.

"Energy beams from the big ship, sir. They just burned off a layer of paint on our hull, but no other damage. Everything out there is hardened or armored. The fighters fired at us on their pass, but the screens kept us safe."

"Just a touch hostile, aren't they, Jim?"

"I'd say so, sir."

A few minutes later, the mother ship launched its main assault. Barrett's voice climbed an octave as he read off the battle sensors. "Anti-ship missiles, captain! Four of them, wide spread, supersonic speeds. Impact in one minute."

"You'd better do something about that, Jim. I'd hat to lose the ship this early in the expedition," Fletcher said, struggling to maintain his calm scientific detachment as the ship's company heard him bite through the stem of his briar at Barrett's report.

"Aye, aye, sir," Barrett replied as he activated the ship's laser battery. He punched the commands into the battle computer and a second later four beams lanced out at the four alien missiles and blasted them out of the sky.

"Good shot!" Fletcher exclaimed. "I hope that cools them off. It would be a shame if we had to start making friends by killing off their warriors."

It was not the end of the battle, but the decision had passed. The aliens seemed to have thrown their best punch and failed. The hull of the *Cousteau* crackled from a few more blasts of plasma from the energy beams. The aliens launched another salvo of missiles, but they were detonated only a few hundred meters out of their launch silos.

Then the mighty alien warship fell silent. There were no more attacks. Even the rocket-propelled fighters drifted off in their own unstable orbits, out of fuel and out of fight.

* * *

The battle was over. The angels had won. And now the *Deragathon* silently awaited its doom – nearly all aboard certain that doom was all that could come next.

Word that the attack had failed spread quickly through the *Deragathon*. The mutinies were now complete. The fighting stopped throughout the ship. The renegade fighters who could do so returned to their hangars, hurrying to their docks before the pilots ran out of oxygen.

The bridge crew was in shock. At the moment Admiral Purdee realized the magnitude of his failure his face turned white as the blood drained from it and the color had not returned – nor had any semblance of command on is part. Ensign Pim tried to comfort his father, but he was soon distracted. With his father incapacitated, under Meshkarian law, Pim now became commander of the *Deragathon*.

There was no other choice. Tradition demanded it, and no one dared oppose it. The admiralty board had changed composition radically in the course of the battle. Arkaria, the Blue Monkeys, Birhat, and Suridash all had lost their seats – through treachery, collusion, or defeat. Rikabar was still in favor aboard the warship, but on the surface of Chamal, the Vegetarian Party had not survived the night. Food riots had swept the homelands and where the Royal Onion had once prevailed, chaos now reigned.

That left Meshkar, Kwikorak, and Shipar in control of the vessel – with the cave-apes dutifully keeping the life-support systems operating to ensure their own survival.

Neither Shipar nor Kwikorak could tolerate a commander from the other's camp, Meshkar's officers retained control of *Deragathon*, and the succession of command would follow Meshkarian custom.

What was left of the board ceased its bickering. Even the marines were subdued, now that their leader had broken. Their leashes lay slack against the deck.

Down below, Whirlpitt and Pirr-Click-Wheet came out of hiding.

Tedrak's plan – the plan of the Cult of the Lost Argument – the plan carried out by Zepp and Griddle – had succeeded. The angels tended station four times eighty-eight leagues away from *Deragathon* in close planetary orbit. They continued to broadcast video signals of smiling faces, clasping hands, peaceful gestures. The *Deragathon* was essentially disarmed – it could defend itself, but it could not attack anyone, alien or chamalian.

Admiral Pim's first order was to stand down from general quarters and secure from battle stations. His second order was for all off- duty crewmembers to return to their quarters – each to his appropriate containment and the surviving Rifters to the flight deck until the Blue Monkey containment was secured by the engineers.

And his third order was to return Zepp and Griddle to the brig from which they had escaped – their slow torture and painful deaths to be deferred until a later date.

EPILOGUE

Just about the only one aboard *Deragathon* to take any joy in the failure of the ship's mission was Zepp. His spirits were high, his morale excellent, and his humor unmatched, despite hours in the brig – despite even the effects of close quarters with Griddle. Nothing, not the irregular meals, the uncertain lighting, or the erratic plumbing, could bring his spirits down.

He knew what had caused the defeat of the chamalian warship.

<u>He</u> had.

The admiralty board could argue and debate, pointing the finger at Purdee or the rebels or the Vegetarians or the Blue Monkeys, but Zepp knew the truth. Tedrak's original vision had been true. Griddle's curse had proven to be the tragic catalyst that brought down the terrible venture that Tedrak himself had launched all those months ago.

For the moment, Chamal was safe – if not secure. It had been judged by the impartial tribunal of fate and found guilty of all its sins. The sentence had been swift and devastating. The world had been condemned to life.

The warship that drifted across the sky once every ninety minutes was not quite the threat that Whirlpitt had once feared. For all their terrible power, the angels were indeed the peaceful scientists that Tezar said they were. And the collapse of the Blue Monkey regime in the rift and the demise of the Royal Onion in Rikabar had eased much of the tension that threatened the survival of the chamalian race.

But a whole new set of problems was just beginning to take form. The angels remained terribly powerful, the creatures of Chamal remained terribly volatile. Peace was by no means at hand.

How would the complex confusion of chamalian races deal with the strange race of purebreds? Violence and destruction were not the mission of the angels, but could Chamal withstand the peaceful probing of the analytical minds aboard the *Cousteau*?

These were not questions that bothered Zepp deeply, although he was aware of them – and had plenty of time to ponder them. He was more immediately concerned with other problems. When would the sink in the corner of the cell be repaired. When would he and Griddle get hot food? What was going to happen to them next?

He was not afraid of the uncertain future, but he did have a great deal of anxiety about conditions back home in Suridash. His sisters and his children – were they all right? Had anyone done them harm in retribution for their sins?

If one hair of their heads had been touched, his tribe would pay. They would know his wrath and learn to fear it. After all, he was the assassin of Sheverek and the scourge of the *Deragathon*, who had pulled the world back from the brink of Armageddon with the angels. He was a power to reckon with – and more important than that, he knew it.

He didn't know how he would be received when he returned home – if he returned home. He might have to leave the tribe of Jobe, condemned to an endless pilgrimage like Griddle. Perhaps he could remain in Suridash – despite its shortcomings it was still home. But would the tribe let him remain in the city after violating them most so flagrantly? Would Tedrak and Whirlpitt intervene to solve his dilemma? He didn't think so.

It was with a mixture of fear and trepidation that he greeted Whirlpitt in the morning after being escorted from his cell to the office. At least Tedrak's lieutenant appreciated what he and Griddle had done.

"You have my congratulations, youngling," Whirlpitt said as he dismissed the guards. "Your success was beyond my wildest imaginings. Penetrating the bridge – who would have believed it. Tedrak cannot believe you stared down the admiral himself. By the way, he sends you his best wishes and asks if there is anything be can do for your family."

"Thank you anyway, but they can take care of themselves for now. And when I get back home I'll do whatever is necessary."

Whirlpitt pursed his wide lips and shook his head. "When you get back home ... that is something of a problem."

"A problem? What do you mean?" Zepp asked quickly, little tendrils of fear gripping at his hearts.

"The situation is still quite complicated right now. It is still too early to be sure of much. For the moment, you are prisoners, not heroes. In the long run, things may change. But for now you are safer kept apart from the rest of the crew. The power of Suridash has been limited by the events of the past few hours. There are things that I cannot do. Presenting you as saviors of our race is beyond our means at the moment. The best we could accomplish is to rescue your necks from the headsman. Is that sufficient?"

"Do you want me to thank you? After all, you got us into this, didn't you?"

Whirlpitt's eyes narrowed in surprise. He leaned back in a new appraisal of Zepp. "The youth has grown spirited with success," he said.

Zepp ignored him. "How do things stand with the angels? Have they begun destroying Chamal's cities or have you put them off with your clever lies?"

"Lies are seldom clever, youngling, and we are prepared to tell the angels only as much truth as will serve our ends. And no, they have not begun destroying Chamal's cities."

Zepp noticed a stiffening to Whirlpitt's back, a hesitation before he continued. Something was up and Zepp braced himself for the worst.

"The angels must know we have had a mutiny aboard *Deragathon* – and that it contributed to our failure to destroy them upon our first meeting. But we cannot afford to remain powerless before them. It is not good for our world and it is not good for the plans Tedrak has made. As things stand now, we – you, me, Tedrak and Suridash – are all traitors to our race. We have a lot of company in that status, so there is no immediate threat to our survival. But in order to recover our position, we must show that the decision to prevent a decisive battle with the angels was a correct one. We still have to vindicate our actions. Perhaps then you can return to Suridash as heroes, but certainly not before then."

Zepp should have been disappointed, but strangely he was not. "And when do you expect that will be?" he asked sternly.

"That is hard to say," Whirlpitt replied carefully.

"Is that another truth designed to produce false conclusions?"

"No, it is not," Whirlpitt said. "Let me be honest with you. The immediate danger has passed, that is true, but as long as the angels remain above our world, the threat remains."

"The angels have shown their power and it frightens even me. They are much more advanced than we are, much more sophisticated in the use of power. They are delicate and sensitive while being forceful and immovable. It is a strange counter to the casual brutality of Chamal. It upsets all the equations, opening up grim possibilities. Even I cannot predict what creatures like these angels will do. They may remain benevolent – but they may also turn out to be a deadly menace to Chamal at the same time."

"None of this scares me, Whirlpitt. Let them destroy our world – and you and Tedrak along with it – for all I care. What is your point? How do we fit into your plotting? Are you planning to make use of us once more? Because if you are, you had better change your thinking. You have lost your leverage over us as well. You hold no more threats against me – I have lived through the end of the world and faced death more times than I can count. And there is little you can do to coerce Griddle – at least without risking your own life. Tell me what you have planned so I can laugh in your face."

Whirlpitt seemed stunned by Zepp's boldness. Zepp could see it in his eyes. That made him feel good, although little else did at the moment. He had a feeling that something terrible was about to happen. And yet, at the same time, he had a feeling that was not bad at all – the feeling that no matter how terrible the future might be, he could deal with it, overcome it, and emerge triumphant in the end.

"Come on, froglegs, hit me with it. What have you and Teddy cooked up for us? It must be bad or you wouldn't take so long to get around to it."

Whirlpitt smiled. "Very well, Master Zepp. Here it is, and I think you'll find that it is not so terrible after all. I'll wager that you accept our proposal willingly – even vigorously. You and Griddle are going to be granted a great honor – one of the highest honors that has ever been given a member of our race."

Zepp sneered in disbelief.

"You are to become our first emissaries to the humans, to go aboard their ship and live among them. Just you and Griddle. You know what that means, don't you?"

Zepp surprised Whirlpitt just a little then as he began to laugh. He laughed loudly and uncontrollably, as if for the first time in his life, until tears ran from his eyes and his sides began to ache.

"Yes, yes," he said gasping. "You're right. That I will do for you. Just in case the angels change their minds and decide that they do want to destroy our world."

* * *